# HER
# CRUEL
# DAHLIAS

## CANDACE ROBINSON

To those who sometimes feel broken

A midnight black dahlia was a rarity, yet not rare enough for a murderous bastard to leave five behind on Cricket's bloodied corpse. As her body lay dying, the last thing she remembered seeing were two obsidian dahlias coming down across her eyes. The gentle weight of two more pressed into each of her palms. And finally, as if offering the dead a bite of food, a flower was placed into her mouth, its flavor sharp and bitter against her tongue, the last thing she was sure she would ever taste.

Flexing her fingers, Cricket sighed. She tried not to think about that horrific day if she could help it. But ever since she'd been brought back to life by a necromancer, Cricket had been waiting for her inherited gift to manifest itself, a peculiarity unique to her—a curiosity to entertain the masses flocking to Mistress Eliza's Carnival. She'd been told that her skin was supposed to become translucent at will, her skeleton to be seen beneath her layers of flesh, then bright crimson roses were meant to bloom across her skin. The necromancer had foreseen this before she'd restarted Cricket's heart once more, and she'd never been wrong in the past. Only, each time Cricket practiced, struggling to discover her gift, nothing happened. No roses, no translucent skin, no skeleton. Her mortal body remained stubbornly normal.

Cricket's curiosity needed to surface soon, as the necromancer, her mistress—Eliza—had demanded. But she *tried*. Every blasted day since she'd awoken. She wouldn't ever take the stage in Mistress Eliza's Carnival if she couldn't call on her gift at will. Tonight was meant to be her second week to perform her hidden curiosity in front of an audience. To *dance*. But it wasn't quite in the cards for her yet. Instead, she was helping the other performers or cleaning up rubbish left behind on the carnival grounds by visitors.

The fiddler's music filled the air, his pace picking up to a delightful and quirky tune that was pleasant to her ears. Pulling back the thick black velvet curtain, Cricket peeked out toward the audience, who watched with mesmerized wide eyes as Wilder—the Wooden Man— removed his left foot, then his right hand by using his teeth. He waggled his eyebrows while his fingers and toes fluttered, bidding a hello to the crowd. Above him, two female acrobats, wearing tight, sparkling black costumes and silver masks covering their entire faces, spun within ivory silk fabric, forming a cocoon around themselves before dark leathery wings burst from their backs.

The audience oohed and aahed, clapping harder when Wilder balanced on the stump of one arm. His skin appeared wood-like, with lines etched into his brown flesh.

"So," a deep voice purred from behind Cricket. "Have you been practicing?"

Her heart skipped a beat and she whirled around to find Zephyr leaning on a rail, his arms folded against his broad bare chest. "In my caravan," she said with a frown, yet her gaze unintentionally swept up his lithe and muscular physique. The dark collar he always wore rested around his throat and black trousers slung low on his hips. Zephyr's onyx hair was drawn back in a knot at his nape while his bright hazel eyes, lined in kohl, danced with playfulness as they studied her beneath long lashes.

"You should come out more often and stop hiding inside your caravan," he said with a grin.

She pretended to observe her nails. "I'm out right now."

Since joining the carnival, she'd remained in her caravan when practicing and only crept out to bathe or when Mistress Eliza required it. Before her murder, seeing Zephyr this close would've made her heart gallop, and even though she hadn't truly known him at that time, in a way, she blamed him for her death, for everything she'd lost.

"For luck." Zephyr reached for her hand, and she didn't pull away as he pried open her fingers, then tucked something cool against her palm.

Cricket peered down at a silver coin, her frown deepening.

"Perhaps you can come to my caravan after I perform, and we can practice for the rest of the night," he drawled, the edges of his lips curling up in amusement.

Frustration stormed inside her veins, and she clenched her jaw. "If you think I'll spread my legs for you in return for one bloody coin, then you'd be wrong. It would take much more than that."

"So it's not a no, then?" He arched a brow, a low chuckle escaping his pouty mouth.

"You're such a—"

With a grin, he pressed his finger over her lips, silencing her before she could curse him. "Now, now, children are out there." He let his callused finger fall from her mouth. "Besides, it was only an invitation to *talk*. Get to know one another since you've been avoiding everyone as if they have a plague. I think it'll help Mistress Eliza get off your back for a bit."

Cricket thought about it for a moment—that might be true. "You think it would?" she asked, biting her lip.

"One way to find out." He shrugged, dipping toward her, his woodsy scent caressing her senses.

Cricket's cheeks heated and she turned back to the stage before he could see. Wilder finished his act, the wood of his skin vanishing, leaving only a deep brown as he raked a hand through his hair. She focused on the next performer—Inara—as she made the crowd laugh by pulling a multitude of lacy hats from her head, one hidden beneath another and another. Long purple tentacles sprouted from Inara's legs and arms, and she slowly crawled in a circle on the stage. Cricket desperately wished her curiosity would unfurl from within her so she could finally experience it, but perhaps Zephyr was right. Maybe talking to someone would help her hone in on her ability more easily. But as she turned around to take Zephyr up on his offer, a dark-haired female, maybe ten years older than him, wrapped her arm around his waist and whispered in his ear. Autumn, with her beautiful, cat-like golden eyes, who was able to contort her body into any position she wished. And Cricket was certain Autumn had been in Zephyr's bed on more than one occasion.

Cricket slipped to the far back of the tent, brushing past two performers: Sylvia, a pepper-haired female who held the ability to expel fire beneath water, and Virgil, a middle-aged man who could tap nails anywhere along his body, including his eyes. She tucked herself into a corner, hidden away from everyone, then pressed her back against a rail and inhaled deeply. A little over a year ago, Mistress Eliza had brought her back from the dead—only things hadn't gone as they had with the other performers. Instead of waking with a gifted curiosity that would bud and grow, Cricket had been asleep until a month ago. During that time, she'd performed as the Sleeping Darling, a woman who remained asleep, no matter how loud her surroundings became.

Everyone who worked at Mistress Eliza's Carnival had once been dead like Cricket, only they'd awoken as soon as the necromancy magic restarted their hearts, and they were able to practice their gifts. Before her death, Cricket had ventured to the carnival, watched Zephyr touch leaves, then sprout vines from his bare back. She'd thought it the most beautiful thing in the world, even more so than the other talented performers. Over the years, every time the carnival came, he'd been the one she'd wanted to see the most, had wished to dance on the very stage where he and the others performed. However, fate decided to answer her prayer while whispering, *Be careful what you wish for.*

"Where's Cricket at?" The snapping voice of Mistress Eliza interrupted her thoughts as the wood creaked beneath the woman's limp. Cricket sighed, knowing Mistress Eliza was in a foul mood—as she'd been unable to raise anyone from death. Not since Cricket's murder. The bodies of the deceased, including animals, would no more than twitch before falling dead once more. Sometimes, or on most days, Cricket wished the necromancer hadn't ever brought her back.

Perspiration coated Cricket's palms, and she wiped them against the waistband of her short tulle skirt. Cricket's heart thundered in her chest as she watched Mistress Eliza limp out the back entrance, her long wool dress swishing and her graying hair loosely plaited down her back. The necromancer refused to use a cane, no matter how rough of a day she was having with her limp.

The crowd cheered for Inara's performance, their clapping akin to the roar of a thousand doors slamming.

Cricket snuck a glance around the corner, cursing herself as Zephyr caught her, and a grin spread his lips. He winked at her while Autumn giggled, her finger trailing across his collar. Zephyr casually moved Autumn's hand away, and Cricket drew back, realizing she was still holding his coin. Even though she wanted to toss it back at him, she slipped the coin into her bodice.

As violins started to play deep and lovely, signaling a new act was beginning, Cricket released a breath and pretended she was the one taking a step onto the stage. *Cricket Wakefield.*

Ever since she was a young child, she'd always wished to become a dancer. Each night, she used to perform in front of her mirror back home, knowing she wouldn't be able to live out her dream and travel, not when her parents wanted nothing for her but a suitable man to take care of her.

Music poured from the instruments, the pace of the bows across the strings increasing, brushing exquisitely against her eardrums. Cricket stepped forward and closed her eyes before lifting an arm above her head. She pointed her toes as she elevated her leg to the side. Once, twice, she spun in a clockwise circle. On her third pirouette, she thought about the blade digging in between her collarbones, slashing toward her stomach, the hot blood spilling down her flesh. The dahlias against her eyes. She stumbled as she inhaled sharply, her lungs begging to drink in more air.

Raucous laughter spilled from the crowd. The sound wasn't aimed at Cricket, but it felt as though they could see through the curtain to where she'd hidden herself, that they were all laughing because they could see her fears, her grief. Cricket's wretched heart thrummed faster, aching to shatter her rib cage.

She peered at her hands and squinted to focus on her curiosity. A bead of perspiration slid down the back of her neck, and for the first time, fluttering wings seemed to caress her arms. She watched as her hands turned translucent, the ivory bones beneath her skin exposed in the dim lighting.

"Come on, Cricket," she pleaded, a small smile tugging the edges of her lips. "You can do this." Even though Mistress Eliza had foreseen her curiosity, Cricket hadn't entirely believed it to be true. Yet now she was *unearthing* it.

Something clawed beneath her skin, as if insects were

begging to make their way from the deepest depths of her being. Cricket's lower lip wobbled when she studied her arms, where not red spots dotted them, but black. She glanced down at her stomach, her legs, finding the same dark-shaded spots there too. Black roses?

A flower bud broke free from her bicep before its petals burst open—a dahlia, black as night. Cricket gasped, her body shaking as fright spread through her. More dahlias tore through her flesh, and she couldn't stop her trembling. She was unable to halt the tormented thoughts that rushed forth at the sight of them—so like the dahlias placed along her dying body.

"Stop," Cricket whispered to herself while balling her hands into tight fists to draw the devilish things somewhere else. But they wouldn't disappear from her sight. She stared in horror as she grasped a velvety one at her wrist and attempted to rip it away. Pain shot through her, and she clenched her teeth while the flower remained.

With shallow breaths, she let her feet carry her forward as the clawing beneath her skin continued. She looked up, and her gaze locked onto Zephyr, who was now alone, his eyes widening in surprise.

"Cricket?" he rasped.

"I don't know what's happening!" she shrieked. And she knew he couldn't help her—she needed to find Mistress Eliza.

Cricket spun on her heel and fled out the back entrance of the tent to find Mistress Eliza. But the necromancer was already gone. The cool breeze tickled Cricket's flesh, and the torches flickered against the starry night.

The clawing turned painful as if thorns were buried inside her muscle and sinew. Zephyr rushed out of the tent, searching the night for her, and Cricket ran, not wanting him to see her as a monstrous garden of dahlias, a reminder of a murderer who had once left the same flower behind.

Cricket remained in the shadows behind the carnival tents, avoiding the crowds as she bolted toward Mistress Eliza's caravan, all the while pleading with the flowers to go back to the depths from which they came. But the dahlias' only answer was to ignore her. For more to unleash their heinous selves as the wind wrapped its delicate hands around her.

The world surrounding her spun when she entered the caravan area, where a few performers laughed while she darted past them, seeming to believe this was all a jest, a *performance*.

"Cricket, just stop!" Zephyr shouted, his voice inching nearer.

She skirted between the painted caravans, when her foot caught on a rope and she toppled forward. Cricket caught herself just as she was about to strike her head against the ground. Sharp pain radiated up her arms, and she couldn't see a single sliver of her pale skin. Another flower bloomed inside her mouth, on her tongue, tasting of death.

A whimper tore from her throat as she pushed herself up from the ground, but she fell again, her eyelids fluttering from exhaustion. Pressure ignited on her lungs where yet more flowers bloomed, consuming her. She could feel the torturous things *everywhere*. When she attempted to scream, only a hoarse sound escaped her mouth.

A shadow knelt beside her, and she looked up to find Zephyr looping an arm around her to scoop her up.

As Cricket turned her head toward a caravan, an oval stage mirror propped against its side caught her attention. But not the object itself—her image reflected in the glass. She gasped, her lungs weighted. Large black petals unfurled from her skull, covering her entirely, all but her eyes, which were wide and full of panic.

"Breathe," Zephyr said, his voice steady as he held her close.

*I can't*, she tried to get out, but the words were trapped in her mouth, her chest tightening. The crackling flames of the torches dimmed as dahlias slipped out from her eyes, darkening the carnival. Her body slumped against Zephyr's firm chest, and she was too tired to fight, her oxygen stolen away by the vicious flowers.

2

*T*he sky above darkened to a deep gray, and Cricket needed to hurry home before it poured. She didn't want to ruin her new shoes, or at least more than she already had.

Cricket had finished walking her closest friend, Anika, home from the carnival, and as she left, she couldn't stop thinking about the performances. How every year she would go as soon as Mistress Eliza's Carnival came to the city and opened, to be the first to catch a glimpse of each of the curious and alluring acts. Necromancers were even more rare to find than witches. The story was that the performers were all brought back to life after suffering a violent death, that their curiosities were indeed real. However, they all looked as though they'd never experienced such a terrible fate, especially Zephyr.

She thought about him, her favorite of the performers, the way he winked at the audience as he juggled swords. The sensual smile that spread across his lips when he would press a leaf against his *tongue before thick green vines grew from wherever he wished, sometimes his arms, other times his torso or back. They didn't need a single flower blooming across them to be beautiful. He was perhaps a couple of years older than her nineteen years.* Stop thinking of him. *Bram was the one courting her, a man whose kindness she had fallen for nearly two years ago.*

*As small drops of rain pelted her skin, Cricket drew to a stop and stared up at the storm-filled sky, letting the rain fall into her eyes. She didn't worry about rushing home any longer, not when she remembered how much her younger brother, Felix, had loved this weather. He passed eleven years ago at the tender age of four from the plague, yet she still thought about him every time it rained, the way his laughter would echo. She wondered what he would've looked like now if he'd lived, if he would've enjoyed coming to the carnival as much as her. He would've turned fifteen a few weeks ago.*

*A twig snapped behind her, and before Cricket could glance over her shoulder, hands wrapped around her throat, fingers squeezing like a steel trap. She writhed as she fought to escape the stranger's clutches, but the person's grip didn't slacken. They finally spun her to face them and shoved her against the nearest tree. Her gaze met two brown eyes and a young man's face she recognized. She'd gone to school with him, but they never once talked to one another. His name was Clancy.*

Why, *she mouthed as her breath was cut off, her muscles weakening. Cricket's knees buckled, and Clancy lowered her to the ground, almost delicately, like a doll made from straw.*

"I just want to see what it's like to murder someone. You could've been anyone," *he cooed, his eyes sparking with madness and glee.*

*Cricket mumbled a curse, her limbs like jelly. She felt the press of a cool steel blade between her clavicles, and she jerked upward as the knife pierced her flesh, then ripped down to her navel. Pain*

12

*coursed through her, shattering her entire being.*

*As she peered up toward the sky, at the dark clouds, drops of rain hit her eyes. Then two shadows appeared, onyx dahlias, coming down from Clancy's black-gloved hands. Two more pressed into her palms, then one tucked inside her mouth. She didn't have the strength to spit it out while she lay broken and dying.*

*Cricket jolted and a rack of coughs barreled through her as if she hadn't breathed in days. She drank in the cool air, finally able to peel her eyes open to the night sky above her, its stars twinkling like diamonds.*

*"Oh my! You're awake!" a young woman gasped, her tight red curls spilling down to her waist. Cricket squinted, unsure if she was imagining this performer from the carnival. One she'd seen over the years. Juniper. "Mistress Eliza," she shouted. "Cricket's awake!"*

*How did she know her name? Cricket's limbs were heavy and she couldn't gather the energy to push herself up.*

*"I was just about to have Zephyr carry you to bed," Juniper said with a warm smile.*

*Zephyr? To bed? What in all the stars above was happening here? Her head swam, dizzy as she attempted to recall where she'd been before this. Had she been drinking at the pub with Anika?*

*"The Sleeping Darling's awake? It's about damn time," a deep voice drawled, then a face with a strong jaw and chiseled cheeks stood above her, holding a lantern. Zephyr... This close, he was just as enchanting as he was on the stage. The kohl lining his eyes, the dark collar circling his throat, his chest bare.* Bram, *she thought.* Focus on him. *To look and not touch was perfectly acceptable—she would swear that to the grave.*

*A small crowd gathered near her, and another woman broke through it, limping toward her. Cricket's pulse accelerated as she attempted to push herself up, to get away from this strange situation. Half of the woman's face was covered in shadow, and the other half was lit by the orange glow of a lantern, exposing deep lines around her brown eyes and wide mouth.*

*"Give her a moment," Zephyr said as he spoke to the small crowd, his voice calm. "Go to your caravans for now. She needs space." The crowd backed away when Juniper pressed a hand to Cricket's back and helped her sit up. She was in a wooden box with only a black velvet pillow and blanket. Dark hair swung forward and she tugged on the locks, drawing off a wig. She frowned at it and her heart pounded faster. What had they done to her?*

*"I'm Mistress Eliza. It's all right," the woman said.*

*As if someone shook her to recollect her memories, they returned to Cricket in a rush. Her walking home, being attacked by Clancy … his strong hands strangling her, the blade slicing through her chest, the dahlias drifting down over her eyes as she lay dying. But no pain lingered, and if anything, she should be dead. "Why am I at the carnival? Why am I in a box and wearing a wig?" Cricket asked, her voice shaky.*

*"We have much to discuss," Mistress Eliza answered softly. "You've missed out on quite a few things since I saved you." As the lantern caught more of her face, she found the woman to be perhaps the age that Cricket's grandparents would've been if they were still alive. Two graying plaits hung past her shoulders, and a violet cloak hugged her curvy form. She pointed to the two performers as Cricket shivered. "This is Zephyr and Juniper. They work here at my carnival. I'm a necromancer."*

*Cricket swallowed the lump in her throat, knowing precisely what direction this was now taking. "You're the one who gives the performers a home after bringing them back from the dead. It's not a story, but real, and that means..."*

She had died, truly died. Yet her heart beat beneath her rib cage and pounded in her ears as if it had never once stopped at all.

Mistress Eliza nodded, her expression grim. "My necromancy called to you a little over a year ago after your death. We found your body near the woods, but it didn't go as planned when I attempted to revive you. You didn't rouse right away, and I thought you wouldn't, yet days later, after you were buried, I felt your pulse thrum to life. Even when we dug your body from the earth, you didn't awaken. You have been in a deep slumber, and I wasn't sure if you would ever wake, so for the time being, you've been here at my carnival as the Sleeping Darling."

"A year? I was dead and then slept for a year?" Cricket gasped, holding up her hand, inspecting it. She was no longer donning a simple blue dress, but a silky crimson gown with lacy sleeves. A gown fit for a fancy ball. "And you had me placed inside this box as a spectacle? As a doll? For people to see and mock?"

Zephyr clucked his tongue. "I told you she wouldn't be pleased about that once she woke."

"What else did you expect me to do?" Mistress Eliza spat at him. "If you stay here, you have to perform. You know the rules."

Cricket couldn't focus on the fact that she'd been dressed and undressed like a doll for an entire year while asleep, only on how she'd been murdered and that so much time had passed. She needed to find Bram, Anika, and her parents, tell them how Clancy had murdered her, if they hadn't discovered what he'd done already.

She clasped the edge of the box to shove herself out and stumbled forward on wobbly legs. Zephyr caught her around the waist just before she fell to the grass.

"I need to go home," she whispered.

"Wake up now!" Mistress Eliza snapped, shaking Cricket by the shoulders.

As she opened her eyes, darkness surrounded her still.

"Chew the rose petal," the necromancer instructed. "It will keep your curiosity from rising for a little while." The petals... Mistress Eliza had given her some several weeks ago, and she'd carelessly forgotten all about them since her curiosity had never come. But she also hadn't expected *this* to happen.

A hint of floral swarmed Cricket's mouth, and she moved her jaw, chewing the dried rose petal, letting it relax her, calm her. Her muscles were heavy, her skin tight when a tugging sensation pulsed beneath her flesh, returning the devilish dahlia blooms to somewhere beneath her skin, deep into her bloodstream. She wished she could yank them free, then watch them burn to ash.

Pipe smoke filled the air as Cricket's eyes cleared, and she wasn't certain where she was at first, but it must've been inside Mistress Eliza's caravan. The small area was cluttered with fabrics, spools of threads, herbs, crystals, and a table covered in jars and cups. A velvet purple curtain split the room into what she could only assume held her bedroom behind it.

"You're lucky Zephyr brought you to me in time," Mistress Eliza said, a hint of annoyance in her voice. "You know good and well I wouldn't have been able to bring you back a second time, not with my necromancy unable to work properly. I've told you to carry the rose petals on you in case your curiosity got out of hand the first time. I brought you back for a purpose."

"Oh yes, to be a spectacle in your carnival, just as I was before I awoke. I know," Cricket rasped, her chest heaving, sweat slicking her pale skin.

"Ungrateful child." The necromancer sighed, brushing a lock of wet hair behind Cricket's ear. "Would you have rather stayed beneath the ground?"

Cricket wasn't ungrateful, nor was she a child. Mistress Eliza and the performers could've unburied her, then taken her home instead of using her. But she understood the reasoning a minuscule amount—because what if Cricket had never woken? Would she have truly wanted Bram and Anika to spend their lives waiting for her to? Her parents? A selfish part of her did … then maybe they wouldn't have moved on.

Her chest tightened as she thought about what she'd discovered a month ago. Bram had married Anika, her parents had packed up then left the city without a trace, and Clancy had been caught and hanged. And so Cricket had chosen to return to Mistress Eliza's Carnival, the only place left for her. A place she'd dreamt of performing in. A dream she wished with all her heart had never come true, not when her curiosity was blooming wicked reminders.

"Why did the black dahlias blossom? You told me they would be red *roses*," Cricket hissed.

"You somehow did it to yourself, twisted your curiosity. You have to move on from your past." Mistress Eliza pressed a comforting hand to Cricket's shoulder. "Tomorrow, you will practice more, *focus*. You need to be trying here."

"You don't think I've been *trying*?" Cricket bit back,

incredulous. "I have. Every day. Nothing happened until these little bastards decided to consume me with their vicious garden tonight." The only part that had gone right was when her skin became translucent, and her skeleton was visible.

"I give you shelter and food. You need to try harder."

"Why not just send me back to the pits from which I came?"

The necromancer narrowed her eyes, sharp as blades, at her. "You're testing my patience, child."

When Cricket died, she couldn't recall if her soul had gone anywhere before Mistress Eliza brought her back. Had she remained tucked in her body until her pulse restarted, or had she been in an afterlife? Perhaps she'd been a spirit cloaked in eternal coldness, hovering in the woods in Nobel, not remembering who or what she was. She shivered at the thought. Mistress Eliza was demanding, yes, wanted her way, most certainly, but she was giving and fair to her performers.

Cricket blew out a heavy breath. "I'm sorry. It's just quite a lot of things to get adjusted to."

Mistress Eliza patted Cricket's back and nodded, then clasped an oval, silver locket around her neck. "Should you need one, this holds a few petals so you don't forget them. Now, go help Zephyr pack up the carnival. I made him wait outside. You're lucky I allowed you in here."

Zephyr was still outside? Waiting for her? "Thank you, and I will."

"As you know, tomorrow we're traveling to Nobel. Will you be able to pull yourself together?" Mistress Eliza studied her with a pinned gaze.

Cricket did know. Going back to Nobel was

something she'd hoped would never come to fruition. She didn't think she could face Bram and Anika after their last encounter a month ago. Just because her heart wasn't as broken as it should've been about them moving on together, it didn't mean she wanted to be reminded of what could've been.

As she stood, her strength returning, Cricket bit the inside of her cheek. "What if the dahlias come again?"

"Don't allow them to," Mistress Eliza said simply.

Perhaps it was the one time. *Please let it be*. She would rather fall back into a deep sleep than see them again.

"Drink plenty of water," the necromancer added, limping to the table and grabbing a canteen for her.

"Yes, to feed the roses," Cricket mumbled. She grabbed the canteen and drank the liquid until her throat was no longer dry.

"Let's hope so."

Cricket left Mistress Eliza's home and stepped out into the cool night. A shadow leaning against the caravan caught her attention just before Zephyr pushed into the silvery light casting down from the moon.

"Glad to see you're awake and not running away anymore," he drawled.

Her gaze lifted to his, locking on his bright hazel eyes. "You didn't have to bring me to her. I know I looked like a monster." She remembered the image of herself reflecting back at her from the mirror before she ventured into darkness.

Zephyr ran a hand over his dark hair, the wind tousling the ends of a few loose strands that had broken free of his leather tie. He stepped toward her, leaning in close as if he was going to tell her a deep secret while he whispered, "You know, if you let some of us in, you might make a friend."

She frowned and drew back from him. "I was never that great at making friends before. I only had one that was close." Anika.

"And I take it you saw them when you went to Nobel last?"

"I did. After the initial fear of her believing I was a ghost, she was happy to see me." So incredibly happy— it was Cricket who wasn't. She hadn't wanted to stay and have Anika worry that Cricket would try to reclaim Bram, even though she'd wanted to. No one in the carnival knew the man who'd been courting her had married her closest friend. No one knew she'd been courted by anyone, and she preferred her past staying where it was. They knew about Clancy's hanging, though. The bastard.

Zephyr bit his lip, glancing up toward the flickering stars. Around them, the performers were packing up to travel to Nobel the following morning. In the distance, customers' laughter dwindled as they trickled out. Once they were all gone, the tents would be taken down and packed away for the journey.

A moan filled the air from outside a nearby caravan, startling Cricket. She turned to find two women groping each other, one with light brown hair, the second dark auburn. Stormy and Louise.

"Get to work!" Zephyr called with a grin.

"Fuck off," Stormy shouted, her lips pulling into a smile when her gaze landed on Cricket. "You look to be luring someone to your bed right now. Who is it?" She craned her neck to see. "The Sleeping Darling? It's about time she gets some pleasure!"

Heat rushed into Cricket's cheeks, and in that moment, she would rather be a pile of weeds inside her caravan.

"Mmm, if only." Zephyr chuckled and winked at Cricket when she scowled. "By the way, you did well tonight. Your curiosity finally came."

"Did well?" she asked, incredulous as they started walking. "I was almost consumed by dahlias that should've never come at all."

"But one was a red rose," he said seriously. "Not all dahlias."

Cricket's brows lifted, hope igniting in her chest. "Truly?"

"A small one, hidden beneath the others, but I saw it, only for a second before it tucked itself back into your chest."

She blinked and prayed that maybe, just maybe, the dahlias were a fluke, that if she could hone in on her curiosity again, the red roses would answer her call.

A few moments later, they stopped in front of a black and white striped tent and kept quiet as they folded up the curtains from inside. Or mostly quiet since Zephyr whistled a song she hadn't heard since childhood, one that reminded her of her mother when she used to hum it to Cricket and her brother. They helped several of the strong men, who'd inherited strength as their curiosity, stack the poles so they could easily load them.

Cricket opened her mouth to ask Zephyr what she needed to assist with next when Autumn rushed up to them, her dark hair like silk as it swished around her.

"I've been looking all over for you, Zephyr." Autumn dipped her fingers into the waist of his trousers, pulling him toward her. "You haven't been to my caravan in a while. How about you ride with me on the way to Nobel?"

Zephyr gently removed Autumn's hand, then leaned forward and whispered something in her ear, making her giggle. Cricket rolled her eyes, not wanting to listen to whatever their conversation would entail, so she slipped away and weaved between the caravans.

A female cursed softly as a wicker basket collided with the ground, the trinkets spilling across the grass. Cricket spotted bright red curls and hurried to help Juniper scoop the trinkets back into the basket.

"Do you need help with anything else?" Cricket asked as she handed Juniper a brass candlestick holder.

Juniper's lips parted, her emerald eyes widening in surprise. "You're wanting to know if I need help?"

"Yes…" Was that such a difficult thing to assume Cricket would ask? She supposed she had been distant from everyone at the carnival, even though she had always yearned to be a part of it. Instead, she'd spent most of her free time hidden in her caravan, begging her curiosity to unleash. Although her prayer tonight had been answered in a way she hoped would never occur again.

What she knew about Juniper was that she was quiet, sweet, and lingered around Zephyr more often than not. It was quite obvious that Juniper was in love with him while Zephyr flirted with anyone with breasts.

"Then I'll take all the help I can get." Juniper smiled. She tilted her head to the side and peered around at the ground. "Hmm, I suppose we finished, though." Before Cricket could turn to walk away, Juniper grabbed her by the arm. "Wait, why don't you come in for a little while? I saw what happened to you earlier, and I can pour you some of my delicious tea."

Cricket didn't want to see the hopeful expression leave Juniper's face, and to be quite frank, she didn't want to go home and think of how dahlias had bloomed from her flesh tonight. How they were the same type of flower that had been on her dead body... "I suppose I can."

# 3

Juniper took a decorative metal art piece of a stag with six legs from the wall and placed it into a box in the corner of her room.

"I like this one," Cricket said, scooping up a different metal piece with a conjoined butterfly. Purple and black spots painted their ivory bodies.

"I make them in my spare time. Just a simple pastime." Juniper shrugged, dismissing her creations as nothing special, but Cricket was always attracted to any form of art and could tell these had taken time.

"Well, it's beautiful. All of them are." Cricket smiled and rested the conjoined butterfly neatly into the box. As for her belongings, she didn't need to worry about putting anything away for the short journey to Nobel since she'd never hung anything on her walls. They'd been in Sorel since before Cricket had woken, one of the carnival's longest visits. Other times their stays might only be a week—Mistress Eliza had told her—depending on the crowds.

"You can have a seat," Juniper said, plonking down on a knitted quilt, then patting the spot beside her. Cricket hesitated before sitting on the lumpy mattress and leaning against the wall. The room was cozy with a pink and black color pattern, one of the walls checkered in the same hues. The sweet aromas of sugar and pastries lingered, both pleasant and comforting, reminding her of when her mother used to bake pies.

Juniper hopped from the bed and grabbed a porcelain pot from her vanity. "I forgot the tea. It might not be as hot now, but it will do." She poured them both a cup, then carefully sat back on the mattress and handed Cricket one. Cricket took a slow sip, letting the lovely liquid glide down her throat while savoring the flavors of honey and chamomile.

"It's good," Cricket said, tipping the cup back once more.

Juniper polished off her tea before grabbing a leather bag from the floor and setting it between them. "Hungry?" she asked as she drew out a cloth napkin containing a few pieces of dried meat, cookies, and sugary pastries.

"Famished," Cricket said, inhaling the mixture of delicious scents. Until then, Cricket hadn't realized how much energy the spell with her curiosity had truly taken from her. Her stomach growled as she peered at the pastries. "Where did you get those?"

"They were gifts that some of the visitors left tonight. They've already been inspected. No poison." Juniper grinned, handing her two pastries with grape jam in their centers.

"Oh? You're lucky. I would dance all day for pastries if I could." Cricket bit into the first one, tasting cinnamon mingled with the grape.

"When you perform, you'll get plenty. Flowers aren't as lovely as sweets, but they are wonderful too."

*Flowers...* Cricket didn't want to think of a single flower at the moment, and she was relieved Juniper didn't have any in her caravan. She studied Juniper, her soft and delicate features—she couldn't be more than nineteen. The age Cricket had been when she'd died. She missed an entire birthday, not that it should matter. But it mattered to her.

Cricket wanted to think about something else, anything else. "I doubt you noticed me with such big audiences, but I used to come to the carnival every year and watch you perform. How long have you been here?"

Juniper's brow furrowed, seeming to mull over her answer. "Ten years now. Zephyr and I came to the carnival together. He was twelve, and I was nine."

She'd come with Zephyr? That meant they'd died around the same time... Had possibly been friends before... Cricket then thought about Autumn, her fingers slipping into the waistband of Zephyr's trousers. Maybe right now, he'd even taken her somewhere more private... "I think you deserve someone who will love you the same. From what I've seen of Zephyr, he's..."

Juniper wrinkled her nose, studying her in confusion. "*What?*"

"You and Zephyr. He's always flirting with other women and—"

"One moment." Juniper held up a hand, a snort escaping her. "You think I'm in love with *Zephyr*?"

"Aren't you?" By the way Juniper was now staring at her with wide eyes and only blinking, perhaps she'd been wrong.

Juniper slapped the mattress, and hysterical laughter poured out from her mouth. "Zephyr and I are *not*, nor will we ever be, lovers. I think I may lose my stomach now for even thinking about something so atrocious."

"I…" Cricket's cheeks flamed as they always tended to do when she grew uncomfortable. "Forgive me. My mistake."

"I know we don't look much alike—or at all—but he's my brother."

Cricket winced. *Brother…* She'd misread things by a lot, and Juniper was right—they didn't look alike in the slightest. But now she could see how their affection for one another would seem more akin to siblings. How Zephyr would playfully tug Juniper's hair in the way a brother would with a younger sister, and the way Juniper would gently shove him at his teasing. "Ignore my foolishness. I'm sorry." If Anika was here, Cricket wouldn't have felt as embarrassed, but she wasn't—she was in Nobel with Bram.

"No, no." Juniper laughed again. "It's all right. Although, it's something we will never speak of again. I mean, I've never even had a lover. She wouldn't—" Her lips snapped shut, stopping herself from continuing.

"You fancy someone else here?" Cricket grinned, her curiosity piqued. "Who is *she*?"

Juniper stared up at the ceiling as if she wasn't going to answer her, but then she released a long sigh. "Don't tell anyone. But Stormy. Not even Zephyr knows."

Stormy, the acrobat who could make iridescent scales appear across her body. Who did happen to have a lover. She'd seen her and Louise's earlier dalliance when Cricket had been with Zephyr.

"It's—"

A knock came at the door, interrupting Cricket. Juniper set down her pastry and hopped from the bed to answer it.

"Look what I found," a familiar male voice said.

Cricket wished there was another door to sneak out of as Zephyr stepped inside and handed Juniper a silver brooch. He halted when his gaze met Cricket's, staring at her as if he didn't believe she was truly there. "I wondered where you snuck off to. You listened to my advice after all." A smirk formed on his face, and Cricket wanted to slap the cockiness away, even though her heart beat a tad bit faster as she studied his taut muscles.

"We're having a lovely chat here, so how about we talk later?" Juniper grabbed her brother by the shoulder, leading him out of the caravan as he chuckled. After shutting the door, she turned back to Cricket, then placed her hands on her hips. "Sorry about him. He can be a nuisance."

"He most certainly can be." Cricket found herself softly laughing, then sobered as she wondered about something else. "Can I ask you a question?"

"Of course."

"Did you ever have trouble with your curiosity when Mistress Eliza brought you back from the dead?"

"This?" Juniper held up a hand and flexed it. Beads of deep crimson seeped from her pores like glistening ruby pearls. The blood trailed down her flesh briefly before she tightened her fist, reining the crimson droplets back in. So easily. So effortlessly. "I don't think anyone here would want my ability, though." Juniper sighed.

"I rather like it," Cricket said in awe. She hated to admit it, but she was envious that she couldn't manipulate her curiosity the same way. The dahlias that had sprouted unwillingly only reminded her of death. Blood could feel like death, but it was also life, what one needed to thrive.

Juniper smiled. "It took me longer than everyone here to master mine. Perhaps a week."

"It's been a whole month for me, and today was the closest I've been. Even then, it was tragic." But there was something hopeful that Zephyr had told her, how he'd seen a red rose peek out for a moment before vanishing.

"Someone always screams during my performances and believes I'm truly bleeding to death." Juniper cackled. "I shouldn't laugh, but I do now. At first, I didn't—I'd wished that any other curiosity here was mine, but it's grown on me. Especially when I'm given the pastries. Yours will eventually come the way it was meant to. When you were asleep, everyone thought you to be an enchanted princess and wanted to kiss you awake."

"Please tell me no one did." Cricket recoiled. The thought of crowds staring at her, wanting her to wake with a stranger's kiss, made her stomach churn. She was grateful that no visitors knew she was the Sleeping Darling once she woke. Everyone believed the mysterious woman had awoken and left the carnival. After a few weeks, they finally stopped asking about her.

"No, the performers protected you. Zephyr punched one man who said he could pleasure you awake. He'd

29

asked me if he should use his tongue or his length on you to do it."

Cricket scowled as blood boiled in her veins. "I would've kicked him between the legs if I'd heard his disgusting words." The performers hadn't known her, yet they'd protected her, and since being awake, she had avoided everyone like a deadly plague instead of getting to know them. "If I may ask, how did you and Zephyr come to the carnival together?" The answer would be grim—that was for certain. Everyone's story was, even if she had yet to learn how death had come for them.

"No, no, it's fine." Juniper waved a hand in the air, then took a deep breath. "We were traveling with our parents to our aunt's manor when our carriage was attacked by thieves. Papa fought back, and that only made the situation worse. The leader and his band of men killed the four of us. Mistress Eliza felt something that day, and after reviving me, it was still there in Zephyr, and she was able to rouse him too. It's a rarity to raise two as she did, but she saved us both even though I hadn't wanted it at first. Her necromancer ability doesn't call to just anyone, or she would've raised my parents. Even though I begged her to do it, she wouldn't, and I accepted her reasoning long ago."

The mere thought of someone murdering children sickened Cricket, and she couldn't imagine how someone became so vile. Why couldn't the thieves have just taken the stolen goods and fled? "I hope all the bastards are dead."

"All five of them were found and hanged, thankfully. After all these years, it isn't enough—my parents are still dead." She paused, staring at the window as if attempting to see the sky above. "I had a home then, but this is my home now. This is your home, too, if you allow it to be."

Home… The home she once had with her parents was no longer theirs, and the carnival could potentially be that… But not if she couldn't hone in on her curiosity. "I think I better take rest in my caravan since we'll be leaving soon."

"Stop by any time. And take another with you." Juniper smiled and placed a sugary pastry in Cricket's palm.

As Cricket ventured into the night, she walked between caravans, passing several strong men and performers preparing for travel. She thought about Nobel, unsure if she could face her old city again. A murder of crows cawed above her, and she glanced up at their shadowy forms beneath the crescent moon before stepping into her caravan. Everything was ready for the journey—the bed and vanity bolted to the floor, her few sacks nestled into the corner of her room. In the morning, the strong men would bring the horses to the caravans and drive them to Nobel.

Slipping off her leather boots and changing into a long white nightgown, Cricket fell back on the mattress and studied the ceiling, the chipped gray paint. She rolled on her side, wondering what she would do if she couldn't get her curiosity to work properly and was banished from the carnival. If that happened, she supposed she would just drift from place to place until she died of old age or the dahlias chose to come back and consume her.

Cricket took one of the horses to Bram's manor, courtesy of Mistress Eliza. After visiting Nobel, she promised she would return it, that she would come back and work at the carnival, yet it had been a lie. She just needed to get to Bram—she'd been in hibernation for over a year. He believed her to be dead, not knowing she'd been dug up from her grave to be a spectacle.

The manor was the same as always, with a beautiful and lush green garden. Cricket drew the horse to a halt, then carefully slid from its back. She knocked on the door with a shaky hand, and when no one answered, she tried again. A familiar face greeted her, one of the servants, Nettie, most of her gray hair hidden beneath a cap.

"Miss Cricket?" she asked, her voice trembling.

The click of shoes against wood sounded, and the door opened wider. Nettie slipped away as Anika stood in the servant's place, her dark hair in a bun at the nape of her neck. Her deep brown eyes widened in surprise. "Cricket?" she gasped. "You died. A ghost. You're a ghost."

Cricket threw her arms around her friend. "I'm not a ghost, Anika. I'm warm. See? But yes, I was dead after that bastard Clancy murdered me. I would've come sooner if I hadn't been in a deep slumber for the past year. The carnival necromancer saved my life when she resurrected me." Releasing her friend, she took a step back.

A set of heavy boots echoed through the hallway, and Bram entered the room, appearing almost the same except for a golden chain from a watch hanging out of his pocket. His clothing was still neat, his hair swept back, and he wasn't looking at her but at Anika. "Your tea's ready," he said with a smile.

Anika bit her lip and shifted to the side, her hands trembling. "Can you grab another? We have a guest."

*As Bram's gaze met Cricket's, the cup fell from his grasp, shattering to the floor, tea slicking the wood. Cricket noticed something else different about him, a golden ring on his left finger. Heart pounding, her eyes drifted to Anika's hand, finding a gold piece with a diamond in the center hugging hers.*

*Realization struck Cricket, and she couldn't breathe, her lungs frozen. "You're married?" she whispered, stumbling backward.*

*Bram caught her by the shoulders before she could run, run back to the grave where she should've been left in peace.*

*"We'll figure this out," he said, his voice soft. "Don't leave. Just talk to me."*

Cricket bolted up in bed, her chest heaving as the caravan jostled. The strong men must've already tacked the horses to the caravans and started their descent for Nobel.

Her throat was dry, and she couldn't stop thinking about her last visit to the city. Bram had confessed that he'd fallen in love with Anika through grief as they'd both worked together to find the man who'd slaughtered her. It was something Cricket couldn't fault either of them for, even though she'd been dejected.

She'd learned that after she died, her parents abandoned Nobel, unable to deal with another of their children's deaths. Bram had hoped wherever they were, they'd heard that the murderer had been found and hanged for his crime, yet if they did, they never returned.

After promising to come back and see Bram and Anika, Cricket had gone into town to visit a few establishments alone, to think, but then she didn't keep true to her word—she'd chosen to go to the carnival instead. The lie hadn't been to Mistress Eliza after all but to Bram and Anika.

The caravan drew to a stop, and Cricket's pulse sped—she couldn't go home, no matter how much she thought she could. She peered out the door and, just ahead, she found a wheel on one of the caravans was broken. Not bothering to get properly dressed or put on her boots, she pushed open the door and fled. Her bare feet protested as rocks and twigs scraped along her skin, but she ignored the pain.

As she realized she didn't know where she was running to or what she would do when she reached an unknown wilderness, Cricket collapsed to her knees and sobbed into her hands. She'd given up on her dream of performing in the past, and she couldn't let herself repeat the same mistake when given a second chance. The only way forward for her was to go back. So she picked herself up, swiped the dirt from her nightgown, and returned to the carnival.

4

As Cricket drew closer to her caravan, several performers lingered in the open, waiting for the carnival to continue their journey while the damaged wagon wheel was being replaced. Stormy and Louise bickered about something, their words too low for Cricket to hear, but their scowling expressions were more than telling that they were annoyed with one another.

Mistress Eliza stood near Cricket's caravan, her back turned, barking orders to two of the strong men. The beads of the necromancer's bracelets clanked together on her arms as she motioned at them to hurry. Cricket silently approached, hoping to sneak back into her caravan without being noticed. But Mistress Eliza glanced over her shoulder, her brow arched as she met Cricket's gaze.

"I suppose you decided to return, did you? Two of the

performers caught you running away," Mistress Eliza huffed, placing her hands on her hips while turning from the two men and limping toward her. "How was your temporary leave?"

Cricket held her head high and inched toward the woman, sarcasm lacing her tone as she spoke, "It was fine. I got a good look at the lovely scenery, but I'm back. I didn't like it as much as I thought."

"Will you be running off again?" Mistress Eliza cooed. "Or will you be focusing on honing your curiosity? The carnival doesn't need fickle people who aren't dedicated."

Cricket didn't fault Mistress Eliza for her reprimand. If she were in charge of a carnival, she would want performers who put their entire hearts into their craft and not give up when they believed they couldn't handle a situation.

"That even includes ones with *wondrous* potential," Mistress Eliza added, her lips tilting up at the edges.

Cricket blinked. Wondrous? The necromancer believed she had that sort of potential? Even though part of her still wanted to flee, she knew wherever she went, her curiosity would be attached to her regardless. And so she needed to try harder, do it for herself. "I'm here to focus."

Mistress Eliza gave a curt nod. "Good. Let's keep it that way."

"Do you think you'll be able to use your necromancy again?" She couldn't imagine how difficult it must be to have had such an ability and lose it.

Mistress Eliza blew out a breath. "Perhaps. Perhaps not. I haven't even been able to raise a single animal, which used to be a simple task. As a child, I was told to raise the loved ones of the wealthy, but as I gained independence, I did things my way. I only bring back those I see in my visions, those who call to me. However, over the past year, after Ingrid died, there have been no calls when there should've been. Now, even when I can feel the life waiting to be reawakened within the dead, my efforts are useless. Unfortunate decisions will have to be made to keep this carnival going. It's infuriating, yet for now, we'll make do."

Ingrid had been the carnival's longest performer who'd passed away while Cricket was dormant as the Sleeping Darling, but several others were also aging, tiring more easily.

Mistress Eliza met Cricket's gaze, and for the first time, pity shone on the woman's face. "There's something else."

"What is it?"

"Something harrowing has been happening in Nobel, and I hope you don't run away again once you hear it."

Cricket faced death itself before, so she promised herself she would face whatever came her way. "If it's a sickness spreading, I'm not worried about that." Yet she couldn't help but think about her little brother's death from the plague. How boils had covered his frail body, his lungs barely pumping.

Mistress Eliza sighed, shaking her head. "No, nothing of that sort. But a little after you left my home last night, Stormy informed me how she'd overheard a group of visitors discussing a recent murder that happened in Nobel. Not only one but three similar cases in the past couple of weeks."

Cricket furrowed her brow. "There's always a murder

here and there in the busier part of the city, more so on the poorer side." Before she could think about Clancy's gloved hands squeezing her throat, she shoved that damning day back into the depths of her mind.

"Unfortunately, that's true." Mistress Eliza tapped her chin and looked behind her at the performers milling about. She met her eyes once more, then whispered, "But not murders like yours."

Cricket froze, taking a deep swallow as her heart struck against her sternum. "What do you mean?"

"Three women have been found dead. All left decorated with black dahlias." Mistress Eliza held Cricket's gaze, the necromancer's grip firm on her shoulder, as the world went cold.

Cricket held back a gasp and dug her nails into her palms. "Clancy's dead. He was hung."

"Is he?" Mistress Eliza asked. "You were dead once. What if another necromancer came out of hiding?"

Her words were like a knife to the heart. Had someone brought Clancy back to life? Or was it someone else imitating him? But why would they do that? "I don't understand. It seems awfully strange. In this case, I'm certain that someone in Nobel would've dug up Clancy's grave to see if his body was still buried." Unless another body was placed down there to appear like it was his… No, it had to be someone else.

"I'm sorry, child. I should've told you before we left, but you were already frightened of the dahlias your curiosity brought forth. If this changes your mind about continuing, I need to know now. I understand if it would."

Three murders with dahlias left in their wake. It most

likely was someone imitating what Clancy had done, but why? If it had been within the past couple of weeks, it had started sometime after she'd been to Nobel. Word had to have spread that she was alive after she'd visited a pub and a couple of shops where she'd been recognized. Bram would've also told the other authorities since he'd joined law enforcement as soon as he was old enough. But why would that make someone want to start imitating murders? It didn't make sense, and she believed Bram would have the situation handled as he had when uncovering that Clancy murdered her. She wouldn't hide from her problems again. It would be cowardly for her to run and just as cowardly for her not to find out more. "I'm staying."

"I'll take your word for it then. And I'll send Wilder to the authorities once we arrive to find out if Clancy's grave has been checked." Mistress Eliza patted her arm, the most comforting she'd ever been toward her, before leaving her alone.

Cricket leaned against the caravan and stared up at the gray sky, the bloated clouds, just as they'd appeared when she'd been walking home the day she was murdered. She thought about the dahlias from the night before, the scratching, but she couldn't feel her curiosity inside her now.

A tall shadow slipped around her caravan, and her gaze fell on Zephyr. He didn't say a word as he rested beside her against the caravan, a hint of his woodsy scent brushing her nose. He wore a white shirt with several buttons unfastened and a black vest over it. The usual dark collar hugged his neck.

As she studied his sculpted face, she was glad for the

distraction from what Mistress Eliza had told her. But then her mind turned into another dark direction— Juniper and Zephyr being murdered as children, how they'd come to the carnival together. A bright side to the darkness was that they'd at least had one another.

"You look like you could use something," Zephyr said, pressing his head to the caravan as he peered at her.

She rolled her eyes. "I'm keeping my clothing on, thank you very much."

"Now that's a damn shame. A nightgown is easy to remove," he purred.

"Zephyr." She glared but couldn't control the corners of her lips from curling up a fraction or wondering what it would feel like to have his hands slide up her body while peeling away the one layer. *No*, she scolded herself.

"I was only teasing. *Maybe.*" He nudged her with his shoulder and drew out a silver flask from his trouser pocket. "I meant this. Here."

Cricket stared at the flask momentarily, then took it from him, needing whatever was in it. She didn't care as she tossed the liquid back, perhaps a bit too much, and a rack of coughs barreled through her.

"Easy now." Zephyr chuckled, reaching for the flask and taking a long sip.

She laughed once she stopped coughing. "You could've warned me it was strong."

"I didn't know you planned to suck it almost dry in one swig. It's a special liquor I make." He grinned, taking another sip before handing it back to her.

"I might die tomorrow then," Cricket teased and drank another swig—this time, the liquid went down smoothly. She hated to admit it, but the liquor was one of the best she'd had, and the anxious feeling that had pulsed in her veins was now soothed for the time being. Her gaze lifted to his collar, and she boldly brushed a finger against the leather, not knowing if it was the liquor making her do something so foolish. "Why do you always wear this?"

"Nosey little thing today, aren't you?" He bit his lip and smiled. "If you're wondering if my head falls off when I remove it, I promise it doesn't."

"Now, *that* would be a terrifying sight," she said, amused.

"Wilder does it every performance, so nothing special." Zephyr chuckled, his hazel irises dancing playfully. "Anyway, did you hear the news from Mistress Eliza? I suppose that's why you were in such a *lovely* mood."

Cricket's stomach sank, and she slowly nodded. "I suppose it's hard not to be. She told me about the murders."

He arched a brow. "What murders?"

"Oh, the news must've not made it your way yet. There have been three recent murders in Nobel, and the victims were all left with dahlias. Like I was." Her voice remained steady, yet inside, she was anything but.

"Didn't they hang that bastard?"

She blew out a breath. "They did. I don't know what's happening." If it was Clancy who had risen from the dead, she would make sure to send him back to that state. Anger pulsed in her veins, and she needed to concentrate on something else for now. "So what's the news then?"

Zephyr smiled wide. A smile that she hated to admit lit up his handsome face. "Mistress Eliza said you're to practice a routine with me, regardless if you can get your

41

curiosity to come out and play."

Cricket's heart hammered in her chest, her eyes like saucers. "You're jesting."

"Afraid not." His smile somehow grew even more as if he took pleasure in seeing her bewildered. "Meet me when we arrive in Nobel and be prepared to practice. I'm not going easy on you." With that, he sauntered away, leaving her scowling at his back.

Cricket spent the remainder of the journey reading an adventurous story and was nearly to the last page when they arrived. She closed the book and took a brush from the vanity drawer to run through her tangled hair.

Soon the carnival would begin setting up in the same place where it always was—in a field near the cemetery. The cemetery where Cricket was once buried... A shiver crawled up her spine at the thought, and she bit the inside of her cheek until it bled to focus on the pain in her mouth instead of lingering in her mind.

The first performance wasn't for three days, but she and Zephyr still had to practice as much as possible. She knew she could learn the routine—she'd always been blessed at quickly remembering dances she'd created.

A knock came at the door, and she stopped brushing her hair to answer it. As though being summoned by her thoughts, Zephyr stood there, an eyebrow raised. "You were supposed to meet me, *remember?*" he purred.

"We literally just arrived. I still haven't set up my things." Which was practically nothing, and Zephyr knew it too as he peered inside at the lack of boxes.

"Mmm, I believe a ghost has more possessions than you."

"And you would know how? Have you seen a ghost before?"

"Quite possibly." He chuckled, luring her forward with a finger. "Now, follow me."

Cricket grunted but walked beside him as they trekked toward the wooded area. The horses had mostly been untacked and led to the lake to drink. From another caravan, the strong men were unloading the poles for the tents.

She and Zephyr ventured through the brush and passed several bushes blooming red and blue berries. The sparkling lake came into view, the sun reflecting off its rippling surface. A few performers filled up their canteens beside the horses as they drank. Zephyr didn't stop there—he led her farther away to an area with a few boulders and enough space for the two of them to practice.

"Looks like we have this spot to ourselves." Zephyr waggled his brows, taking his large satchel from his body. "I knew you probably wanted to be away from everyone, so I picked this place for us." She shouldn't have been surprised he would know this about her.

Zephyr knelt beside his satchel and fished out five silver juggling rings. He then brought out a couple of cloths and polished them.

"You really like performing?" Cricket asked, crouching beside him and taking a ring and a cloth from the ground to help.

"I do, but it wasn't something I'd dreamt about." He

shrugged. "I didn't know how to juggle before joining the carnival. At first, I would just stand on stage and let the vines snake out. It was pitiful, really."

"Not pitiful at all. Your vines are extraordinary, regardless if you were to stand as still as a statue," she said softly, peering down at her hands as she remembered this was where she'd seen him perform on the day she died. That murders like hers were happening again.

"A compliment from you? I'll take it." He chuckled, and when she didn't glance back up, he lifted her chin so their eyes met. "What is it?"

She swallowed, not having the strength to pull away from his gentle touch. "It's just … we're back in the town where I died."

He let out a breath and nodded slowly as he released her chin to run the fabric across a ring. "I understand. We were just in Sorel. It was where I was murdered. You can talk to me about anything—I won't judge." He returned to polishing his rings, waiting for her to speak.

Juniper had told Cricket about her and Zephyr's deaths, but she hadn't confessed that they'd been in the same city where they were murdered. Perhaps she'd wanted to pretend she wasn't, just as Cricket wished to do so now. "Last night, Juniper told me what happened. To her, to you… I'm so sorry, Zephyr."

Zephyr stopped his meticulous movements with the fabric. "She told you?"

"She did. I hope you're not angry with me for mentioning it." Cricket had never been the best at keeping secrets, only with Anika. There had been so many between each other over the years, and she would continue to hold them even now.

"No, I'm not—just surprised, is all. Juniper doesn't talk about what happened to us to anyone. But again, neither do I."

Even though everyone at the carnival knew about her death, because of her unusual circumstance of not waking right away, she'd never discussed it with any of the performers, only Mistress Eliza on one occasion.

Zephyr's serious expression became playful once more. "Are you ready to get close to me and practice?"

She rolled her eyes. "I suppose… What do you want me to do?"

"Spin for me."

"Simple enough." Cricket pushed up from the ground and brushed the dirt from her trousers before turning in a slow circle. Zephyr cocked his head at her, clearly unimpressed.

"I think you can do better than that pitiful spin." He smirked. "A little birdy told me you were a dancer before."

The only person it could've been was Mistress Eliza, and she wished the woman wouldn't have. "Yes, but that was before..." Cricket thought about the days of practicing in her bedroom, dreaming of joining a stage at the carnival, moving like flowers drifting in a breeze.

Zephyr stood in front of her, his tall frame hovering above her as he placed a hand around her waist and drew her close, his warm breath mingling with hers. "And this is now. Spin, but remember how you felt about dancing then. Bring the passion into your performance."

Cricket blew out a shaky breath, avoiding looking at Zephyr when he stepped away from her, his fingers leaving her waist. She brought one leg back and lifted an arm toward the sky. Then she spun, as he'd asked, pretending as if a piano was playing, the ivory keys being pressed harder, faster, the song chaotic, creating a wonderful frenzy.

Zephyr raised his rings and tossed them high above him, catching one after another. He plucked a leaf from a tree and placed it between his lips. She flicked her gaze away from his pouty lips to twirl. Thick green vines slipped out from his arms, and they grasped his rings, continuing to do what his hands had been.

She paused, arching her back as she stretched. Farther away, shriveled flowers caught her attention—thoughts of death swirled in her mind. Scratching stirred beneath her skin, and clawing broke through her veins. She stilled, unable to move or scream. Zephyr didn't seem to notice as he continued with the rings.

Cricket finally willed herself to move, telling herself the roses would come out when her skin became translucent, the bones peeking through. She spun slowly, building faster, ignoring the perspiration dripping down her neck. Her muscles prickled, the clawing burning, black dots freckling her pale skin. Not a single red spot in their wake. She tripped, falling to the hard ground after two dark dahlias bloomed.

Zephyr's silver rings dropped to the dirt, and he cursed as he came to her side. "Focus on your curiosity. Rein them back in and think of crimson."

The foliage spun around her, even though she was no longer moving on her legs. She remembered the dried rose petals and brushed the locket at her throat, to place one into her mouth.

Cricket's numb fingers fumbled to open it, and her

eyes fluttered. As Zephyr scooped her into his arms, everything turned black.

Like death.

5

Flaming orange lit the backs of Cricket's eyelids as she chewed a dried rose petal. It took a moment for her to open her eyes, the world becoming brighter. The sun shone above, the sky no longer gray.

Cricket took a slow breath, swallowing herb-infused air, her gaze meeting hazel irises.

"There you are," Zephyr whispered, brushing back a wet lock of hair stuck to her forehead.

"Let there not be a third time you frighten us like this." Juniper sighed and squeezed Cricket's hand. Mistress Eliza hunched beside Juniper, her lips set in a tight line as she smoked her pipe.

"I'll try not to," Cricket rasped. "I was attempting to get a rose petal from my locket, but my fingers were too numb and weak to open it. Everything came quicker than last time." She couldn't remember when she passed out, only the dahlias bursting from her.

"I didn't know the petals were in there, so I brought you here," Zephyr said. They were crouched at the foot of Mistress Eliza's caravan steps.

"I was going to have you perform on stage with Zephyr." Mistress Eliza frowned, trailing a hand down her cheek. "I thought it could possibly help your curiosity, but perhaps you're not ready."

The practice wasn't only to provoke her curiosity to come to fruition but to prepare her to *perform*. Even if it was a simple task, such as being a piece to Zephyr's act, it was a start and would be much better than standing behind the stage helping the other acts or cleaning up rubbish. "I can perform with Zephyr."

Mistress Eliza tapped her chin, studying Cricket hard. "I'll give you a chance, but start small. No dancing just yet. He can do a chair act with you and attempt to build up from there. Either way, I still need you to practice getting a hold on your curiosity so it doesn't murder you. Do you understand?"

The thought of dying from suffocation made Cricket brush a hand to her throat where Clancy's firm grip had been. But starting small could get her used to the stage, perhaps even gradually calling on the roses.

"I can do it." Her chest heaved, though her voice was determined.

"If this goes well," Mistress Eliza said, "we can slowly add in more, but if you can't harness your curiosity, then I'm afraid you can't travel with us anywhere else until you do. This carnival is not a charity. Unless you can contribute in an extraordinary fashion, like every one of my other performers, I'll have to let you go, Cricket. With a murderer leaving black dahlias on victims, we can't have you going around showing them, accident or not."

"I'll work harder, Mistress Eliza," Cricket murmured, hating to admit that she understood her reasoning.

"I want you to stay with Juniper for the night. Let her watch over you in case this happens again."

Cricket had mostly been taking care of herself while at the carnival, but after the past two days with the dahlias and hearing about the new murders, she didn't think it would be a good idea to spend the night alone.

"Wilder went into town to find out about Clancy. I'll let you know what he uncovers," Mistress Eliza said, taking another puff of her pipe.

Cricket nodded, and as she attempted to push herself up on wobbly limbs, Zephyr's strong arms came around her waist, helping her to stand. He steadied her when she stumbled, and even though she wished she could walk on her own and not appear like a newborn fawn, she leaned into his chest, letting him guide her away from Mistress Eliza's caravan. A breeze blew past them, the wind becoming chillier.

Zephyr turned to Juniper as his arm firmly held onto Cricket and asked, "Can you collect our bags from the east side of the lake? I'll bring her inside your caravan."

"Of course." Juniper took off toward the woods, her bright red curls bouncing behind her.

"So." Zephyr smiled as they walked toward Juniper's pink and white painted home. "Looks as though you're stuck with me."

She was thankful for his light mood, that he wasn't acting overly protective about what had happened or telling her she needed to practice harder.

"It appears so," she drawled.

Zephyr winked at her as he opened Juniper's door. Cricket left his arms and sat on the edge of the lumpy bed, the sweet smell of Juniper's home comforting. He handed her a canteen of water, and she drank half of it down, then slowed her pace. A few moments later, Juniper stepped inside, her cheeks flushed from the wind. She placed their bags beside the bed and ran a hand through her tangled curls.

"I better help set up before Mistress Eliza comes squawking about." Zephyr smirked. "Do you need me to stay?"

"Go so she doesn't become a grouch. I'll get you if needed." Juniper grasped her brother by the arm and led him out before turning to Cricket with a warm smile. "I'll go make us some tea and leave the door open. You can shout if you need me."

Cricket lay her head against the pillow, her eyelids too heavy to keep open. "I'll be fine," she said. But really, she didn't know if that was true.

Cricket tightened the short black silk skirt over the crimson sleeveless one-piece at her waist. She added red powders to her eyes and a matching shade of gloss to her lips, then accentuated her cheekbones with a stroke of rosy pink on each side. Cricket had stayed with Juniper for one night before returning to her caravan. Wilder hadn't found out anything important besides Clancy's body still being below ground, but did that mean it was his? She thought again about how a rotted corpse could easily be replaced with another. Pushing the thought away, she focused on getting ready, hoping her nervousness would subside. Just as she finished styling her hair into a plaited bun at the nape of her neck, a knock sounded at the door.

Adjusting her skirt once more, she drew open the door to find Zephyr standing there with his lips tilted up to one side. His leather collar stood out against his bare chest, his dark wavy hair brushing his shoulders instead of pulled back. He looked like a devilish delicacy, luring her in as he held out a hand to her. A hand she hated to admit she wanted to let ground her at that moment.

"We go on soon. You look … you don't want to know the words I'd use to describe how you look," Zephyr purred.

Cricket's blasted cheeks heated, and she took his hand, her own shaking as she stepped down the few steps. "I'm nervous." She hadn't planned on telling anyone, but it was quite obvious by how she trembled as they walked.

"Really? I wouldn't have even known," he lied, distracting her from her thoughts, and her lips tilted up a smidge. "If something happens, I know where your rose petals are this time."

"As long as the locket opens, I'll be fine." She was now at ease enough to release his hand when they passed the other caravans to the main area of the carnival. The flags at the tops of the tents cracked against the wind. The tantalizing aromas of roasted meat and sugary pastries drifted around her, making her mouth salivate. Perhaps she would treat herself to a taste of them if she made it through the performance.

Patrons milled about, eating caramel apples, chocolate bananas, and popcorn. A cacophony of metal and bells filled the air as children tried their hands at the many games. A hammer struck a metal piece, followed by a shrill ding when the bell rang. *Winner.* Other guests paraded around in small groups, laughing and chatting while couples held one another close, pointing to their surroundings with their mouths open in awe. No one seemed frightened or worried that three similar murders had occurred in Nobel recently. Most likely because it was no one they were close to.

As she gazed around, Cricket couldn't help but search the faces of the crowd, wondering if any of these people were secretly a killer. But the outer layers of a person weren't where she would find her answer—it was inside them, their thoughts, and she was no mind reader. A few familiar faces caught her eye that she'd seen before in town or back in school, and she turned away, hoping to go unrecognized.

Above the flaming torches, the stars flickered in the sky. For the past couple of days, Cricket had practiced both with Zephyr and alone. Her curiosity hadn't once appeared, nor had it stirred beneath her flesh. She needed it to come and behave so she could remain with the carnival.

They approached the white and purple striped tent in the center of several black and red ones. Zephyr pushed open the thick fabric of the back entrance, then held it up for Cricket to walk through.

Inside, Juniper knelt beside a fruit basket, riffling through it until she lifted a pear and stood. She wore a black leather bodice and a matching skirt flecked in silver beads that exposed her skin well enough so her curiosity could be seen thoroughly. Biting into the fruit, Juniper wiped her other hand across the perspiration dotting her brow.

"I just finished. You're almost up." Juniper smiled. Not a single speck of blood lingered on her freckled skin from her performance.

"Where's the chair?" Zephyr asked as he tilted a board back in the corner.

"Autumn needed to use it, but I told her to leave it there once she's finished." Juniper shrugged.

Cricket glanced behind the velvet curtain at the stage, watching Autumn stand on a wooden chair, lifting one leg behind her until her foot rested atop her head. She then brought her leg back down and stepped inside a small clear box. Blowing a kiss to the audience, she bent backward and peered through the glass at the crowd as piano music played.

Above Autumn, two female acrobats, wearing deep purple tutus and onyx masks, swung across the stage, hanging from the metal rod by their legs. Cullen, an older man with white powder on his face and black diamonds painted over his eyes, pretended as if an imaginary rope was pulling him across the stage before placing the glass lid over Autumn's box. He sat atop it, tapping his chin in playful boredom while Autumn feigned a huff.

The crowd's boisterous laughs echoed in the tent at the act, and Cricket stepped back. She needed the performance to go well for Zephyr—all she needed was for the black dahlias to remain at bay. The rest would be simple. And if everything went well, she wouldn't receive another reprimand from Mistress Eliza.

Even though she'd partially blamed Zephyr for her attendance at the carnival over the years, she would never want to ruin his wondrous performances. Part of her old self was creeping out, the piece that would've been ecstatic to align herself with him in an act.

Zephyr adjusted his collar and took three swords from Juniper.

"No rings tonight?" Cricket asked, her gaze roaming across the shiny jeweled blades.

"Nope." He grinned. "Tomorrow I'll practice the swords around you."

"As long as one doesn't slice me, I won't have to return the favor. And with that favor, I'll choose where precisely," she drawled.

"I like this side of you, *Cricket*." He smirked just as the audience cheered. Her heart lurched at how her name rolled off his tongue, but she became distracted when the performers stepped off the stage.

Autumn sauntered by last, running her palm across Zephyr's abdomen. "Good luck," she said to him, then glanced at Cricket with a smile. "You too."

Cricket's frown left her face, replaced by surprise. Zephyr didn't lose focus as his hand pressed against Cricket's back. "Ready?" he asked when the piano began a new song.

Her stomach coiled tight, but she nodded, letting him lead her onto the stage to the wooden chair resting in the middle, waiting for her. Black lacy fabric hung around them like gossamer, and beds of nails lined the back of the stage. Same as in their practices, Cricket sat while Zephyr stood behind her. Her gaze roamed the silent audience, their expectant gazes. No face mirrored

Clancy's, and as for everyone else, she couldn't see behind their expressions. Sweat gathered on her palms, her upper lip, the back of her neck.

As a violin accompanied the piano with a slow and deep melody, Zephyr's hand fell to Cricket's clavicle. He'd told her what he would do, but they hadn't practiced this part because he said it should be natural, like a first kiss. His callused fingertips sensually trailed up her throat, lifting her chin until her eyes connected with his. Her heart beat faster, but not with fear, as something warm stirred within her chest, dipping lower.

He winked, signaling her next step. Cricket slipped a leaf out from the front of her one-piece and placed it between his lips, lingering for a moment, feeling the fullness of them against her digits. A few whistles came from the audience, and she caught the twitch of Zephyr's mouth. She held back from rolling her eyes as his vines grew from beneath his flesh, her heart slamming against her rib cage.

Cricket remembered his words during practice. *"I won't do anything you don't want,"* he whispered. *"If you want me to stop, just say my name, and I will."*

The vines curved around her, groaning, creating a barrier as they drew closer. Zephyr released her chin, stepping back and allowing the vines to fold around her. Their texture wasn't rough as expected but soft like silk, surprising her when they cradled her in a way that felt like they were caressing her. She didn't study any of the audience's faces again yet instead looked toward the back of the room to tamp down the fear that her dahlias would break free. That the audience would scream in fear.

Zephyr's vines lifted her from the chair, and even

though she hadn't practiced the next part, she was prepared from his words. Cricket gasped, pretending to be frightened, as she clamped onto him briefly. His vines tossed her up into the air, and a thrilling rush barreled through her stomach when she fell, but he easily caught her. The vines tilted upward, and she rolled down them straight into Zephyr's warm, awaiting arms. A scratching sensation came beneath her skin, and her eyes grew wide—she couldn't force the smile she was supposed to have. So instead, she pulled Zephyr's face to hers and kissed him on his cheek, distracting her.

The scratching within her halted, her shoulders relaxing as she drew back.

Zephyr smiled at her and whispered, "Kiss me anytime you want." He set her on her feet, winking at her once more. "I'll see you in a moment."

Cheeks heating, Cricket twirled across the stage to her exit, the closest to dancing she would get for now. The audience clapped, and a sense of home flowed through her as she reached Juniper.

"You did it!" Juniper chirped with a big smile before handing her a canteen.

The scratching didn't stir again, and now that she was off stage, Cricket wished it would, just to see if roses would blossom. "I need to do it with my curiosity though." Taking a swig of the water, she watched as Zephyr effortlessly juggled the swords. She couldn't juggle one ring by herself without it hitting her in the face, let alone swords.

Juniper pressed a hand to Cricket's shoulder. "You'll get it, I promise. An almost skeleton that blooms roses, who twirls like you just did, will be a beautiful performance indeed."

Her heart swelled at that. "You truly think so?"

She nodded. "If I could bloom flowers with blood, it would be sensational. I'm going to grab a sweet treat. Do you want anything?"

"Not yet. But soon." Cricket smiled, recalling how delicious the food in the carnival had smelled.

The audience cheered again as Zephyr bowed to the crowd, his vines no longer out. He strode off stage with his hands in his pockets. "You're still here." He grinned as he approached her.

"Oh, was I meant to leave?" She supposed she looked like a lovesick fool waiting there for him.

"I'm glad you stayed. You did great out there." He tucked the swords in a bag hanging at the back of the stage.

She tilted her head to the side and pointed at him. "*You* did all the work."

"Not the kiss to my cheek," he purred, shifting closer, his woodsy scent becoming enticingly stronger.

The tent's fabric rustled, and Mistress Eliza slipped through the back entrance. "That was good, Cricket. Now, you just need to continue focusing like that. But not like molasses," she added before limping away to tell another group of performers how they could improve.

The necromancer was right, though. Cricket had spent a year at the carnival while asleep, helping to bring in paying customers. And now that she was awake, it was one less curiosity act that could draw in a crowd. Some carnivals dolled up their performers to pretend to have oddities, but Mistress Eliza wouldn't be a part of that. Everything needed to be authentic.

Zephyr gently grasped Cricket's arm and motioned his head toward outside. She let him lead her into the cool night breeze, where he circled his arm around her waist, pulling her closer. "Come to my caravan tonight?" he asked, his voice thick.

"I don't think that's a good idea." She smiled, ignoring the wretched part of herself that yearned to give in.

"Are you sure about that?" He lifted her chin, his eyes hooded as he peered down at her. "I don't only want to know what your kiss feels like on my cheek, but on my lips, my neck, my chest, my stomach... I want you to feel what mine are like when I kiss you any damn where you please."

"That *kiss* was all part of the performance." Her cheeks warmed again, and she wished she could control that tell-tale sign of her lies. "Goodnight, Zephyr."

"You're flushed," he said in a gruff voice. "I like that color on you. That I'm the one who put it there."

Cricket tried not to glance back at him as she walked away, but she did, finding him fighting a grin. She whipped her head around and went toward the caravans. Juniper sat on the steps in front of her home, eating a caramel apple while she watched Stormy drink whiskey and spin beneath the moon near a small crackling fire. Her gaze never drifted to any of the other performers in that way. If Juniper hadn't confessed the name of the woman she was attracted to, Cricket would've easily guessed it now. It was how her lips were parted and how her fingers dug into her dress as she continued studying Stormy.

"Try not to be so obvious about it unless you plan on telling her how you feel," Cricket murmured in Juniper's ear while crouching beside her. She thought about the first time she'd told Bram how she'd felt about him, the first time she'd ever confessed how she felt about any man. At first, Bram sputtered out his tea, but then he'd lifted her hand and kissed her knuckles. However, his courting her hadn't lasted…

"It's not obvious." Juniper's eyes widened as she pinched her lips together.

"It very much is." She shrugged.

"Stormy has been on and off with Louise for a long time. Tonight they're off again. Louise slapped her over something and left." Juniper blew out a breath, then took another bite of her apple.

Cricket arched a brow. "Sounds like they could remain off if a slap was involved. I say, go talk to her."

Juniper stood from the stairs and fluffed her curls with her free hand. "I'm only going to warm myself by the fire."

"Yes, just warming yourself by the fire. That's *all.*" Cricket grinned, finding herself liking that she'd allowed herself to make a friend.

Juniper gave her a soft shove, then handed her the rest of her caramel apple before nearing the fire. Cricket took a bite of the perfectly sweet delicacy as she glanced up toward the sky—a feeling that had been nagging her since arriving in Nobel slithered back. She wondered, should she go into town and ask about the murders?

6

Since last night had gone well, tonight's act would require Cricket to perform more. The thought of dancing like she'd never done before sent a nervous thrill coursing through her.

A light knock sounded at the door as she finished curling her lashes. It wasn't Zephyr coming to get her but Juniper dressed in black ruffled trousers and a shimmery ivory corset.

"Where's Zephyr?" Cricket asked, peering past her but only spotting two performers practicing a routine on wooden stilts.

"So you would've rather had my brother come?" Juniper grinned, causing Cricket's cheeks to flame. *Such a tedious thing.*

"I'm only teasing," Juniper continued. "He's backstage in one of the tents fixing loose floorboards.

Arthur twisted his foot when he fell through one. Lucky he didn't break it, or Mistress Eliza wouldn't have been pleased."

"She would've found a way for him to still perform." Cricket snorted. "Zephyr seems to genuinely care about the carnival."

"He does. Thankfully, he's not as overprotective with me as he used to be."

Cricket smiled, wondering what the siblings were like when they were younger, not what they'd become now, but how they truly were behind the face of the carnival before death came for them.

"Give me a moment and I'll come with you." Cricket pressed a bobby pin into her curls. With her blonde hair styled this way, it fell just past her chin instead of down her shoulders. Two pink circles were drawn onto her cheeks, her face pale with powders, black kohl rimmed her eyes, and a red heart was etched over her lips. She wore a black dress held together by felt buttons, its ruffles barely reaching mid-thigh, white lace peeking from capped sleeves.

She grabbed her collar from the vanity and put it around her neck as she walked beside Juniper toward the performance tent. Birds chirped above them, and the sun was starting to descend, bathing the sky in pinks, oranges, and yellows while making room for the night.

"By the way, I like your makeup," Juniper said as a breeze ruffled her red curls. "You look just like a marionette."

"That makes me less nervous, at least." Cricket smiled, fidgeting with her black lacy gloves. Laughter and music burst through the carnival, the aroma of buttery popcorn drifting through the air, yet she wasn't steady enough to think about food. She'd attempted her curiosity earlier, and she hadn't felt anything except for a small twitch, but the petals in the locket still rested at her collarbone in case she needed them.

As they approached the tent, one of the strong men with a bushy beard exited and held up the fabric for them.

"Thank you," Cricket and Juniper both said as they entered. On the stage, a performer, Kyrie, pedaled a unicycle while playing the flute and making snow swirl around him. Behind him, an acrobat went across a bed of nails on her hands, a dark mask hiding her face.

Once two acts had finished, Zephyr still hadn't shown up. Cricket was uncertain what she would do if he didn't arrive in time. But then Zephyr walked through the tent, his shoulders relaxed. He met her gaze and smirked before glancing at his sister. "The floor's fixed. Your precious feet will remain safe and won't fall through it."

"With my luck, I would've broken something, so thank you," Juniper said, hugging her brother. "I'll see you two later."

Zephyr pinned his gaze to Cricket as Juniper left, his hazel eyes slitted. "Are you ready to be *my* marionette?"

Butterflies swarmed low in her stomach at his deep baritone, and she forced herself to break their staring spell. "*Your* marionette?" She arched a brow as the piano music picked up.

He winked and lifted her, making her gasp. "It's time. Now, become still in my arms, and as much as I want you to hold onto me like you did last night, don't." As if he couldn't help himself, he added, "But after, you can touch me as much as you'd like."

Cricket rolled her eyes and let her body become limp while he carried her out on stage. Her head tilted toward the audience, peering at as many faces as she could. She attempted once again to see anything in those expressions, if possibly a murderer was present, but she saw nothing besides the stares of the visitors waiting to be entertained.

Deep green vines unfurled from Zephyr's back, and they lifted Cricket from his arms before gently resting her on top of a glass box. She sat in an upright position, and she let her head lull to the side, her limbs wilted. Zephyr brushed his fingers beneath her chin, then placed leather cuffs with strings around her wrists and ankles, all while his vines collected silver rings from a small table and juggled them.

Out of the corners of her eyes, she watched as rings went up and listened to the swishing sound they made while they cut through the air. When he was finished placing the last cuff around her ankle, he caught a ring in his hand. A vine ripped it from his grasp, and he cursed, making the audience bark with laughter.

Zephyr disappeared behind her as the vines lifted the strings of her arms and brought her to her feet. He pulled Cricket's arm back, her right leg mirroring it before she performed a simple spin and halted. This was where the marionette was supposed to come to life. Her head jerked up, and she studied the audience, her gaze landing on a single face. A mistake, she realized. Before her was a man she knew all too well. She attempted to blink him away, pretend it was a horrible dream. Though it wasn't, and her heart pounded furiously. It wasn't Clancy who sat there watching her, but Bram wearing a bowler hat and sitting alone. Anika wasn't at his side.

The scratching sensation stirred within her muscles, like a pack of wolves ready to rip her apart. Her skin paled, turning translucent until the bones were visible. The audience gasped. If the dahlias showed themselves, it would be more catastrophic than running off the stage.

But the scratching somehow faded, her skin returning to its normal shade. Cricket didn't look at Bram again and broke away from her binds, the strings tearing. She spun in a circle, one pirouette after another. Zephyr's vines joined her, caressing her stomach and back, adding momentum to her spins.

She slowed to a stop, then slumped forward, her eyes trained on the floor, not once peering up at Bram. If anything, it may have just been her imagination.

But she knew it wasn't.

Zephyr scooped Cricket up and carried her off the stage as the crowd clapped and cheered. A few loud whistles echoed.

Once behind the curtain, Zephyr ignored the other performers congratulating them and brought her to the corner.

"What happened out there?" Zephyr asked as he set her on her feet. "You froze as if you'd seen a ghost just before your curiosity slipped out."

"It's nothing. No dahlias, at least. I need to grab something really quick. I'll be back." But she wasn't going to fulfill that promise tonight.

"Cricket—" Zephyr started, yet she didn't stay to hear the tail end of it as she ran out into the dusky night. She couldn't remain in a tent where the first man she ever loved currently was. She would go to her caravan and stay there until the carnival ended.

Her heart thundered, and her hands shook as light scratching caressed her insides. She closed her eyes, concentrating, praying her curiosity wouldn't come right then. Gradually, the sensation faded. Taking a breath of the fresh air that smelled of strawberry desserts, she opened her lids before rounding the tent and bumping into a firm chest.

"Sorry," Cricket mumbled, avoiding looking at the person, but the stranger's hand grasped her wrist before she could go.

"Cricket?" he said, and she stilled, recognizing Bram's voice instantly.

She slowly lifted her head, her eyes meeting his brown ones. He was dressed in his finest as always. A white button-up collared shirt with a black jacket and matching trousers, his chestnut hair hidden mostly below the bowler hat.

"What are you doing here?" she stammered.

"You never came back to say you were leaving," Bram said, his brow furrowed as though he were hurt.

"I know," Cricket whispered. Their past stormed through her, but her heart didn't beat for him as it used to. Perhaps it never had in the way it was meant to. Regardless, as of now, it only beat for herself. "I decided to join the carnival."

"I wish you would've at least told Anika. She's been worried sick. Especially now…" A vein ticked along his square jaw. "I need to discuss something with you in private. It's about what's been happening in Nobel."

Cricket nodded. "Walk with me to my caravan." She knew precisely what he wanted to discuss. The murders.

He wouldn't know whether or not she'd heard about them yet, but worry shone in his gaze. Since he was here and she hadn't ventured into town yet, there were questions she needed to ask too.

Neither spoke as she led him toward the caravans, even when they passed several performers who watched them with curiosity. *Yes, I once was outgoing enough to be courted and taken to bed. Now stop looking,* she wanted to shout.

Words continued to remain trapped inside Cricket and Bram's mouths, the silence uncomfortable to the point she wanted to shatter it. She ached to slice a knife through the quiet to see if it would scream or bleed. She'd never felt this way around him before, and even though only a month had truly passed for her, over a year had gone by for everyone else.

Cricket unlocked the door to her caravan and motioned him inside. "Sorry, the space is small, and I have nothing to offer you besides whiskey." She lifted the flask from her vanity and took a swig. "Sit wherever you like."

"It's fine." He held up a hand, not bothering to take a seat as if the act would be too intimate.

Cricket sank down in the vanity chair and drank another sip, letting the strong burn of alcohol soothe her. "I've already been informed about the murders, but since you're here, I do have questions." She hated how stiff she sounded and how rigid her shoulders were.

"So you know then?" he said, running a hand along his jaw.

"That there are mutilated bodies decorated in dahlias? Yes, I know those details. Is it Clancy? Just because his body was dug up doesn't mean it wasn't replaced or that a necromancer didn't bring him back." Her voice came out harsh, but if she spoke any other way, she would break down, and she didn't want to cry in front of Bram. Not again.

"It's not Clancy," Bram said, his voice assured. "I verified the body was his. Same chipped front tooth and another missing near the back. His hair was still there too. It's someone else doing this."

"Who then? Who would imitate how he killed me, and why?" she whispered, concern filling her.

"That's what we're trying to find out. But that isn't all." He paused, taking a breath. "All three victims are young and blonde. Did you hear that part? That their eyes are blue too, like yours."

Cricket frowned. "I didn't know that. But almost half the people in Nobel have blond hair and blue eyes. It isn't as if it's up north where it's less common."

"It could be a coincidence, but I don't think so. After you died, I never gave up searching for the killer, and with Anika's help, we caught Clancy. I'll find this one too," he vowed.

Cricket leaned back in the chair, thinking. "This didn't start until after I came back to town. Do you think it has something to do with that? That I'm still alive?" She fought the memories swarming through her—the choking, the blade, the dahlias.

"It's a possibility. A high one." He sighed, his voice concerned like the authority he was. "Carefully and without drawing any attention to yourself, let me know if you see or hear anything out of the ordinary. As much as I don't want to involve you, I may require your help."

Her? She couldn't even solve a riddle, much less a crime. But she could let him know if she spotted something suspicious. "I'll watch the visitors closely and do the same during performances. What about flower shops? Have you checked all of them? I know midnight black dahlias are rare, but maybe they were purchased there, and the shopkeeper could remember who bought them." That was how Clancy was discovered, but then he'd tried to leave the city before Bram and Anika found him.

"No luck with any of the flower shops. There's another thing, though. This isn't going to be pretty to say, Cricket, and I don't want to dredge up more pain for you. But each of these murders is worse than what Clancy did to you. Their rib cages were torn open, and dahlias were placed inside. Always one over the heart."

Nausea bubbled up Cricket's throat, the taste of acid on her tongue. Anger boiled within her veins as she thought about what kind of wicked person would do something so sickening. She pushed up from the chair and stood in front of him. "I'll do anything necessary, Bram."

"Thank you." He nodded and wrapped his arms around her, drawing her close. "I'm glad you're safe. I'm sorry for everything."

Tears pricked her eyes as she hugged him back, inhaling the comforting leathery smell he always carried with him.

Blowing out a breath, he took a step back. "How about you come over for tea tomorrow after you wake, and we can thoroughly review the details? Anika would love to see you."

Even though she couldn't think about drinking or eating anything after hearing about the victims, she would go to find out more. Besides that, she should see Anika. Her mind turned toward the past, wondering if she hadn't been murdered, where would she have been now? Would she still have been with Bram? The one married to him? Or would she have decided to live out her dream and find somewhere to perform, away from Nobel? "Of course, I'll be there. Why didn't Anika come tonight?"

He pursed his lips as if this was an answer he didn't want to give. "She's ... not feeling well."

"Is everything all right?" Her chest tightened at the thought of Anika suffering or having something worse, like a fatal illness.

"She's with child and has been quite nauseous as of late," he said softly.

Cricket's eyes widened, and she swore her heart stopped beating for a moment. A child... Anika was pregnant with *Bram's* child.

"Congratulations, you'll be a wonderful father," she finally said, the words true. The thought of having children was something Cricket never wanted, and if she'd stayed, if she had married Bram, that would've taken from what she'd desired to do in the now. "She'll be in my prayers tonight. I shouldn't have left like I did."

"I understand why. If I'd known you were alive, I would've come for you. I feel like such a bastard, but I love her. I love her so damn much, Cricket." His eyes grew glassy, and Cricket clenched her fists, digging crescent moons into her flesh to keep her tears at bay.

Cricket knew how much he loved Anika even when she'd first come back to him. She sighed and folded her hand over Bram's. "I know. I was angry, saddened, lots of things. But now I understand, and I'm also happy for you both. You worked together to find Clancy and fell in love through so many different emotions. It's beautiful, really. Even under the circumstance. A better story than ours. If we'd stayed together, I believe wholeheartedly that I would've always yearned for something beyond this town."

Bram gently squeezed her hand as the corners of his lips pulled up. "Because you love to dance. Your performance tonight was miraculous, the way you made your skin translucent."

"Thank you." She wasn't going to discuss her current curiosity predicaments with him—it wasn't his concern when there were more important matters at hand.

"I better go and check on Anika. She really wanted to come," he said, releasing her hand.

"Tell her I wish her well, and I'll see you both tomorrow." As Cricket drew open the door, she caught a glimpse of Juniper and Zephyr as they walked by, each carrying a wicker basket.

With a smile, Juniper gave her a wave, yet Zephyr held a neutral expression that didn't seem right on him. And she hated to admit that she missed his usual smirk.

"Watch your back, and keep this on you at all times," Bram said, taking a small knife in a sheath from his pocket and placing it in her palm.

Cricket folded her hands over the blade and stood quietly as he walked away. She shut the door, then pressed her back to it, inhaling slowly. If there was a reason the women were blonde and blue-eyed, and it had nothing to do with her, what else could it be? Perhaps they just wanted to continue Clancy's legacy. Or they may have even had an obsession with an ex-lover and murdered women who looked this way as a sick sort of pleasure. But she went back to Clancy's original reason—how he'd picked the first person he saw. That chilled her the most because that meant a victim could be anyone.

$C$ricket woke with a yawn, and when she sat up, a slight headache pulsed above her right eye. Once she and Bram parted ways, Cricket wasn't able to sleep well after hearing more about the murders, that the victims hadn't only been left with dahlias the way she had, but their bodies held common characteristic traits. So she'd tossed and turned, polished off her whiskey, and when she did manage to find sleep, she was consumed by nightmares filled with women, their bloody chests sliced open, black dahlias blooming from their eyes and mouths.

Shaking away the images, she threw back the covers. Her hair and nightgown were damp with sweat. She peeled the cotton fabric from her body before fumbling through her small wardrobe. Most of the clothing consisted of performance costumes and about ten pretty dresses she'd purchased in the previous town after waking. Mistress Eliza had given her payment when she'd woken for performing as the Sleeping Darling, but Cricket had almost used up all the coin. Not having time to bathe until she returned, she chose a deep blue dress with a high collar and pearl buttons down the front of the bodice. The simplest of the dresses so as not to appear as though she was there to impress Bram.

Cricket slipped on the comfortable fabric and fastened the front. She studied her reflection in the vanity mirror, not knowing what to do with her hair. The curls had fallen out, leaving a tangled bird's nest. She combed out the golden locks and quickly plaited her hair but decided to forgo the rouge to her cheeks and gloss to her lips.

Bram's manor wasn't far from the carnival, so she wouldn't bother asking Mistress Eliza if someone could take her or if she could borrow a horse.

As Cricket slipped on her boots, a knock came at the door. She tucked the knife Bram had given her into the lacy black garter around her thigh.

Zephyr stood outside, his leather bag draped over one bare shoulder as the sun cast a warm glow on his broad tan chest and handsome face. A lazy smile spread across his lips, the neutral expression from last night no longer there. "You're not dressed for practice," Zephyr drawled. "You're dressed as though you're going to afternoon tea somewhere."

Cricket couldn't help but smile. "That's because I *am* going for tea. Or morning tea with an old friend. I was going to tell you I won't be able to practice until later."

"Oh?" He arched a brow. "Would this friend be the same rigid man who was here last night?"

She rolled her eyes and collected her satchel from beside the door. "Yes, he will be there, amongst others. And he isn't rigid."

"He doesn't seem suited for you in the least." She could've sworn she'd heard a hint of jealousy in his voice.

Cricket blinked as she stepped into the morning light and shut the door behind her. "Oh, I didn't realize you were a fortune teller." She placed her hands on her hips. "And just who do you predict to be my perfect match?"

Zephyr pressed his hand to the caravan so he was partly caging her as he leaned in. His intoxicating woodsy scent enveloped her, and a part of her wished he would put his other hand up, caging her in completely.

"Someone who can easily match your hidden wildness, make those pretty lips of yours part in pleasure," he purred, his pupils dilated. And then he did what she wanted—lifted that other hand to fully cage her in.

Cricket swallowed, her gaze shifting away from his as warmth spread through her. Pushing away whatever *this* was, she forced herself to duck down and out of his cage. "Not that it's any of your business, but Bram and I are no longer together. He courted me before I..." She trailed off, the words trapped in her throat. And she was glad for it because she didn't know why she admitted the part about him courting her before aloud.

Zephyr's face softened as he finished what she'd intended to say. "Before you died. And he's with someone else now? That's why you came back to the carnival seeming different, melancholic, after visiting Nobel. Why you never spoke of him or anyone. Why you avoided the performers."

She remembered when she'd seen Anika and Bram together last. How he'd so easily come into the room, staring at Anika as though she was the force to his heartbeat before he'd discovered Cricket was there at all. The things he'd admitted about Anika last night, the things she secretly wished someone would say about her one day.

"He's now married to my closest friend." She shrugged as if she had poured herself a cup of tea and had given it to her friend instead of drinking it. "They are a good match, and I'm happy for them. But sometimes…"

"You wonder what might have been," he finished for her.

Cricket slowly drew in a breath and nodded. "Yes, this past month, I did that more times than I'd like to admit. But it's been different recently, especially after the chat with him last night. If I were to think about it at this very moment, I see that if we had one day married, it would've led to regret. Performing and traveling are things I always wanted to pursue. Even though I've come to terms with Bram and Anika being married, I must admit I'm still nervous about seeing them together today while I'm alone. If only I could get these blasted nerves to go away."

Zephyr stepped toward Cricket and lifted her chin, her eyes meeting his again. "If you wish, I can help ease your nervousness. Whether you want me to make you come quick or drag out the pleasure, I promise it will relax you."

At that moment, she wondered what it would feel like to have those callused fingers of his hike up her dress, then trail them up her bare thighs to touch her— "I think I'd rather sleep in a bed of snakes." But it didn't come out as haughty as she would've liked.

He smirked. "Oh, we can make that happen while I spread your—"

"Just stop talking," she cut him off, flames licking their way through her and into her cheeks. She couldn't decide if she wanted to pull him closer or shove him away with how frequently she blushed when around him. "Anyway, Bram is with the authorities working on finding the Dahlia Killer. It for certain isn't Clancy miraculously brought back to life."

Zephyr cocked his head and studied her face. "You're not going to meet him only for tea, are you? You're going to discover more, so you can search too."

"No," she drawled, and even though it was only a single short word, she could hear the lie in her voice.

The playfulness disappeared from his face, and sincerity shone in his light hazel eyes. "You don't have to bottle this up inside. You can talk to me."

For the past month, since leaving Nobel for good, Cricket had felt like she had no one, even though the performers had been kind and attempted to talk to her. But it was her fault—she'd been too focused on the past, on having her curiosity come out. She wasn't the only one who'd faced death at Mistress Eliza's Carnival. Zephyr had been through a murder too—all the performers had, yet he was the one here now, and she desperately needed to confide in someone. Not only that, but each time she'd sprouted the black dahlias, he'd been the one to help save her by bringing her to Mistress Eliza.

"All right," she said, motioning for him to follow her away from the caravans and toward the road. They passed a small crackling fire where Wilder was skinning the fur from a rabbit beside Autumn while two of the strong men roasted meat. Arthur took out a flute and began to play a slow melody.

Once they broke away from their homes, Cricket continued, "Last night, Bram told me that not only were the victims being murdered and left with dahlias, but they are all young women with blonde hair and blue eyes. Like me. At first, I thought it was a coincidence, maybe. But since it's not Clancy, there are several directions the reasoning could go into. However, I don't know precisely what it could be."

Zephyr rubbed the back of his neck. "With Clancy, you were the only one and random at that. With these, coincidence doesn't seem right, especially since there have been multiple murders all using the dahlias. Perhaps the killer just so happens to like blondes. I know I do."

"Zephyr!" Cricket hissed and shoved his arm.

"Just trying to lighten the mood while we think about the gory details," Zephyr said, brushing the crease between her eyebrows away with the pad of his thumb. "Whoever is doing this will be found, same as Clancy was. I find it rather pitiful that someone is mimicking a murder instead of at least being original." He held up his hands and stepped away just as she tried to shove him again. "I'm not saying I agree with murders, but don't use what someone's done before, is all."

She sighed. What he said did make sense, yet she wouldn't admit that aloud. "My rib cage was still intact— these victims' aren't. I suppose by breaking open their rib cages and placing a dahlia over their heart, he's adding his own paltry flair."

"Paltry indeed."

"I think this would've been easier if it had been Clancy. He wasn't the brightest, but perhaps I'm not either if I didn't notice him sneaking up behind me." None of this seemed real to her because she didn't even know the  women's names. It was something she should've asked Bram the night before, but she would when she met up with him at his manor. She supposed her death might not have seemed real to most of Nobel since they hadn't known her. Cricket stopped and stared at the sun high up in the sky as anxiousness crawled through her.

Zephyr stood beside her, gazing up with her. "Hmm, the sun doesn't seem to be one for offering us much advice. What do you say, Sun? Can you let lovely Cricket know who this bastard is?"

She looked at him and shook her head. "Thank you for having a semi-proper discussion about things with me. I better get going, but maybe we can talk more about this when I get back?" Bram hadn't given her a precise time to meet with him and Anika, yet she didn't want to arrive too late.

"Of course, I—"

A shrill scream pierced the air. Cricket's heart thundered in her chest as she froze, unable to move. Zephyr grabbed Cricket by the waist and pulled her behind him.

"Stay here," he whispered before taking off toward the road.

Cricket wasn't going to remain there and do nothing—she pulled herself from her staring spell, then hiked up the skirts of her dress to fish out her blade. Clutching the knife, she darted through the grass, skirting around a few trees until she caught up with Zephyr.

"I told you to wait back there," he said between clenched teeth.

"You don't even have a weapon on you!" she whisper-shouted.

"I carry leaves in my pocket."

Cricket hadn't thought about how easy it would be for him to place a leaf into his mouth and let his vines slip out to shred someone apart. Out of everyone's curiosity at the carnival, he could be the most powerful, the most dangerous, and she'd never thought of it that way until now.

Frantic cries echoed across the morning haze as they broke through the trees beside the dirt road. A woman with dark hair plaited over her shoulder stood in the middle of the road, cupping her mouth as her body trembled.

"Miss, are you all right?" Cricket asked, knowing it was a ridiculous question when the woman had just been screaming.

"No. Over there," she stuttered, pointing toward the trees across the road before she released a choked sob.

Zephyr didn't hesitate as he pressed a leaf onto his tongue and walked to the road's edge. He halted just where the grass dipped down.

Cricket hurried to his side, and she gripped the knife harder when she discovered what rested in the swale.

A limp body, with arms and legs sprawled at unnatural angles. Blood rested beneath the still form, matting the woman's golden hair, coloring the shallow pools of water crimson. Nausea churned in Cricket's stomach when she peered at the two black dahlias over the victim's eyes, the next peeking out between her blue lips. As her gaze swept down the shredded silk dress to the torn-open rib cage, dahlias also rested inside, twisted in a macabre fashion and drenched in scarlet. Two more lay in the woman's dead hands. Cricket's gaze flicked back up to the ones covering the victim's eyes, and she knew that sky-blue irises would be hidden beneath, even without lifting away the dahlias.

The same blue as the other victims. Just the same as hers.

8

Seeing a dead body wasn't a new experience for Cricket or one she would shy away from. When she was a child, and the plague had come, dead bodies littered the streets, covered in pustules oozing sickness. Her younger brother had suffered that same fate, his little heart and lungs unable to battle any longer. But she'd never seen a death like this before, one where not only the flesh was sliced but ripped open, exposing organs inside of a bloody, cracked rib cage. The woman's body had been mutilated, then decorated with dahlias as though her murder were a celebration.

Cricket's heart pounded, and her lungs tightened while she clenched her rib cage. She didn't scream or sob like the other woman who'd found this body had done, only stared, time freezing in place as something clawed beneath her flesh.

Even then, when a dark dahlia bloomed from her hand, she couldn't move. Zephyr noticed, and his fingers remained steady while opening her locket to pull out a dried rose petal.

"You have to part your lips for me," he whispered as he held the petal in front of her mouth, the rose scent taking away some of the metallic odor from the victim's blood.

Cricket blinked and opened her mouth, knowing she didn't have the strength to attempt to reel her curiosity back in and would surely fail if she tried. So she let him slide the petal onto her tongue. As she chewed, the rose flavor consuming her senses, the scratching halted, then, like the sun dipping beneath the horizon, the dahlia hid somewhere back in her bloodstream.

"I was on my way home from an inn." The dark-haired woman sobbed, stumbling beside Cricket. Zephyr caught the woman's arm just before she toppled into the grass. She yanked away from his grasp, seeming to not want to be touched. The woman reeked of alcohol, and her eyes were glazed red. She looked as though she'd spent most of the night at a pub, and judging by the smell of her, she'd spent most of that time drinking. Cricket didn't fault her for it—after this, she might need to drink until she passed out herself.

"Did you see anyone on the road at all?" Zephyr asked.

The woman squinted and rubbed her temple. "Not near here. No." Tears streamed down her cheeks, and she looked away from the victim.

Taking a breath, Cricket searched around for any footprints near the slain woman without getting too close but couldn't see any against the weed-covered ground. She glanced at Zephyr. "I don't know how long she's been here, but we need to get the authorities."

"Can you have someone take a horse into town to get them, then bring Mistress Eliza here to see if she can try her necromancy on the victim?" Zephyr asked. "I don't want you to have to wait out here with the body, and I can see if maybe this woman missed something before the authorities come."

Perhaps the victim had seen something, could tell them precisely who had done this horrific misdeed if she could be risen. Cricket prayed that Mistress Eliza's necromancy would finally work, that she could close up the wounds, make them disappear as if they'd never been there at all, the way she had for Cricket.

"All right," Cricket said as she stood, relieved he'd asked her to go instead of stay. She hurried through the trees and back toward the field where the caravans were. More performers had gathered around the fire to eat, ignorant of the horrors just beyond their sight, their cheerful music having drowned out the unfortunate passerby's screams.

"There's been a murder!" Cricket shouted to them, and the music halted—everyone focused on her. "Near the road. Can someone take a horse into town and get the authorities?"

"I'll do it," Wilder said, setting his food bowl beside Autumn.

"Thank you," Cricket rushed the words out as she hurried to Mistress Eliza's.

When she reached the necromancer's caravan, Juniper stood beside her, chatting. Mistress Eliza's eyes met

Cricket's, and she furrowed her brow. "Why do you look so pale, child? Did the dahlias come again?"

One did, but she wasn't going to discuss her failed curiosity now. "Another woman has been killed. There, beyond the trees," Cricket said between panted breaths. "She was left … gutted. And … her body is decorated with dahlias. Wilder is taking a horse to get the authorities, but maybe you can bring her back to life for answers."

"A body?" Juniper gasped.

"I can certainly try. But no promises," Mistress Eliza said as she removed the three ruby stones from her pouch. "Is it someone from the carnival?"

Cricket shook her head and motioned them to follow her. "No, it isn't a performer, and I've never seen her before." She didn't run as quickly as she would've because of Mistress Eliza's limping, but the woman moved a bit faster than she'd ever seen her, though she winced, struggling to keep up.

"Do you think it was a customer from last night?" Juniper asked.

"It could've been, but there were so many faces."

Cricket's chest tightened as she remembered her conversation with Bram the night before. How the victims' hair and eyes matched hers. The body was so close to the carnival, and she knew she had to tell them, even though she would've rather kept it bottled up inside so she wasn't to blame if the killer was doing this because of her.

"I spoke with an old friend last night. Bram is also one of the authorities," Cricket started. "He told me that the victims of the Dahlia Murders have certain traits in common with me. All of them are young, blonde, and have blue eyes."

"That doesn't necessarily mean it has anything to do with you," Juniper pointed out.

"Let's not jump to wild conclusions and make ourselves hysterical. I need to focus on this woman, and this woman alone, if you expect me to help her," Mistress Eliza said, her gaze trained on the road once they pressed out from the trees. A small crowd of performers had gathered around the body as if it were an act they were watching and not an innocent woman who'd been slain by a murderous monster.

"There's no time to stand around gawking like a bunch of fools," Mistress Eliza snapped, breaking through the crowd to get to the victim. "If you didn't witness anything, return to your caravans!"

None of the performers argued as they turned to walk away, muttering and gossiping under their breaths to one another. Only Zephyr, Juniper, Cricket, and the frightened woman remained alongside Mistress Eliza as the necromancer knelt beside the mutilated body. Water and blood gathered at the hem of her skirt.

"Wilder already left on horseback, so it shouldn't take long for the authorities to come," Zephyr said, then turned to the woman who had discovered the body. "Sarah tried to recall if she saw anything suspicious, but nothing came to mind."

"Let me see if I can get us some answers." Mistress Eliza took a breath, seeming to gather her strength. No matter that the woman's necromancy had faded, Cricket chanted prayers inside her head that it would work this time, that the victim's heart would beat once more.

"What is she doing?" Sarah asked, wrinkling her nose

as she observed Mistress Eliza.

"She's a necromancer," Juniper said, waving her off. "Now, keep quiet while she works."

Cricket studied the victim's round face, her delicate features, and the dahlias covering her eyes like coins given to the dead for their safe passage into the afterlife. She still didn't recognize her, but perhaps she'd passed her in a shop or on the streets as one did, simply not noticing each face in a crowd.

Mistress Eliza placed a hand on the woman's blood-speckled shoulder, the other clutching the stones. She closed her eyes as her lips moved in a silent chant. Cricket had never seen her bring another to life, only her failed attempts on animals. From what she'd heard, no smoke or glittery magic filled the air—they just awoke, and any wounds they may have suffered from were gone. Physical ones, anyway.

Cricket trembled as she looked on, then Zephyr's arm wrapped around her waist, steadying her. The victim's body twitched, and Sarah gasped at the same moment Cricket's heart galloped. Hope coursed through her while she continued to watch.

Mistress Eliza chanted faster, her fist shaking as she held the stones. The victim's hands fluttered, then lifted slightly before falling back into the puddles, the dahlias in her palms. Her hands and her body unmoving, yet Mistress Eliza didn't relinquish her grasp on the young woman's shoulder. She whispered, her words drifting on the wind and becoming audible, commanding the woman's chest to close up, for her to wake, to speak. But the victim remained still, any secrets she carried gone, taken with her where no one could follow.

A harsh cough spilled from Mistress Eliza's throat, and she released the woman's shoulder to grip her chest as though in pain. "I can't get her to rise, damn it. She's gone." The necromancer sighed, her breathing ragged.

Cricket and Zephyr rushed to Mistress Eliza's sides to grasp her arms as she shakily stood.

"I hear someone," Juniper said, stepping back and peering down the road. "Wilder and two authorities are coming on horses."

Mistress Eliza brushed Cricket and Zephyr off and straightened as she limped to where Juniper waited. The hooves of the horses pounded the road, coming closer. She recognized one of the authorities when they approached—Charles. A lanky man with gray peppering brown hair and a matching mustache. He'd been the one to train Bram as soon as he turned eighteen. The other young man was possibly a few years older than her, with his hair trimmed short.

The two authorities stopped in front of them. "You may return to the carnival," Charles said to Wilder before sliding down from his horse. He then turned to face them, his gaze meeting Cricket's, and he motioned her toward him while the second authority began questioning the others.

"Bram told me the news that you were alive about a month ago," Charles muttered as she approached him. "It's curious how you were brought back to life after being buried. You know it's a crime to disturb a body without consent." What she knew about Charles was that he loathed when the carnival came to town and had never believed necromancy should be allowed.

Cricket frowned, not understanding what this had to

do with the murder that had just occurred. "I crawled out of the grave myself," she lied, then pointed toward where the victim's body rested. "It's not me we should be concerned about here, but this poor woman instead."

He followed her closer, and his mouth formed a tight line. "Dahlias again… Just as they were on yours. It's strange how someone is mimicking an old murder. And you saw nothing?"

Cricket shook her head. "None of us did. I wasn't the one who found her, so I have nothing else to say."

"Hmph." Charles clucked his tongue, then motioned the other authority to his side. "Miles, come here."

Cricket couldn't hear their conversation as Charles pulled Miles toward the victim. But then Charles barked, "Someone disturbed the body."

"I did." Mistress Eliza narrowed her eyes. "I tried to see if there was any life left in her to get answers."

"There clearly wasn't," Charles grumbled.

The sound of creaking wheels filled the air when the coroner's carriage approached. Soon they were pushed back as the authorities took over, beginning their investigation in earnest. Miles removed the dahlias from the victim's eyes and lifted one lid. They were indeed a light shade of blue.

They discussed matters for a little while longer between one another when Miles offered to take Sarah home, and Charles finally said, "I would suggest closing the carnival for a few days."

"A few days?" Mistress Eliza cried. "We're not closing the carnival for that long. No crime was committed inside my carnival. There is no reason for my performers to suffer a loss. Unless you plan to cover our expenses yourself."

Charles's lips curled into a sneer. "One day this time, then. But it will be longer if we find out the victim was at the carnival."

"Of course," Mistress Eliza agreed and turned to Juniper. "Round everyone up. I'll inform them the carnival will be closed. For today only. We'll reopen tomorrow evening."

"Yes, Mistress Eliza," Juniper said, clutching the skirts of her dress and darting through the trees.

"Take as much time to yourself today as you need." Mistress Eliza patted Cricket's shoulder before limping away.

Bram wasn't with the authorities, and he would discover what happened soon, but she was supposed to have already been there anyway.

Cricket started down the road when Zephyr caught up with her. "You're still going for tea after *that*?"

"I don't think I'll be able to drink tea at all today," she said as she continued walking. "But I want to let Bram know what happened and uncover a few things anyway. He doesn't live far from here."

"Let me at least take you there." Concern filled his eyes as he looked at her.

After seeing a victim's body, going alone probably wasn't such a good idea. "I'll take your offer, then."

Cricket glanced over her shoulder to find Charles watching them with a scowl as the victim's body was wrapped in sheets to be loaded into the carriage.

9

The town center was busy as usual. An older woman in a pale green dress watered plants outside the flower shop while two men got their shoes shined in front of another. Through the food market window, a bald man cleaved apart a large chunk of bloodied meat. Cricket turned away in disgust, reminded of the dead woman's open rib cage. Instead, she focused on the lovely smell drifting out from the bread and pastry shops.

Zephyr walked beside her down the bustling streets, close enough to where his woodsy scent cocooned her. Word of the recent murder hadn't made it to the town yet, but it would soon.

She kept alert, searching for anyone who might seem suspicious or keep their eyes trained on her a beat too long, but stares only lingered on Zephyr, with his kohl-lined eyes and exposed chest. He'd slipped on a vest he'd pulled from his bag, unbothered that there wasn't a shirt to wear beneath it.

"All the women are looking at you," she whispered. And something akin to jealousy swirled within her, making her frown.

"There's only one woman I want looking at me," he purred as they turned the corner, and a blush crept up her neck. "I always like when the carnival visits Nobel."

"Because of the attention you get?" She arched a brow.

"Partly." Zephyr grinned. "Though it's mostly because people are so welcoming here. In other cities, not so much. You'll see."

"If Mistress Eliza allows me to stay." She sighed, remembering how, once again, her curiosity had reared its ugly head with a devilish black flower instead of a rose. "Are you going to mention the dahlia slipping out to her?"

"What dahlia?" he said slyly.

Cricket smiled and grasped his upper arm, drawing him to a stop as they rounded another corner. "Thank you."

"I think you just wanted me in this back alley." His playful expression softened. "But seriously, how are you? I know it wasn't easy seeing that."

"It's worse than a nightmare. I'm going to help Bram in whatever way I can, though." Being bold and desperate for a drink, she slipped her hand into his pocket and fished out the flask. "May I?"

Zephyr nodded, his gaze hooded. "Mm-hmm. Reach in there any time you bloody well wish."

Rolling her eyes, she took a swig of the liquor and let

the burn ease her tension. Before she could put it back, he drank from the flask.

"Come on, we're almost there." Cricket led him down a winding road to a neighborhood with several large manors, lush and beautiful gardens decorating the front of each one.

Zephyr chatted about mundane things like the reason why the sky was blue, and she knew it was to keep her distracted. She was thankful for it too.

A gust of warm wind blew past them, carrying the salty scent of the sea that lingered on the other side of the cliff behind the manors. Bram's palatial home came into view—gray stone, tall windows, and perfectly manicured gardens beneath the dancing rays of the sun surrounded a majestic fountain of a stag with a stream of water falling from its mouth.

Anika used to come here as a child when her mother worked for Bram's parents, which was how Cricket had met him.

"This is Bram's home," Cricket said as she pointed at the black iron fence. "I can ask him to take you back to the carnival with the carriage if you don't want to walk."

Zephyr blinked, his face neutral—she now understood it to be a way of him wanting to hide how he felt. "No, I'm fine with walking. I didn't expect an authority to be so wealthy. This is a manor fit for a damn prince."

"It belonged to his parents, but his father passed away during the plague, and his mother's lungs weren't great after. She was bedridden until she didn't wake up one morning three years ago.

His face softened at her words. "No parents. Seems

we have that in common."

"And kind hearts." She smiled, her voice gentle. "You both have that."

Zephyr's expression washed away, replaced by something more playful. "Well, I have a kind heart that can make you feel good any time you want."

"That can make me come as many times as I wish?" Cricket let out a small laugh when Zephyr's eyes widened in surprise. "Seems you aren't the only one who can say unexpected things at inappropriate moments. I'll see you back at the carnival, and thank you for accompanying me here." She walked through the gate, glancing back as she padded up the garden pathway. He continued to watch her, and she knew it was to ensure she safely made it inside. Her heart gave an extra thump as she looked away from him, passing around the water fountain.

Behind the manor, a fine mist drifted up from the sea, and she loved the days when it would pour in over the garden as if this place was meant to be in a mystery story. She bit the inside of her cheek, reminding herself that she was currently in one.

Two servants, Nettie and Ebba, tended to the flowers and weeds in the gardens near the front of the manor. They looked up as she passed, their eyes blinking in surprise.

"Hello." Cricket smiled at them like she always used to, and they both waved. She wondered if they were uncomfortable that she'd once been dead, the way Charles had been around her earlier. But she and the other carnival performers weren't immortal—they would all die one day just like them.

The various-colored rose bushes were in full bloom,

and she brushed her fingers across a bright red bloom, hoping it would somehow get her curiosity to start behaving by bringing her the flowers she needed.

On either side of the door were potted succulent plants, something Bram's mother always had, saying how one never knew when aloe vera might be necessary to help heal a wound. Cricket and Anika hadn't grown up wealthy, but that had never mattered to Bram. Just as it hadn't when Bram's father married his mother.

Cricket's heart pounded faster as she lifted her fist to knock, the deep rumble loud in her ears. Perhaps she should've asked Zephyr to accompany her further, but she didn't want Mistress Eliza to get annoyed with him when she needed him back at the carnival to help. She wished he didn't have to be a part of these murders, yet after today, they both were.

As her nerves ticked inside her, she prayed the wicked dahlias wouldn't sprout unwillingly, but her locket with the dried petals rested against her collarbone if she needed one. Even then, no scratching brushed her muscles while she waited.

She reached up to knock again when the door opened to a servant wearing a simple black dress and a white apron around her waist. The woman's blonde hair was plaited back, her face unfamiliar.

"Hello," Cricket said, her voice shaky. "I'm supposed to meet with Bram and Anika for tea. I may be later than expected."

"Miss Cricket?" the woman asked, her smile bright and pleasant.

She nodded, fidgeting with the skirt of her dress.

"They've been expecting you. Come inside." She shut

the door behind them before gesturing her toward the long hallway. "Just take this all the way down to the drawing room, and I'll let them know you're here."

"Of course." Gilded-framed paintings still hung along the crimson silk wallpapered walls of the hallway. Lavender sat in tall vases across the wooden floor, and the scent tickled her nose. Besides the last time she'd visited, the manor was always comforting, quiet, peaceful. Before Bram's mother passed away, she always had the servants decorate the home in lavender.

The hallway opened to the spacious drawing room with an unlit fireplace at the back. A blue chaise, two velvet red chairs, and a settee rested in the center. Between them, an ornate rug lay beneath a carved wooden table, a vase of lavender decorating it. Cricket recognized Anika's artwork on the walls and smiled. She would know her friend's style anywhere, the way she layered the colors and curved the lines.

Footsteps sounded from above, and Cricket glanced up to find Anika walking down the staircase, wearing a yellow dress with capped sleeves and white lace around the collar. Her feet were bare, and Cricket's smile grew wider. Anika had always hated shoes.

Anika's black hair hung to her waist in thick curls, and her stomach cast a small bump, barely noticeable. If Bram hadn't admitted that Anika was with child, Cricket would've never guessed.

Cricket's gaze lingered on Anika's stomach a beat too long before meeting her dear old friend's deep brown irises.

Anika smiled wide, and it lit up her eyes. As soon as she stopped in front of Cricket, her smile fell. "I've been worried sick. You took off without so much as a goodbye."

"I did. I'm sorry." Cricket bit the inside of her cheek, knowing she must've seemed like a wounded, envious shrew at first. After what Bram had told her, how Anika had always wanted children, her heart swelled, and she didn't have to force herself to smile. "Congratulations."

"Thank you." Anika chewed on her lower lip, always her sign of anxiousness. She took a deep breath before speaking, "I should've told you when you were here last, but I was frightened. I didn't want you to hate me more than you already did. If I had known you were alive, I never would've let Bram court me. Perhaps I shouldn't have, even if you'd never returned."

Cricket's chest tightened, her friend's words ringing true to her ears. She didn't want to take away any of the happiness, even if it had been at Cricket's expense. "Fate led us on this path. I know you love one another from the little while I saw you two together." Setting away the last remnants of the hurt hidden deep within her, she placed her hands on Anika's shoulders. "The world pushes us in directions we may never have found otherwise. You knew I always wanted to perform more than anything. And now I am." She wouldn't tell her the whole truth, that she hadn't mastered her curiosity, that she only recently was allowed on the stage, and even then, it was her barely doing a few pirouettes. "At least we know the child will be beautiful."

Anika released a choked sob and folded her arms around Cricket as though she might disappear again. "I missed you so much. My days aren't the same without you," she sniffed.

Cricket lifted her arms and held her just as tightly. "You have Bram."

"Oh, you know how men are. Sometimes we need our closest female friend to gossip with." She grinned as she drew back, tears gathering on her lashes and streaking her cheeks.

And then the true reason she was here washed over Cricket. It wouldn't be about catching up over tea or learning more about the murders, but a discussion over the recent victim that Cricket had seen herself. "There's something important I need to discuss, and it won't be pleasant."

"Is everything all right?" Bram asked, his voice concerned as he rounded the corner.

Cricket turned to find him dressed in a button-up white shirt and black trousers, his boots shined to perfection. "A woman's body was found near the side of the road, not too far away from the carnival," she said.

"Another one?" Anika gasped, cupping her mouth with both hands.

Bram pinched the bridge of his nose and cursed under his breath. "Did the authorities already come?"

"Yes, Charles and Miles showed up, then the carriage to take the body to the coroner's followed suit. I had to—" Cricket was interrupted when Anika's hand fell to her stomach and her face paled.

Bram circled his arm around Anika's waist, holding her up. "Are you all right, darling?" he asked.

"I'm feeling nauseous again, and not only because of this news. I'm well now, though." Anika stood straight and blew out a shallow breath when she brought a trembling fist to her mouth. "On the other hand, no, I'm not. This blasted morning sickness won't stop."

"You can lie down, Anika. I won't be long," Cricket said, worry lacing her tone. "I'll come another time for tea and hopefully under better circumstances."

"All right, I'll see you soon." Anika's eyelids fluttered, her face becoming a shade of red as she held back nausea. "I've got it, Bram. Thank you." She squeezed his hand and ascended the staircase. Bram watched her the entire way up, as did Cricket, afraid her friend might collapse, but she made it just fine.

Cricket glanced at Bram, concern swarming through her. "How often has this been happening?"

"Daily, but the doctor says it's normal for some women to experience this. She's better than yesterday morning. Her mother is normally here to help, but she's visiting a relative. She's due back today or tomorrow, though."

Cricket didn't want to know what Anika had looked like the day before.

"I'm afraid I need to go and see the coroner about the victim," Bram said. "Would you like to stay here, or should I take you back to the carnival? I'm sincerely sorry."

She glanced toward the empty staircase, thinking about her friend ill and alone. "No apologies. I'll stay for a little while. I'd like to check on Anika after you leave."

"Will you finish telling me first-hand what happened?" He grabbed a hat off the rack and placed it atop his head.

"Of course." Cricket detailed the recent events, beginning with Zephyr walking with her and them stumbling on the screaming woman near the slain victim.

How she retrieved Mistress Eliza and the necromancer's failed attempt at bringing the victim back to life. The color of the woman's hair being blonde, and her eyes blue. "No one saw anything, not even the woman who discovered the body."

Bram ran a hand across his jaw, then tapped his fingers against it. Cricket wished these murders had never occurred, that she could've run into Anika in town before deciding to have tea together. They would've had the same conversation as earlier and could've moved on from the past, then laughed and chatted about everything else. But that wasn't how it was.

"Anika isn't blonde," Cricket started, "and I know she doesn't like to be a caged bird, but keep her safe."

Bram gave her a half smile. "Anika does what she wants, just as you always did. You are both strong-willed women."

Cricket needed to ask him the main question that nagged at her before he left. "Can you tell me the names of the victims? Maybe I knew them?"

"About three weeks ago," Bram started, "Georgia Davies was the first to be murdered, and she was discovered in front of the Royal Oak Pub. Elanore Jones was found ten days later, not far from the library steps, then Phoebe Brown's body, the most recent, was left in the alley near the western church. I went to school with Elanore, but we were never close."

"I don't recall ever having heard of any of these women. Did any of them work together?" Perhaps if they all danced like Cricket, it would mean something.

"No, their trades were all different. Georgia was a baker, Elanore a school teacher, and Phoebe didn't have a profession but was engaged. None of them lived near one another or were friends. They had nothing in common besides their age, hair, and eye color."

She bit the inside of her cheek and nodded.

"If there is anything you need, all you have to do is ask one of the servants, and they can fetch you some tea or anything else. I'm taking a horse, so if you want the carriage to bring you home, it's there."

The thought of tea still made her stomach churn. "Good luck, and thank you."

"One more thing. If you need a place to stay, if this becomes too much to bear, Anika and I don't mind you taking a room here in the least."

"I'll keep it in mind," Cricket said as he hurried out of the room. If she stayed here, she would be pampered and have the softest of beds. It was quite tempting, but she'd grown used to the caravans and would miss the lumpy mattress and the sounds of the performers practicing.

Cricket wanted to check on Anika, so she went up the staircase, then turned down the hall, stopping at the first door. She knocked lightly. "May I come in? It's Cricket."

"If you can ignore the smell," Anika groaned.

Cricket opened the door, and only a light smell of sickness permeated the air. Bram's room looked less bare than it used to, and it was obvious it had a woman's touch to doll it up. The floral curtains and matching rug, the vase of daisies and daffodils sitting on the desk.

"Bram left, but I wanted to stay with you a while. I suppose I couldn't resist seeing your pretty face." Cricket smiled, taking a seat beside Anika on the bed.

Anika opened her mouth to say something when she hurried to reach for the metal bucket beside the bed to expel her stomach.

"Tell me what happened earlier since I missed it," Anika said, wiping her mouth with a cloth.

"Certainly, but only if you promise to show me where the baby's room will be before I leave."

"I promise."

Cricket reached for a clean cloth on the night table and soaked it in a bowl of cool water. She squeezed the cloth out and set it atop Anika's forehead before telling the dreary story once more. Unable to stop there, she confessed the truth about what was happening with her curiosity, the dahlias nearly consuming her.

"I want whoever is doing this hung. Just like that bastard Clancy," Anika said when she finished.

"Me too."

"As for the dahlias, you'll get them to turn into roses. I may not know anything of these necromancer gifts, yet I will always aid you in any way I can. Even if it's to help you fight the flowers off. However, I do hate to admit this, but I agree it's best to hide them from any audiences for now."

After Zephyr caught wind of her earlier spell with her curiosity, Cricket hadn't planned on telling anyone about it, yet she'd always confided in Anika. "If I knew how to get them to appear right now, I would show you, but they are beastly things." Things she wished she would never have to see again.

# 10

Cricket had stayed with her friend for hours until Anika fell asleep, leaving her to return to the carnival. Though it was closed, Mistress Eliza stood near her palm reading booth, ordering acrobats to improve their routines. Her gaze fell to Cricket as she approached, her lips turning into a thin line. "When I said to rest, I didn't mean go traipsing around town." The two acrobats went inside their tent, seeming relieved by the disruption.

"I wouldn't have been able to rest anyway," Cricket replied. "Besides, I was supposed to have tea with Bram and his wife today. Since he's one of the authorities, I went to tell him what happened. I'm going to practice now, though."

"Tomorrow, you can practice. Today, you rest," Mistress Eliza said, her voice firm.

"All right," Cricket relented. She was tired anyway,

not enough to sleep, but enough to sit by the fire or in her caravan and not have to focus.

"After this morning, some of the performers are worried the town will think the murder had something to do with the carnival." Mistress Eliza sighed, pinching the bridge of her nose.

Cricket shook her head. "The carnival wasn't even here when the murders started, so if they believe that, they are bloody fools."

The edges of Mistress Eliza's lips tilted up a fraction, a rare smile coming from the necromancer. "You have a mouth on you when you want to use it."

"Sometimes." Cricket cracked a small smile in return. "I do think having the carnival reopen tomorrow is the right decision. It's an escape for people, whether it's forgetting about an awful trade, a not-so-great home life, or a way to have a good time. As a child, when the carnival would arrive, it let me escape the life my parents hoped for me instead of what I really wanted."

"And what kind of life did you want?" Mistress Eliza cocked her head and pressed a hand to her hip.

Cricket remembered those days of twirling in front of the mirror when her parents couldn't afford dance lessons, so she'd taught herself the best way she could. She would sneak in with Anika to performances at the theater or flip through books that held illustrations and descriptions about the art. "To dance, but mostly to perform at this carnival."

Mistress Eliza's face softened. "Tomorrow, you'll practice, and we'll see from there. Necromancy is all I know, and with it not wholly there, it feels like a part of me is missing. But if you tell anyone I said that, I'm sending you off somewhere else."

It was a small confession, yet one she didn't expect the woman to reveal aloud. "Your secret is safe with me. I'll pray tonight you'll get it back."

"I don't believe in prayers, but maybe yours will change my mind." Mistress Eliza turned on her heel and limped into her tent.

Every night before bed, Cricket had continued to say her prayers, whether someone answered or not. But she believed someone was always listening. Tonight, Mistress Eliza would try her necromancy once more. Only, Cricket wouldn't tell her just yet. During the carriage ride home, the names of the three other victims had repeated over and over inside her head, then she'd thought about how Mistress Eliza had attempted to bring the recently murdered innocent to life. She needed the necromancer to attempt it again since she didn't know another who could try. But she first needed someone to help her dig up a body.

An arm draped around her shoulders as if that someone had heard her call. "I've been waiting for you to come back," Zephyr said. "Did everything go all right?"

"It went as well as could be expected. Bram went straight to the authorities, and I stayed with Anika for a while. She's pregnant and hasn't been feeling well." Cricket blew out a breath. "I need to ask something of you, but can I have a drink first?"

"So secretive. I'll do anything you ask." He smirked as he fished out the flask from his pocket.

"I believe you're going to regret that," Cricket said, relishing the liquor's warm burn while it traveled down her throat, taking the edge off her frayed nerves. "Now, follow me." Bringing the flask to her lips for another sip, she led Zephyr past the lake to his practice spot.

"We're here, and no one is around, so let me know your delicious secret." Zephyr folded his arms and relaxed against a tree.

Cricket handed him his flask, knowing he would need it after hearing what she wanted. "When night falls, I was wondering if you'd go to the cemetery with me."

"The cemetery?" He arched a brow. "For pleasure?"

"No!" she hissed. "If I wanted pleasure, it wouldn't be on top of land with people buried beneath! Bram gave me the victims' names, and I need you to help me dig up one."

"My dark imagination can lead me to wicked places sometimes, but that wasn't quite what I had in mind, Cricket."

"Come on, please. I want to see if Mistress Eliza can try her necromancy again, to possibly get answers, but I can't tell her now, or she'll say no. I have no one else here who will agree, and I can't dig fast enough alone," she begged, clasping her hands together even though she hated doing it. Anika would've helped her, yet she wouldn't ask her, not when she was ill and pregnant.

Zephyr drank from his flask as his eyes stayed pinned to hers, dancing with curiosity. "Is it just the one? I don't think we'd have enough time to dig up all three."

"Just one *teensy* corpse," Cricket said. "I promise I won't ask you to do another if this fails."

"I'll do it, but you owe me."

Cricket rolled her eyes. "I'm not going to tumble you in exchange."

"When I bring you pleasure, it won't be in exchange

for something." He smirked.

"You say it as though it's happening," she drawled.

Zephyr chuckled. "I like to be optimistic."

"I'm glad that's sorted then." Cricket sank down on a large rock. The night would descend soon, but she didn't want to stay here where it was quiet, where she would think about how the body from earlier had looked. But wouldn't the one they were digging up haunt her just as much, if not more?

Cricket needed another distraction, so she held out her hand and squinted as she studied it. She wanted to see if she could get the first part of her curiosity perfected, to make her skin turn translucent.

"You're trying too hard," Zephyr said and pushed off the tree. He sat beside her, and his alluring woodsy scent relaxed her.

"It doesn't come when I will it, so I need to try harder."

Zephyr grasped her hand, then interlaced their fingers before holding them up. "Now."

Cricket's eyes remained open as she squeezed his hand. And then, something stirred beneath her skin, like moth wings caressing her palms. Her skin became lighter, exposing muscle and blood until they turned translucent, leaving her ivory skeletal system in their wake.

Cricket waited for the scratching sensation to arise, but it stayed at bay. "Look," she squeaked. "And no flowers."

"Brilliant." He grinned, releasing her hand.

As if being covered back up with a blanket, Cricket's flesh held a peach hue once more. This time, she tried it without Zephyr's touch. The color of her flesh faded, and the bones shone brightly. The flowers still didn't claw their way free, and perhaps it was better this way since the night was already descending.

"I think we should start now. I'm not sure how long it will take," Cricket said. "We need to get shovels."

Zephyr stood from the rock and helped her to her feet. "We'll grab some from the tool caravan, then go to the cemetery."

"Easy enough." As they trekked back through the woods, the moon took its place amongst the stars. Between the gaps in the trees, the torches' flames blazed, lighting their way.

Once they neared the tool caravan, laughter floated around them. A smoky aroma brushed her senses as Zephyr went inside to collect the shovels. Nearby, the bonfire crackled, and she spotted Juniper wearing striped trousers with suspenders, her tight red curls free and blowing in the wind. She stood beside Stormy, listening to her talk about something. Juniper grinned, appearing happy, and that brought a smile to Cricket's face. Beside them, Wilder tackled Autumn to the ground, tickling her sides as she giggled and cursed him at the same time.

"I found them," Zephyr said, hopping down from the top step. She reached to take a shovel, and he tugged them back. "Let me be a proper gentleman and carry them to our secret rendezvous."

"You're so… I can't think of the word at the moment, but fine," Cricket grunted. Although she was thankful for his calmness. If she'd attempted to come alone, she would've been too anxious, her heart thumping more rapidly than it already was.

After grabbing two lanterns from her caravan, they

walked toward the cemetery. Cricket wondered if the victim from earlier had been identified yet. And if so, had her family been notified? She thought about her parents, how they'd left when they believed Cricket was dead. Once the murderer was found, she would search for them, let the burden of death lift from their shoulders. She wished she knew where they were so she could send word that she was alive, that they didn't have to believe both their children were gone.

Zephyr pushed aside a tree branch and held it for her to slip past. Cricket lit her lantern and raised it to reveal rows and rows of headstones. She stepped before a crumbling one, barely making out the date from centuries ago. Her body trembled as she thought about all the bodies decaying beneath the ground while their headstones stood watch. How her own grave marker might still be resting out here... A scratching sensation rustled within her, burning beneath her flesh. She held her breath, and a hint of a dark dahlia emerged at her wrist.

"So, who is the lucky lady?" Zephyr asked, startling her.

Cricket shot him a glare as her heartbeat lessened, the dahlia tucking back inside her.

"What? I don't *pleasure* the dead." He shifted closer to her and handed her a shovel, his eyes sparking with mischief. "I mean, unless they are revived, that is."

"Enough of that." Cricket fought a smile, but he caught it and grinned.

"Did that help you feel better?" His voice grew serious as his hazel eyes pinned to hers.

Cricket slowly nodded, thankful for his distraction and that the dahlia could go away without a rose petal.

But once they focused on digging, nothing would distract her from knowing what they would unbury.

"We can start searching. What are the names?" he asked.

"If they are indeed buried here, Phoebe Brown was the last victim before the one today. Georgia Davies and Elanore Jones are the other two—the freshest graves will be near the back. Let's hurry." She waved him on, and they quietly began their search.

They held up their lanterns and ventured down separate rows, reading name after name. As she padded across graves, she noticed the dirt on some of them was much harder than it was on others which could pose a problem if it delayed digging.

"I found Phoebe," Zephyr called, kneeling in front of a headstone on a row in front of hers.

Cricket stepped around a grave and crouched beside Zephyr, running her fingers over the engraved letters and numbers. "This is recent, so it has to be hers."

"Well, what are we waiting for then?" Zephyr stood and studied the dirt where a bushel of wilted flowers rested. "The earth's still soft, which is a good sign. Unless snatchers were here first and took the body."

"Please don't tease like that," Cricket said, pushing herself up beside him.

"I wasn't teasing. If it were thieves, the body should still be here." Zephyr set his lantern beside the headstone, then struck the earth with his shovel and scooped out the first clump of dirt.

Cricket had heard about snatchers stealing bodies, then selling them to schools that practiced medicine. But as Zephyr said, if it were thieves just being thieves, then they stole for their own gain, and the body would still be there. If Phoebe's body wasn't below ground, they would have to wait until the following night to start on another.

Together, they continued to dig, only taking a small break to take a swig of liquor. As the buzz of insects grew louder, she thought the process would never end. Her muscles ached, and her throat was dry. She wanted to retrieve water for the two of them, but they were too close for her to want to stop.

And then, finally, her shovel struck something hard. The *coffin*. Zephyr shoveled faster, lifting the dirt away until there was enough room to open the wooden box. He pulled the lid back, and the earthy smell around them filled with something putrid.

She covered her nose as she gazed down at the corpse in the lantern's orange glow. Phoebe was still beautiful, her impossibly pale features not yet decayed, her delicate lips parted in death. But then a beetle crawled free of her collar, its ebony shell shining as it traveled along her chin. She then noticed maggots, not teeth, lay within her mouth, trailing over one another in a happy feast.

Cricket pushed down the bile rising up her throat. "I'll get Mistress Eliza."

# 11

Cricket broke through the trees, following the torches leading to the caravans, their smoke billowing toward the starry sky. The bonfire was nothing but ashy embers now. A few lanterns lit performers' windows, though most homes were dark for the night, their curtains drawn tight.

Mistress Eliza's window was completely darkened, hidden behind black fabric as always, yet Cricket banged on the necromancer's door anyway, her hands shaking in nervous anticipation.

The woman yanked open the door, wearing a long white nightgown. Her face lay in shadows before she lifted a lantern that illuminated a table covered in tarot cards behind her. "What are you doing here so late, child?" Mistress Eliza asked, her eyes puffy with sleep. "Is something the matter?"

The blood in Cricket's veins sang wilder than ever.

There was still a long while until the sun rose, and it wouldn't take much time for the necromancer to try to rouse the victim. "I need you to come with me to the cemetery," she said hurriedly.

"The *cemetery*? At this hour?" Mistress Eliza hissed. She brought her lantern forward, letting it rise and fall, the orange glow sweeping across Cricket's form. A deep crease formed between the necromancer's brows. "Why are you covered in dirt?"

The woman wasn't going to like this, but it needed to be done, regardless. "I dug up one of the victims' bodies from the Dahlia Murders."

"You *what*?" Mistress Eliza whisper-shouted and yanked Cricket inside the caravan. The spicy herbal scent of the necromancer's home enveloped her. "Are you trying to get the carnival banned from performing? Or are you attempting to get yourself thrown into a prison cell?"

"Zephyr and I—"

"*Zephyr*?" Mistress Eliza spat. "Why are you dragging one of my star performers into your chaos?"

Cricket didn't want to get Zephyr in trouble, yet Mistress Eliza would see him the moment she arrived at the cemetery. "I know how this sounds. But if anything could help the authorities find an answer about the murderer, this could. You were able to get the victim from this morning to twitch a bit, so maybe you can get this one to rise, even if only briefly. You tell me I need to practice my curiosity every day—now I'm giving you the same advice." She didn't like the way the words sounded coming out of her mouth, as if the victim's body was only something to be tested or practiced on. But if there was a chance, no matter how slight, that they could catch whoever was hurting these women, Cricket was determined they should at least try.

"Dead animals work just fine to practice on. Besides, you didn't have to dig a whole body up for me to see if I could get her heart to start." Mistress Eliza glared.

"Maybe not, but it would be stronger if the body were closer, right? And if it did work, it would be better for her to be above ground than below." Even though Cricket didn't remember being buried in a wooden coffin deep in the ground, the thought still haunted her. Suffocation, claustrophobia, and being alone without an escape. Cricket had wondered if Mistress Eliza hadn't felt her pulse, what would've happened down there when she did awaken? She shuddered at the thought.

After a few moments, Mistress Eliza sighed and reached for the cloak hanging beside the door. "Fine, show me where the poor woman is. You will not unbury another, understand? I will feel the soil if needed on anyone else."

"I understand," Cricket said, going down the steps with Mistress Eliza following closely. The necromancer fastened her cloak as she limped beside Cricket toward the cemetery.

The necromancer gritted her teeth. "Sometimes I wish I could get around faster."

"May I ask what happened?" Cricket had never once heard any of the carnival performers talk about it. Everyone was used to seeing that aspect of Mistress Eliza just as they were used to seeing the color of someone's hair.

"Being the stupid child I was, I climbed a ladder when my father told me not to and fell on my leg wrong. It's a part of me now, but I certainly can't run if needed. Not that I ever liked running anyway."

The corners of Cricket's lips turned up. "Running is something I prefer not to do, too, if I can help it."

"Glad we have *that* in common." Mistress Eliza held her lantern higher as they neared the woods.

Cricket pushed a branch to the side, finding Zephyr leaning on a shovel, the lantern's flame flickering atop the headstone. When they approached the unburied grave, Cricket wondered if she truly had gone mad for doing this. But perhaps it required madness to solve these murders.

"You allowed this, Zephyr?" Mistress Eliza growled, shaking her head.

"I couldn't let her get caught out here if someone came, now could I? Two digging is faster than one." Zephyr shrugged.

"I should ban the both of you from the carnival," Mistress Eliza grumbled. "But if I can get this girl to rise... Help me down there, Zephyr." She unclasped her cloak and passed it to Cricket before placing her hands into his. He lifted Mistress Eliza, then lowered her into the darkened grave. Cricket knelt to the earth and held the lantern above the necromancer.

Earlier, when distracted by the maggots and beetles, Cricket hadn't paid attention to what Phoebe was dressed in. A golden pendant rested around her neck, and she wore a beautiful lacy blue dress with a high collar. It easily hid the stitches that would've been used to seal up her destroyed chest cavity before the burial.

Mistress Eliza opened the pouch at her throat and let the three ruby stones fall into her palm. She then crouched to press her other hand to Phoebe's shoulder. A soft incantation spilled from Mistress Eliza's mouth, just as quiet as the one had been that morning. The moon shone above, casting eerie shadows that danced across the ground. Cricket looked around the cemetery to make sure they were still alone. No graverobbers or authorities, only the peaceful sounds of the night.

Mistress Eliza's knuckles were tinged with white as she dug her fingers into the woman's limp shoulder. The necromancer's lips continued to move, her words coming faster. A ragged groan filled the air, and Cricket's breath caught as she stared at the victim. Phoebe's eyes twitched behind her closed lids, and Cricket prayed she would open them, that she would have no fear of dahlias obstructing her sight. Phoebe wheezed, her body shuddering as maggots continued to feed on her.

"Come on, damn it," Cricket pleaded. She watched in horror and hopefulness while wishing the woman's breaths would become steady.

"It's all right," Zephyr called to Phoebe, his voice soft. "Open your eyes. You're safe now."

Phoebe's wheezing ceased, just as Cricket wished, but so did all signs of life as her body lay still. Dead once again.

Mistress Eliza's shoulders sagged and she slumped forward. "It's the same," she rasped, her chest heaving. "A closed door I can't open."

"What about the other two? If we find them here, can you try to rouse them from above their graves?" Cricket asked, brushing the dirt from her dress as she stood.

Mistress Eliza reached for Zephyr's hands, letting him help her out of the grave. "I can," she started, "but the repercussions of what it's doing to them if they don't rise is unknown to me."

"We should probably still try." Cricket bit her lip and exchanged a worried glance with Zephyr.

"Tell me their names."

"Georgia Davies and Elanore Jones."

Mistress Eliza's expression turned hard as she adjusted her cloak. "While I look, you will bury this one back up before you're both caught and cause the carnival more trouble."

"No one will even notice," Zephyr cooed to Mistress Eliza's back as she limped down the row of headstones.

After Zephyr sealed the coffin, Cricket lifted a shovel and scooped the dirt back into the grave. "Thank you for helping me even though my idea was for naught," she whispered to Zephyr as they worked.

"There are only a few people I would've done this for. Even when you were just a sleeping darling inside a box, I promised you things." His hazel eyes met hers, and he smirked.

"I believe you're exaggerating now." Cricket arched a brow while curiosity bloomed in her chest. "What would you have ever promised someone who couldn't answer you?"

"This may sound foolish," he said, dumping a lump of dirt into the hole. "But I would talk to you as if you could hear me. I even once promised you a picnic if you ever woke up."

A fluttering ignited in her chest, and she smiled. "Seems you still owe me that, then. One grand enough for a queen."

"Seems I do." He chuckled.

Cricket looked farther down the row, finding Mistress Eliza kneeling over a grave. The necromancer stood, shaking her head as she continued passing headstones. Not long after, she came back with her lips set in a tight line. "I'm unable to do a damn thing. Finish filling the grave, and don't get caught."

As Mistress Eliza left them alone, they worked faster to cover the grave back up, to provide Phoebe eternal peace.

Once the task was completed, Cricket straightened, and her body swayed. As she leaned forward to grab her lantern, she stumbled, and Zephyr caught her by the waist.

"Is it your curiosity?" Zephyr asked.

It wasn't flowers trying to peek through her but exhaustion. "I'm not feeling well."

"When's the last time you ate or drank something other than a few sips of liquor?"

Cricket mulled it over. "Only the rose petal and a small bowl of stew for lunch when I chatted with Anika."

"Damn it. Don't fight me on this." Zephyr scooped her up, and she gasped, but she didn't have the strength to fight him even if she wanted to. As she swallowed, small granules of dirt scratched her throat. She needed water and should've brought some back when she'd retrieved Mistress Eliza.

Zephyr rushed Cricket to the caravans, the wind mussing his hair as she peered up at him. He opened the door to his home, carried her into the small space, and sat her on a wooden chair in the corner. She hadn't been inside his home, but it was cozy, everything neat, and smelled of woods, like him. On the walls hung various swords and daggers, his own museum of weapons. At his past performances, when she attended with Anika, she remembered how he could easily throw daggers with his vines or hands and hit their marks.

He set a basket of food beside her on the night table and handed her a full canteen. She guzzled down the water until her thirst was quenched.

"I'm getting your chair dirty," she said as she took a piece of jerky from the basket.

"Get anything dirty you want." He smirked.

Cricket rolled her eyes, wondering how many women he'd brought to his bed, whether performers or customers, as she chewed the salty meat. Envy crawled through her, knowing she wouldn't like the answer. But why did it matter to her? "Have you ever been in love?" she asked, wishing she could reel the question back into the nosey depths from which it came.

"Love?" he asked, incredulous.

"It doesn't have to be true love. Just close enough to where you wanted to see the person's face again after they left." She'd always wanted to see Bram's face again, but perhaps it was the same kind of friendship love she'd held for Anika because she'd always wanted to see her face again, too.

He paused, tucking his lip between his teeth. "No, but I suppose I fall into lust easily. I was young when my sister and I came to the carnival, and we travel, so I never saw a point in offering anything beyond a night in my bed. There's been a performer here and there, but nothing serious."

"Like Autumn?" Cricket asked, thinking about how easily her hands had touched Zephyr.

"Not in a long time. She's only a friend." He moistened his lips, studying her with an impish grin. "You're very inquisitive tonight. Makes me wonder if you're growing fonder of me."

"I was only *wondering*." Heat flooded Cricket's cheeks, and she took a plum from the basket, avoiding looking into his curious hazel eyes.

Zephyr's fingers brushed her chin, turning her head so their gazes fastened. "I've never been in love," he said softly. "But that doesn't mean I never will be." He took the plum from her hand, his digits trailing against hers. With a smirk, he brought the fruit to his lips and took a slow bite before giving it back to her.

She didn't shy away as she placed the fruit between her teeth, precisely where he bit. Its juiciness filled her mouth, and she couldn't control her devilish thoughts from imagining Zephyr's tongue tasting the sweetness, then how that sweet tongue would feel against hers.

"I think I better go and get whatever rest I'm able," she said, her voice husky.

"You can always stay here. I'll even sleep on the floor and won't touch you unless you ask me to." His grin grew wolfish, tempting.

Even though she wanted to tell him that would never happen, she couldn't get the words out of her mouth, so instead, she said, "Goodnight, Zephyr. I'll see you tomorrow."

12

Too exhausted to bathe in the frigid lake, Cricket discarded her filthy clothes and fell into bed. For what was left of the night, she took turns staring at the lantern's flickering flame or the ceiling above her, unable to sleep. Cricket wondered if one of the victims had been awoken, would they have seen the murderer as she had with Clancy, or was this person trickier? Her gut believed the second choice especially since there had now been four murders linked to the same person in such a short time frame, and nothing seemed to bring the authorities closer to finding the bastard. Either way, answers wouldn't be coming from the dead any time soon, no matter how much she wished they would, so Cricket decided she needed to come up with something else.

Through the window, the night was ascending, and the day creeping in. Shoving away the blankets, she balled them up in the corner of her room to be washed later. She then sifted through her wardrobe until she found a comfortable, simple dress to wear after bathing in the lake. As she opened the door, an array of bright colors embellished the sky. With all the devilish things going on, there was still beauty in the world, in nature. Unable to stop herself, she peeked at Zephyr's caravan as she passed it. She thought about their conversation from the prior night, how he'd never been in love, how he bedded women on his travels, most only for a single night. Then she couldn't help but wonder if he was still asleep and how he slept. Did he leave his trousers on or off? And did he cover himself with his blankets or let his bare skin feel the air? A sensual feeling pooled low in her stomach. *Enough of that.*

A gust of wind blew past her, carrying the scent of pine and earth. Twigs snapped, and leaves crunched just ahead before Stormy pushed out from the woods, her dark hair in a wet plait. She carried a large satchel over one shoulder, and a black and white checkered full-body one-piece hugged her curvy form.

"The water's freezing this morning," Stormy said, her teeth chattering. "Juniper's somehow managing to stay in there and not turn into ice."

Juniper had been bathing with Stormy? It was nothing new for performers to share a lake or a pond to bathe, but she still fought a smile as she approached the glistening water.

"Don't you dare say a word," Juniper huffed when her green irises met Cricket's. She pressed a finger to her lips as if Cricket might call Stormy back to tease about the situation.

"Dear Juniper, what ever would I be bringing up on this lovely morning?" Cricket laughed softly while removing her boots and peeling her nightgown from her body. An unpleasant smell of sweat hit her senses, and she yearned for the wash, no matter how cold the lake was. She stepped into the frigid water, her body trembling as she clasped her bar of lavender soap.

"So," Cricket continued with a grin as she drew closer to Juniper. "Did you two come together?"

"I was here first." She paused, dipping her head back into the lake so it wet her red curls further. "For a while, actually."

"Did anything, you know, happen?" Cricket's grin widened as she ran the soap bar across her face, then through her hair.

Juniper heaved a sigh. "No, I think she's still in love with Louise. She didn't discuss her, but I'm waiting for them to get back together. Things I wish for don't generally happen. I wouldn't want to be of temporary use either. Not that I have experience with *that*. I'm pitiful, really."

Cricket's expression softened. "Sometimes people may still think they love another because of old feelings, but then they finally realize that's all they are. It's not how they feel in the present, but the past. Until, one day, they notice something that has been right in front of them all along."

"Whatever makes her happy is good enough for me," Juniper said, dipping below the water, her eyes almost melancholic. "Last night, I wasn't able to sleep well after the victim was found near here. And I don't think I have the right when you're back in the town where you were murdered."

A murderer that was mimicking what happened to Cricket… The image of the body found yesterday flickered in her mind—the woman's torn chest, the dahlias decorating her corpse. And then her thoughts turned to the victim she'd unburied with Zephyr—the rotting flesh, the loss of innocence. Cricket had been revived, but she wasn't the young woman she had been. She would never be her again. Still, at least she had a second chance at life—a chance to see where the new door would lead her.

"You have the right, just as much as anyone. I visited Bram yesterday, and he went straight to the authorities, so I don't know if he's discovered who the woman is yet. Though I'm certain we'll hear something soon, especially if she was at the carnival. If the murderer continues on the same path and chooses another victim, they will most likely be blonde with blue eyes. Most of the female performers here have dark hair … or red hair." She tugged at one of Juniper's wet curls. "So I believe everyone here will be safe, at least."

"Except for you, Cricket," Juniper whispered. "You have blonde hair and blue eyes."

A chill ran up her spine, and it wasn't just from the cold water. "I'm all right. The only time I've ventured to town was yesterday when Zephyr escorted me, and then the coachman took me back."

"Just please don't go out alone. Promise me."

Cricket could see the concern flickering in Juniper's green eyes, and she didn't want to worry her further. Even though they'd just been in the city where Juniper and Zephyr were murdered, she hadn't shown a hint of worry, not like now. But there hadn't been a murderer like this on the loose. "I promise. If you find another night when you can't sleep, you're always welcome to stay with me. Unless you would rather stay with *Stormy*?" she drawled.

Juniper's cheeks turned a bright shade of pink, and she splashed water at Cricket, making her laugh.

"I wish I could stop being so shy," Juniper said, her shoulders hunching. "I've always been this way, even as a child, more so when we first came to the carnival. My brother has always been the outgoing one."

Cricket's smile spread. "Really? I *never* could've guessed that about him. But I can be shy, too—it just depends on who I'm around. Like you don't seem quiet around me. So I suppose that means we're good friends now. And when you're on the stage, you're natural and whimsical with a bit of the macabre."

"I've never heard blood coming from my flesh described as whimsical, but thank you." Juniper's face lit up, her radiant smile becoming wider than Cricket's. "My brother likes you, you know."

"He likes that I haven't gone to his bed." Cricket rolled her eyes. She remembered their conversation, how Zephyr had admitted he'd never fallen in love with anyone he'd bedded. Cricket herself had only been intimate once in her life, when she and Bram had shared too many glasses of wine. And though she dreamt of travel and adventure, Cricket had always wanted to fall in love with someone who truly loved her in return, not someone simply looking for a body to warm his bed.

Juniper sighed. "Zephyr is just afraid of losing someone, is all, so he shuts those feelings out and focuses on his performance. Being perfect at it, perhaps a bit too perfect. But I think you're starting to chip away at that piece by piece."

Cricket wasn't certain if that was it or if Juniper just wanted there to be a reason for why he did it. Either way, it was his life, and she would rather not think about it anymore. "How long are we going to stay in here? I'm freezing and starving."

"It's not even cold," Juniper said and swam toward the lake's edge. Cricket huffed and followed her.

A group of performers stepped through the trees to bathe after Cricket slipped on her boots. As she and Juniper neared the caravans, several people were participating in a game of swordplay. Others ate and chatted or watched Arthur play his flute. Wilder poured them each a bowl of grits when they approached.

Cricket took a seat next to Juniper close to the fire. Juniper practically inhaled her breakfast as Cricket blew on the grits to cool it down first. "I think your curiosity may prevent you from being affected by temperature." Cricket laughed softly.

"If only. I—" She shrieked and almost dropped her bowl when Zephyr tickled her ribs. "Stop sneaking up on me!"

"Oh, hush, you should've noticed me. I didn't slither across the ground like a snake," Zephyr said as he plopped down beside his sister. A few smudges of dirt that he hadn't removed from the night before rested on his forehead and along his neck below the leather collar. His gaze drifted to Cricket, lingering on her for a beat too long before focusing back on Juniper. "I have something for you," he said, placing a compact mirror with swirling designs etched in the silver into her palm. "Found it the other night in the tent, and no one's claimed it, so it's yours."

"I love finding left-behind trinkets," Juniper squeaked, staring in awe while rotating it in her hand. She opened the mirror to look at herself before snapping it closed and sneaking it into her bag as if someone would take it from her.

"I better go bathe. Cricket and I had a *long* night last night, didn't we?" Zephyr smirked and Juniper's eyes widened.

Cricket shook her head with a sigh. "A night I'd like to forget."

Cricket straightened her spine in the chair while staring at herself in the vanity mirror. She lifted her hands and watched as her skin turned translucent, then changed back to her peach complexion. In case she needed it, she'd removed a dried rose petal and had rested it atop her vanity beside her powders. No matter how much she focused, the flowers wouldn't come. Not roses. Not dahlias. And not even a slight scratching.

She'd been at it for a long while when a hard knock pounded on the door, startling her. Her lips parted in surprise when she found Bram standing there, his hair disheveled and his face grim. She knew at some point he would come, but she hadn't assumed it would be this soon ... unless the death had something to do with the carnival.

"What did you find out? Did you discover if the

victim had been at the carnival?" Cricket asked, taking a deep swallow.

"May I come inside for a moment?" Bram sighed, his tone off. By the looks of his scowl, he wasn't in a good mood.

Cricket motioned him into her caravan and folded her arms after shutting the door. "Don't keep me in suspense. You know how anxious I get."

"First, thank you for staying with Anika. She's much better today, and I think it's because she had you there." His voice shifted as though he couldn't help but be grateful above all things.

"Of course. I've missed her. Now, what's the real reason you're here?"

"The victim from yesterday wasn't at the carnival. She'd been working at the bakery, then at night, she'd gone to a pub with a friend and left alone." His voice was nearly a whisper, as though he didn't want spying ears to hear him. "You didn't have to go dig up a victim's *grave*, Cricket."

She inhaled sharply through her nose and kept a straight face. "A victim's grave was dug up? Oh my. Those blasted thieves venture to the cemetery all the time."

Bram pinched the bridge of his nose, clearly frustrated. "They do, but it seems quite suspicious that you discovered Phoebe's name yesterday, and then an attendant at the cemetery reported to authorities this morning to say he believed her grave had been disturbed."

Cricket knew Bram, and he would not drop the matter until he heard the truth. "Oh, fine, it was me. I dug up her body, then attempted a bit of necromancy to try and get answers. Put me in manacles if you must." She wouldn't mention Zephyr and get him in trouble simply for helping her.

His brows lifted, and he drew closer. "You mean *Mistress Eliza* tried. Was she able to?"

"Don't you think I would've come straight to you if she had? I just wanted to get answers. Could you possibly locate another necromancer?" Not that any were easy to come by...

"I've tried to get Charles to look for one, yet he refuses. However, I'm going to attempt to do so now. When I was searching for your murderer, I planned to travel to the carnival myself, but I sent a letter to see if Mistress Eliza could try to rouse you. By the time I received a response that she wouldn't be able to, Clancy had already been caught and hung."

She blinked. "I didn't know you did that."

"I didn't know the reason she wouldn't be able to was because you were in a deep slumber either."

"Fate made it all work out, though." Except there was still a murderer skulking around that needed to be put to death, just like Clancy.

13

Cricket knelt behind the stage, untangling a rope that Stormy had used during her performance. The carnival was open once more after being closed for the allotted time—however, Mistress Eliza had put Cricket back on stage duty after the necromancer was questioned by Bram. Zephyr was only performing because Bram hadn't known he'd helped Cricket.

"I can stay back here if you wish. And *perform* with you instead of on stage," Zephyr said, crouching beside her. His warm breath along her neck sent a shiver through her, knowing precisely what sort of performance he meant. But she couldn't stop herself from leaning her head closer to him to inhale his woodsy scent.

"Now, *that* would only make me get in more trouble. So you will *perform* on that stage."

"*Fine*," he dragged out the single word. "I'll miss you

out there, though."

"You'll do wonderful as always." She smiled, unknotting the last of the rope. "And besides, you'll have Autumn."

"I think you and I work better together. And you still owe me something." He winked as he smirked.

"I'll be ready to help you do something that could get us both thrown in prison cells—just tell me when," she drawled, surprising herself at how flirtatious she sounded.

He put a fist to his mouth to conceal his deep laughter.

The back entrance opened, and Autumn sauntered up to them, wearing a sequined gold one-piece, exposing her long legs and elegant arms. Most of her hair was drawn atop her head, and a loose plait fell down her back. She was beautiful as ever, and envy crawled through Cricket that *she* wasn't the one with Zephyr tonight. *Performing.* She shouldn't care if she was the one on stage with him or not, but she did.

"Here's the rope," Cricket said as she handed it to Autumn.

"I'm surprised Mistress Eliza doesn't have you performing with Zephyr. You two have been doing so well together," Autumn mused.

"She's not too happy with me at the moment," Cricket grumbled. Mistress Eliza had made it clear to her that if she told anyone about digging up the grave, she could expect to clean up after the horses and the performers.

"And I assume you know why." Autumn's cat-like eyes slid to Zephyr.

"My lips are sealed." He pinched his mouth together

131

in a tight line.

"You're no fun."

Wilder, donning leather trousers and a billowing black cloak, his chest bare, joined them inside the tent. He backed Autumn into a pole and kissed her as though he'd returned from a lengthy journey to see his long-lost love. Cricket's jaw fell, and she glanced at Zephyr, who was grinning.

"Good luck," Wilder said before leaving, his expression becoming serious like usual.

Autumn straightened and lifted her chin as if nothing had happened. "We're almost up."

The two ice performers set their large hoops against the wall after finishing their act. Autumn inched closer to Zephyr, and they stepped out onto the stage.

Cricket watched their performance—Zephyr juggling, Autumn contorting in flexible positions as his vines lifted her high into the air. It was intriguing, but her chest still tightened with envy once more, wishing it was her in his arms.

Not wanting her emotions to show when their act ended, she went out the back entrance, the cool air making gooseflesh rise on her arms. There was nothing left for her to do backstage anyway, so she decided to go the longer route to her caravan, to pass the visitors as they played the games and ate the food.

Red curls sweeping around her face, Juniper stood in line beside Stormy to get a caramel apple. Cricket waved at her friend, but she was busy chatting with Stormy, which made her smile.

Cricket hurried past Mistress Eliza's tent before the necromancer saw her. A blonde woman walked out with a dreamy smile, meaning her tarot card reading must've gone well. The next in line entered—a young man with a boyish face and his hair swept to the side.

As she neared the caravans, a female voice called her name, "Cricket!" She whirled around to find Anika, lifting the skirts of her light blue dress and racing toward her. Her cheeks were flushed as she stopped in front of Cricket, her chest heaving. "I've been trying to catch up with you, but every time someone blocked my way."

"Why are you running out here in your condition?" Cricket hissed, remembering when Anika could barely get out of bed. "And where's Bram? He's letting you wander around alone?" Cricket searched for his tall form and spotted him near one of the games. He nodded toward them, then went into one of the tents.

"I told him if he stayed a leech at my side while I had a conversation with you, I would make him sleep on the chaise." She laughed softly. "He's going to meet me after the performances. As for my condition, I will run anywhere I please unless the nausea returns. I believe you're the miracle cure that helped me feel better."

"I'm so glad to hear that." Cricket smiled and pointed to the caravan painted in different shades of purple, the roof a glossy black. "That's my home. We can go inside and chat for a while. I know how you like the quiet, and it's as quiet as we'll get out here."

"It looks positively cozy. I love it." Anika beamed, clasping her hands together.

Cricket walked alongside her friend and led her into the caravan. Anika lowered herself onto the chair at the vanity while Cricket sat across from her on the bed.

"Why didn't you perform with Zephyr? I was waiting

to see you. *Impatiently*, I might add." Anika lifted and inspected each trinket and makeup piece resting on the vanity.

"Did Bram not tell you?" Cricket reclined back on her hands. "I dug up one of the bodies to see if Mistress Eliza could bring her back. But that's hush-hush between me and you, or the necromancer will put me out in the stables."

"Oh, I already know. I was just seeing if you would tell me." Anika waved a hand in the air.

"You— If you weren't pregnant I'd throw a pillow at your face."

"I would've caught it before it hit me," she said matter of fact. Her expression grew serious. "How's your curiosity?"

"Well, it's still being quite the nuisance. No roses, only dahlias. On the bright side, I can master the first part of it now. I just need to achieve the second part." Halfway there was better than nothing, at least.

Anika leaned forward, her gaze roaming across Cricket's bare arms in anticipation. "Will you show me?"

"I shouldn't have used the word *master*, but let me try." Cricket drank in the air around her and held out her hands toward Anika. She kept her breath even as the curiosity within her brushed against her nerve endings, touching across her layers, then one by one, pulling back the blankets of her flesh at its will. Her skin grew lighter, fading until it was translucent and exposing the ivory bones beneath.

Anika gasped and clapped her hands, the sound echoing off the walls. "It's brilliant. Beautiful."

"You always did have a morbid curiosity that mirrored

mine." Cricket laughed, remembering every instance when they'd visited the carnival. How afterward, Anika would paint the curiosities on canvases while Cricket danced, pretending she held those abilities that could enhance her performance.

"I'll paint yours and show you when I finish," Anika said excitedly.

"Just not my face," Cricket pointed out, hating having her face painted. She didn't mind how she looked, but it was strange the way people saw others differently than how they saw themselves.

Anika blinked. "So does that mean I can include a head still, or do you want it replaced with something else? Perhaps a skull? Or a rose?"

"Surprise me." Cricket laughed. "Is your mother back yet?"

"She just came home today, and she's been worrying nonstop over my being sick even though I'm feeling better. Overprotective as usual." She paused. "I don't think I got to tell you, but she's been living with us for the past three weeks. I'd always hoped to get her out of our withering house." A horrified expression crossed Anika's face, and she hurried on, "But that's not why I married Bram. I would never do that just for money or a *house*."

"You most certainly would rather live on the streets than marry someone for money. I know you, just as you know me." Cricket smiled at a memory of them as children, holding their pinkies together and vowing to never marry unless it was for true love. And if they'd never met their true love, they promised one another to meet for tea and continue their passions while growing wrinkled and gray.

Anika grasped her skirts as she stood and plopped down beside Cricket on the bed, taking her hand in hers. "I'm glad you're here, even if it's only for a little while. But please come and visit more."

Before returning to Nobel, Cricket had attempted to pretend as if Anika and Bram didn't exist, but it was only a temporary trial that she knew would never last. Anika was more than a friend—she was family. "Once the baby arrives, I'll visit. I promise." She squeezed Anika's hand, tears streaming down her friend's face. "What is it? Did I say something wrong?"

"No," Anika hurried on, straightening her spine. "Not at all. I've been holding in this guilt, knowing it's my fault you died. You walked me home after such a lovely time at the carnival, and then…" she trailed off. "It's as if I've taken over what could've been your life."

Cricket should've discussed this with Anika when she'd seen her last, but her friend had been too exhausted and weak from her nausea spells. "You didn't," Cricket started. "It's not your fault. I've thought about this plenty, and I was never engaged to Bram. Even if he had offered, I don't think I would've agreed. Deep down, I wanted to get away from here, to be on the stage. Sometimes being in Nobel felt as though I were trapped in a cage. I only wanted to travel, to perform, then come back here and visit as I'm doing now." She tilted Anika's chin up so she could see the truth in her gaze. "You love Bram. He loves you. And his eyes never lit up when he saw me, the way they do with you. If a love is true, then it shouldn't fade as much and as easily as it has for me. Yes, I was hurt at first, but then I took it as a blessing. Both of you believed

I was dead, and I'm relieved you had one another, fell in love, because it opened my eyes."

A tear trailed down Anika's cheek, and she swiped it away. "I have a secret I must confess, Cricket."

A sinking feeling swam through her stomach, wondering what other kind of secret she would have. "You can tell me."

Anika took another breath and tangled her fingers in her skirts. "I knew Bram since we were children, and at first, I'd believed him full of himself and stuffy, but he wasn't any of those things. I then always wished I'd had someone like him. Not Bram specifically at the time, but his qualities—someone who was kind and smart, a true gentleman toward women, and didn't care about anyone's station when it came to calling them a friend. After our first *unplanned* kiss, I felt so guilty because you were gone. I pushed him away for weeks, but I couldn't stop thinking about him."

Cricket bit her lip and smiled. "He is all those things and the right one for *you*."

Anika circled her arms around Cricket and held her tight. "With these murders, I'm worried about you. If you wanted to stay with us, at least until the carnival leaves, we wouldn't mind at all."

She knew it would be pleasant to stay at the manor, but she wanted to remain here. Besides that, Anika's mother was living with them, and she feared the woman would worry that she would put a wedge between her daughter and Bram. "Let's take it day by day. But how about I have tea with you this week?"

"Perhaps we can make it through without me losing my stomach." Anika smiled as she pulled back. "I suppose I'll go. Bram is most likely confused by the performances."

"A good reason why we always went with each other." Cricket laughed softly.

Anika stood and looked in the mirror, wiping away a few lingering tears. She glanced over her shoulder with a mischievous expression after she opened the door, her grin widening. "Not only is Bram impatient and waiting for me, but there's someone here to see you. Seems we have even more to discuss over tea."

Cricket's brows drew together, and she padded to the door. Zephyr lingered there, his hands in his pockets, while Anika walked away with Bram, still smiling over her shoulder at her.

"I wanted to give you something before I wash up," Zephyr said, taking his hands from his pockets.

"What is it?" She peered at his empty palms and wrinkled her nose. "You came here to show me your *hands*?"

"If you want to experience them closer, I'm also fine with that." He grinned. "But I brought you my company."

Cricket rolled her eyes and snorted. "Well, do come in and present me with the greatest gift I've ever been given."

"I love the dramatics," Zephyr purred and sauntered inside. He sank down on the floor in front of the bed. And when she sat beside him, he added, "I missed you performing with me tonight."

"Did you really?" No matter who he performed with, it always looked as if he relished the act.

"Really." His voice came out low, seductive.

Her heart fluttered, and she needed to talk about anything else. "Will you do something for me?" she finally asked as she studied the ceiling. "Will you tell me everything that happened in the past year while I was asleep? Even the little things that people believe no one cares about."

Zephyr twirled a lock of her hair around his finger. "Listen closely, and let me tell you a tale," he cooed, his voice full of intrigue. "We begin with the Sleeping Darling and all the magical and grotesque things she missed while unaware."

Cricket didn't interrupt as she listened to every single word that poured from his lips until her head grew heavy and her cheek rested against Zephyr's shoulder. Though she wanted to remain listening to his melodic voice all night, she was unable to keep her eyes open any longer.

# 14

With a yawn, Cricket cracked open her eyes and drew the blankets to her chin. Dawn's light spilled into the room through the slit in her curtains. She was about to close her eyes for a little longer when images from the night before came to her. Zephyr telling her about all the things she'd missed while being the Sleeping Darling. Besides the time that Juniper had told her about a man wanting to pleasure her awake, there'd been ones begging to court her, and another had even brought a ring and proposed. She'd never had that much attention from men while awake. She remembered falling asleep against Zephyr's warm shoulder, his soothing voice continuing into her dreams.

Cricket ripped the blankets away and jolted forward, searching around the room, but Zephyr was no longer there. He must've placed her in bed, fully dressed, then covered her with the blankets.

Today would be more of Cricket working behind the stage. If she could get the roses to bloom, that might satisfy Mistress Eliza enough to allow her to perform, even if it was only to assist Zephyr and not show her curiosity to an audience just yet.

Her boots rested neatly on the floor, tucked beneath her vanity. Cricket smiled to herself at Zephyr removing them from her feet and placing them there instead of leaving them on her.

It was still too early for most of the performers to be awake, including her, but since she couldn't fall back asleep, she gathered fresh clothing and soap to bathe. A gust of wind slammed against her when she stepped out from the caravan, carrying a metallic smell. Cricket froze as her gaze swept across the ground, dropping her clothing and soap. Hoping what she saw was only a nightmare, she inched forward, her legs trembling, but no matter how much she wished the dreadful scene before her would vanish, it didn't.

There, in the shadows between two caravans, lay a woman. Her blonde hair speckled red, her chest torn open, a pool of blood beneath her. Dahlias stared at Cricket in place of the victim's eyes, another poked out from her mouth, others were buried inside her torn chest, and in each palm, a lone flower rested. Cricket bolted to the horrific scene and knelt beside the victim. Her scream remained locked away as the scratching from her curiosity, desperate and wild, clawed beneath her skin, but then someone else released one for her, the high-pitched sound piercing her ears.

Autumn ran toward Cricket, her dark hair billowing

behind her as she covered her mouth. "What happened?" she shrieked, and doors to caravans opened. Performers stepped out, some half-dressed, others in nightgowns.

"Same as what happened to the others," Cricket whispered, knowing if she pinched herself, she wouldn't wake. "Will you get Mistress Eliza? Please."

Autumn turned to the approaching performers. "Stay back!" she instructed, then took off on a heavy sprint just as Juniper broke through the crowd, the only one choosing to come close. A light pink robe was wrapped around her loosely, and her red hair was matted in tangles.

"Cricket!" she gasped, kneeling at her side.

Cricket's gaze pulled back to the victim as if drawn by magnetism. She couldn't stop staring at the slaughtered body—the blonde hair matching hers. Blood, so much blood. The black of the dahlias cloaked their crimson-stained petals. The haunting day of her own death revisited her, the blade pushing through her flesh. Her fingers absently ran up her chest where a scar should've been if the necromancy magic hadn't taken it away. Sometimes she wished the scar had remained to remind herself of what she'd survived, that her murder had indeed happened. Yet the body in front of her now proved that it had, that there was another murderous bastard out there mirroring what Clancy had done.

Cricket ignored the quiet chatter filling the crowd as she noticed something white peeking from the victim's coat pocket. A note of some kind. She drew the paper out and unfolded it.

In a choppy, cursive style, one single sentence was written. *A pity you didn't perform last night, Cricket.*

"What does it say?" Juniper asked, leaning closer.

Cricket could barely breathe, her lungs tight in her chest. "This isn't a coincidence that the victim's body is here. It was meant to be left for me," she murmured, her hands trembling as she slipped the note into Juniper's fingertips.

"Why is everyone lurking around and staring like fools," Mistress Eliza spat. "Someone take a horse and get the authorities." She limped through the crowd, barefoot and wearing an oversized black nightgown. Her lips pursed as her gaze looked past Cricket and Juniper to the body.

Mistress Eliza limped faster, drawing the ruby stones from her pouch, then knelt before the young woman. She didn't seem to take a moment to breathe as she pressed her other hand to the victim's shoulder. Whispered words spilled from the necromancer's lips while Cricket prayed silently that this time, the woman would rise, that her body would mend back together, that she would get a second chance to live the way the others at the carnival had, the way *she* had.

The woman twitched, her hands squeezing the dahlias resting inside them. A choking sound poured from her throat, and Cricket took the flower from the woman's mouth, then removed the ones from her eyes, not caring what the authorities would say about it. Yet the victim's eyes didn't open, and not a single word escaped her lips. Silence reigned along the dawn air, and the woman returned to death once more.

Mistress Eliza's shoulders drooped, her body hunching forward when she released her hand from the woman. Sweat beaded the necromancer's brow as she turned to face Cricket and Juniper. "Did either one of you see or hear anything?"

Cricket shook her head. "No, but I—"

"Neither one of us saw or heard anything." Juniper cut her off, tucking the note in her robe. Cricket frowned as she continued casting glances at Juniper, but she didn't say anything else.

Mistress Eliza tightened her lips once more, then blew out a breath while murmuring, "This isn't good."

Zephyr rounded a caravan, dressed only in dark trousers, and when his gaze found them, he rushed forward. "Are you two all right?" Zephyr asked, his face wild. "Autumn woke me up and told me what happened. Wilder's bringing the authorities."

"They're fine," Mistress Eliza answered and limped toward him. "What I need you to worry about now is making sure everyone remains in their caravans while I get with the strong men to search inside the tents." She then focused on Juniper and Cricket. "And you two, make sure no one tampers with the body more than it already has been."

Zephyr scowled and looked as though he was going to argue when Juniper said, "We're not hurt. Just do what she asked. It will make things easier for when the authorities arrive."

"For you, I'll listen," he muttered.

Mistress Eliza drew Zephyr by the arm, instructing him to get her when the authorities came as they walked away.

After long minutes ticked by, Cricket leaned closer to Juniper, and though no one was around them besides the victim, she whispered, "Why did you hide the letter and not tell them?"

"If Mistress Eliza saw it, she would demand you leave. But what this awful note means is you need us more than ever. We'll keep this between us." With a sigh, Juniper fished out the folded paper from her robe and handed it to Cricket.

Juniper was right—Mistress Eliza would be furious to know that a vicious killer was targeting someone within her carnival. She warred with herself on whether to listen to her friend and ultimately decided to. Even if it was selfish on her part.

Footsteps crunched against the dirt, and Cricket hurriedly slid the note inside her bodice. Zephyr came into view, his voice low as he spoke, "Sorry, I had to get her off my back."

"Did you see anything when you left last night?" Cricket asked.

He shook his head. "I should've—"

The sound of horses' hooves pummeling the earth through the gathering mist soared with the breeze. Cricket jerked her head up, then leapt to her feet, peering between two caravans to catch sight of Bram, Charles, Miles, and Wilder riding their horses toward them.

Zephyr jogged away to retrieve Mistress Eliza. A few moments later, the horses halted and their riders dismounted. Bram raked a hand through his thick hair, a rigid expression on his face. Charles frowned when his gaze met hers, and Bram gave her a brief nod. They kept words at a minimum as they inspected the body.

"I've seen her," Miles said. "Her name's Joanna. She works at the meat shop." A name with a body only made this nightmare more real, especially knowing that her family would soon discover her horrible fate.

Once Mistress Eliza and Zephyr returned, they were each questioned. Charles's eyebrows pinched together when Mistress Eliza admitted she'd tried to revive the victim, which was why the dahlias were no longer on her eyes or in her mouth.

Charles and Miles then went door to door of the caravans, asking if anyone had encountered the victim before today or had seen or heard anything suspicious the previous night. A carriage came shortly after to take the body away to the coroner, leaving only a pool of blood behind.

Bram stepped toward Cricket, his expression grim. "I need to discuss something with you. Will you follow me?"

Her chest tightened as he led her to where his horse lingered. The note felt weighted in her bodice, and she hoped he didn't believe she'd had something to do with this intentionally. As they came to a stop, she turned to him and asked, "What is it?"

"You're hiding something. If you want to help these victims, you can't keep secrets from me."

Cricket sighed and fished out the note from her bodice. "I didn't want anyone else at the carnival to see this."

Without a word, Bram took the note from her hand and read it over. His throat bobbed as he peered down at her. "This letter is specifically for you, Cricket. That body was left for *you*. And you didn't give me this as soon as I arrived?"

Cricket gazed at the ground in silence. "I would've shown you." This was Bram, her friend, an authority she trusted, and she should've given it to him as soon as he'd gotten there, but she hadn't.

"From now on, if anything else is left for you, or you want to do something illegally, come to me. Please. There's only so much protecting you from ending up in a prison cell that I can do."

She frowned. "What do you think the reason is for the note?" The murderer had known she didn't perform last night, which meant they'd been at the carnival as well as the other times when she'd been on stage with Zephyr.

"The murders began a little after you left Nobel, so I believe it was to lure you back here for some reason. But even though you're here now, the murders are continuing. So my theory may not be right, or maybe it needs to be adjusted. I feel as if this case is pushing us in circles."

"Are you going to tell everyone about the note?"

"Only the authorities for the time being. There's handwriting on this, and if we can find a match, that could be the key we need to catch this murderer. If you want to keep silent on this matter from the other performers, that's your decision. They weren't threatened directly, and the letter wasn't sent to them—it was left for you. I can't force you to come to my manor, but the door is always open."

"Thank you, Bram. I'm staying here, though."

He ran his hand across his jaw, his lips tight as though he wanted to argue. "One more thing. Last night, Zephyr was with you for most of it?"

"Yes, I'm unsure of the precise time he left." She narrowed her eyes. "Why are you asking me that? Do you think one of us did it? That I wrote the note to myself? I know how authorities think sometimes."

"You?" he asked, incredulous. "Of course not. But I was going to suggest that you stay with someone at night if you remain here. I think it should be Zephyr since he seems to care about your safety and looks like he could defend you. I believe it necessary, especially after a letter was left with your name on it."

Cricket considered it. "All right, I'll see about it." She would ask Zephyr, but she wouldn't tell him about the letter. There was no need for him or anyone else to worry about her, not when Mistress Eliza had already reprimanded him for helping her the last time. Besides that, Juniper wanted it to stay between them, even though she'd already fractured that a bit by telling Bram.

But the truth was, things were becoming a little clearer, and the victims' murders were most certainly her fault.

15

Once the authorities left, Cricket found Juniper walking away from Stormy toward her caravan. She caught up with her, noticing tears beading along her lashes and worry filling her gaze.

"What is it?" Cricket asked and immediately cursed herself for it. "Sorry, that was a foolish question."

"If I'm to be honest, I'm frightened. But not for me, for you. After the letter…" she finished the last part in a whisper.

Cricket sighed. She would be a liar if she didn't say she was at least a little frightened too. "I couldn't hold onto it—I gave it to Bram. It wasn't hard for him to know I was hiding something. Thankfully, he will see if he can find a match for the handwriting."

Juniper nodded and seemed to fold in on herself. "I should've thought about that. But what about the others?

The carnival will be closed again, so you need to keep quiet about it. Mistress Eliza isn't the only one in a raging mood."

Mistress Eliza wasn't a fool—even without the letter, she would still assume that there was a possible link between the victims and Cricket due to the dahlias, the hair, the eyes... "For now, I'm not telling anyone. However, Bram wants someone to stay with me, and—"

"I don't mind staying with you!" Juniper chirped, her eyes wide.

"He suggested Zephyr, but if you—"

"No, that's perfect. My brother's great with blades and can use his vines to cut down anyone who tries to hurt you."

That was true—Zephyr was great with swords and daggers, could easily hit the center of anything he put his mind to. While his vines could be lethal if he so chose. "Let's hope it doesn't come to that. I know you've been having trouble sleeping, and you shouldn't be alone. Would you want to stay with me anyway?"

Juniper bit her lip. "Stormy actually just offered for me to stay with her, but I told her I was fine."

A small smile curled the edges of Cricket's lips. "I think you should, and not only to protect one another, but maybe to tell her how you feel?"

Juniper's cheeks pinkened. "Now's not the time to discuss *that*. But I suppose I will take her offer. It would be less cramped with two people." She rested a hand on Cricket's shoulder. "Just be careful. Every time I see or hear about death, it reminds me of my parents. So with you seeing this, so close to how you died, I can't imagine what you're feeling."

"I just want this bastard found." It was hard, but other situations had been harder. Losing her brother to the plague was a worse fate. She wondered how often her parents were still thinking about her. No matter what, she promised herself she would one day find them, let them know she was alive as soon as the murderer was caught. With her being taunted, even if she knew where they were, it was better they not discover the truth in case something happened to her again.

As she parted ways with Juniper, she rounded one of the caravans and found Zephyr talking to Mistress Eliza and Autumn. When his gaze locked on hers, Cricket chewed the inside of her cheek and motioned him to walk with her.

"How are you?" Zephyr asked as he sauntered up beside her.

She shrugged, wishing she could get the simple question out.

"Need a drink?" he asked, fishing out the flask and handing it to her.

"I need a favor," she said but took a sip from the flask first, letting the liquor calm her nerves.

"I remember the last time we dabbled in favors—it wasn't good. You still owe me one, remember?" He smirked, tucking the flask back into his trouser pocket. "But I'll allow you a favor anyway."

She rolled her eyes and folded her arms, her tongue like lead inside her mouth. "I was wondering if... This will sound ridiculous, but Bram wants you to stay with me. He's worried about me, and now that I think about it, maybe it isn't necessary since there are plenty of performers near my caravan..." Cricket trailed off, not revealing the true reason why Bram wanted Zephyr to stay with her.

He grasped her arm gently and drew her closer, his woodsy scent steadying her. "Would you want me to?"

"I *suppose* it wasn't so terrible when you were there last night," she murmured, attempting to sound more careless and failing.

"You're going to think me a bastard for saying this now, but I would stay with you under any circumstance." He lifted her chin so his hazel eyes fastened on hers. "*Any.*"

"I think your expectations of staying with me are a bit too high. I'm quite the stickler of where I like things to go." She smiled.

"Then you can come to mine." He grabbed her hand and tugged her forward. "I promise I'll keep my hands to myself unless you ask me not to."

"Stay with you?" She laughed, pulling him to a stop. "I thought you liked having your space to yourself?" Most of the performers had to share a caravan except for a few who brought in good wages from their performances. Cricket was lucky Mistress Eliza hadn't moved her when she'd awoken.

Zephyr held up a finger. "Seems I changed my mind. Besides, my caravan is farther away from where the body was found. Maybe it would be less of a reminder if you need it."

She didn't think the memory would fade for a while, regardless. After another woman's body had been discovered so soon, more than ever, the killer had to be found. She didn't know if she could take any more macabre dead bodies decorated in bloody dahlias.

"I will then, but only on the condition that if I do something ridiculous, like spill secrets in my sleep, you promise not to tell anyone." Cricket smiled, and her shoulders relaxed.

"Secrets, you say?" Zephyr grinned while pretending as though he was sewing his lips shut.

She released a sigh. "Thank you. I'm just relieved Mistress Eliza has allowed me to stay."

His hand glided down her arm, stopping at her wrist, and he drew her close. "It'll stay that way. You'll get a hold of your curiosity, and the murderer will be hung. The authorities found yours before, and this one will be found too."

Some cases weren't solved as quickly—she knew that—but she hoped this one was coming to a close sooner rather than later.

"I think we need a break," he continued. "The carnival will be closed, so let me take you into the city."

She lifted her brows. It would be a wonderful distraction, and perhaps she could find out something about the latest victim, Joanna. "I'll gladly take the offer."

As she grabbed her satchel from the caravan, Wilder and Arthur carried buckets of water, pouring them over where the remaining blood stained the dirt until it was as if a body had never been there at all.

Zephyr met Cricket outside her home, wearing a white shirt that hugged his arms perfectly. He left a few buttons at his chest undone, the collar at his throat on display.

Together they walked into the city, the sun shining brightly above. Thick, puffy clouds that she could easily make animal shapes out of floated slowly across the blue sky.

The shops bustled with life, and a woman carrying a large stack of tomes hurried past them. They approached a white-bricked pub called the Garland that she and Anika used to frequent. Zephyr opened the door, and the smell of tobacco smoke clung to the air. A few men and women sat at tables smoking cigars or pipes. Old, faded maps hung across the wooden walls, and thick green velvet curtains cloaked the windows. At the bar, a familiar face was wiping the counters with a wet rag, her frilly green dress rustling as she scrubbed harder. The young blonde-haired woman, Leslie, turned when they sat at the counter. She halted as she studied Cricket with her pale blue eyes. A chill ran up her spine that Leslie would be a perfect fit for the murderer.

"Hello, Leslie," Cricket said, remembering how when she used to come in here, the young woman would laugh and tell jokes to her and Anika.

"You're back," she stuttered.

*From the dead? Why yes, yes I am*, she wanted to say, but she held her tongue.

"Gossip spread about a month ago that the carnival necromancer had brought you back from the grave. I'm just relieved they caught that awful bastard." Leslie huffed, no longer surprised by Cricket's visit. "What can I get for you? It's on me."

"A bowl of lamb soup and a whiskey," Cricket said.

"I'll have the same." Zephyr passed Leslie a few silver coins, but she batted his hand away before leaving them alone to go into the kitchen.

Zephyr inched closer to Cricket, whispering in her ear, his breath warm against her neck. "I have a confession. A little secret I've been keeping."

"Color me intrigued. What is it?" she drawled.

"I remember seeing you when you would visit the carnival."

She rolled her eyes. "I doubt it. There are so many faces in each crowd and too many performances to remember someone."

"That's usually true," he purred. "But not someone who comes to almost every performance and sits front and center. Your blue eyes were always wide in amazement as you watched each act."

Heat rose up Cricket's neck. She averted her gaze from his and peered down at her hands. "I mean, I suppose I liked the carnival."

"I would've asked you back to my caravan if you'd approached me after the performance, but I'm certain I would've received a slap across the face." He smirked.

"I'm certain." She laughed softly just as Leslie returned with two bowls of steaming soup, the savory aroma delicious.

"You hear about the murdered girl this morning?" Leslie asked as she poured them both a glass of whiskey.

"Only that her name's Joanna, and she worked at the meat shop."

Leslie nodded. "Joanna was here last night and drank so much she could barely walk. When the authorities came in here earlier, I told them that she'd gone to the inn across the road. She'd been staying there a while since it was all she could afford. I always watched her go into it, made sure she was safe. But someone must've been waiting for her inside her room. One of the inn's servants told me she found blood when she came in to make up the room this morning. How Joanna ended up at the carnival, though, is beyond me?"

"She was murdered at the inn?" Zephyr scrunched his face, seeming to mull it over.

"Someone must've brought her to the carnival after..." Cricket trailed off.

"The question is, why do that, though?" Leslie's gaze held Cricket's, and her chest tightened, thinking about the note she'd given to Bram. "Something to think about." She stepped away, grabbed her wet rag, and cleaned an empty table.

"That is quite the conundrum," Zephyr muttered, bringing a spoonful of soup to his lips.

"Quite." Cricket sighed. The body was brought for her to see and retrieve the note. A sick and twisted gift of sorts.

She forced down the soup, even though she'd lost her appetite. Taking the glass, she polished the whiskey off. She wanted another drink, but she needed her head to be clear.

"Watch over yourself," Cricket called to Leslie before they left, and as the woman's blue eyes met her own, she hoped she remained safe.

"Can't help not to. Just wish I knew if there was another reason they're chosen," Leslie said, turning the cloth over and scrubbing a new table.

As Cricket and Zephyr stepped outside, Charles passed them on his horse and stopped in front of the inn across the street.

"Cricket?" Charles said, hopping down from his horse and studying them both. "What are you two doing here?" His voice sounded suspicious.

"Just grabbed a bite to eat after a long day," Zephyr said, narrowing his eyes.

"I suggest going back to the carnival. The town isn't going to take too kindly on what happened." Charles frowned. "We'll be patrolling the road near there from now on."

Cricket pressed her lips in a tight line to keep from telling him that the murder had occurred at the inn and not the carnival, but it wouldn't matter. They were just carnival filth to him at this point.

"Come on, Zephyr. Let's go." Cricket pulled on his wrist, and he circled his arm around her shoulders.

"We don't have to go home just because that bastard tells us to," Zephyr grumbled.

She would've liked to distract herself by walking around the city, but now she just wanted to go home. "It's all right. I just want to bathe a long while in the lake." Zephyr arched his brow. "Alone." She laughed.

The walk back to the carnival was nice, quiet—flocks of birds flew past them without so much as a caw. Once she reached her caravan, Cricket gathered a change of clothing and dropped a bag of her things at Zephyr's before bathing in the lake. A few other performers were washing themselves at the opposite end, so she wasn't alone, which was better—she didn't know if someone could be lingering in the woods somewhere.

Night hadn't fallen yet, but a fire was already blazing. Most of the performers were there, chatting to one another. Mistress Eliza motioned her over with a finger. "If you haven't heard, one of the young authorities, I can't recall his name, but not Bram, came back and mentioned how the victim wasn't murdered here but at an inn. It's quite strange."

Cricket waited with bated breath for Mistress Eliza to send her away. The only one in danger at the carnival was Cricket, but she would be in danger no matter where she went.

"You might want to cover that pretty hair of yours up while we're here."

"I will." She still had a few wigs from when she was the Sleeping Darling. Perhaps she should've worn one earlier when they'd gone into town too.

Night descended, and the stars lit up the sky. Cricket found Zephyr sitting beside Juniper and Stormy, throwing small sticks into the crackling flames. She knelt beside him, her muscles heavy. "Do you mind walking me to your caravan since you have the key? I'm tired."

"It's fine. I'll turn in, too," he said and pushed himself up.

Cricket bid goodnight to Juniper and Stormy before she and Zephyr comfortably walked side by side. Once inside his home, she stood on her tiptoes and kissed his cheek. "Thank you for the distraction today."

His eyes widened, but he didn't say a word as she removed her boots and slipped into his bed.

# 16

The carnival remained closed for a couple of days, and since then, it only opened its doors during daylight hours. Mistress Eliza was in a foul mood about it, but they couldn't arrive at the next town too soon. The authorities patrolled the streets, questioning everyone with any connection to the victims, yet were no closer to discovering the killer. One body being found near the road of the carnival and another inside hadn't kept the crowd from venturing to it, but the same could be said for the earlier victims whose bodies had been found in front of a pub, library, and church. At night, more torches were lit throughout the carnival in an attempt to keep the shadows at bay.

Cricket stood behind the tent, practicing her routine while Juniper watched. She wore the chestnut wig as Mistress Eliza had suggested, only she pinned it up in a plaited crown to keep the locks from overheating her. The necromancer had released Cricket from backstage duties and allowed her to resume her practice. But Mistress Eliza still didn't know about the letter she'd given to Bram. He'd visited once and taken her to see Anika for tea, yet there hadn't been any leads on the murderer. Just because they had a sample of the bastard's penmanship didn't mean he would be easy to find in a city of thousands.

Lifting a hand toward the cloudy sky, Cricket brought her right leg back, then twirled. Even though she and Zephyr temporarily shared a caravan, they hadn't spent much time together since Mistress Eliza ran him ragged with constant demands that he do her errands and complete endless chores. Their bedtime arrangements stayed the same—her on the bed and him on the floor. He remained gentlemanly enough at night, not asking if he could slip beneath the covers with her. If he did, she might be tempted enough to allow it.

A hammer striking metal sounded, and Cricket peeked inside the tent. She found Zephyr still helping Kyrie build a guillotine for his act.

"Focus, Cricket," Juniper said with a smile. "Ignore them."

She released the fabric and held her hands out in front of her while Juniper stayed silent. Her friend promised not to intervene unless she deemed it necessary. Over the past few days, nothing had changed. No dahlias or roses, only her flesh becoming translucent when practicing.

Cricket's heart hammered in sync with Zephyr pounding away behind the fabric of the tent. The easy part came, the unveiling of her bones beneath her skin as the colored layers of her flesh faded. She brought her arms up toward the sky, then stood on her toes and slowly spun. Unlike the other days, the scratching inside her muscles stirred. She took even breaths, praying the red roses would unfurl at the surface.

However, dark marks freckled her flesh, and she continued to inhale gently while her heart raced. This time pain didn't accompany it. *Red. Become red.* As the flowers sprouted, they weren't roses but the same damn dahlias. Her veins thrummed violently while she attempted to tuck the nuisances back in, yet they wouldn't listen. They didn't try to consume her though, only lingered as a reminder of the victims' deaths.

"Focus, Cricket," Juniper repeated.

Cricket couldn't try any longer, for fear someone would see them. She stopped spinning to take a petal from the locket, then placed it on her tongue. The dahlias drew back in as she chewed, her chest heaving, the rose flavor sliding down her throat.

"They didn't seem to want to devour you this time." Juniper clapped, a bright smile tugging at her pinkened cheeks.

"Besides them not being roses, I still couldn't get the blasted things to go away on their own." Cricket tightened her fists, letting her nails dig half-moons into her palms. "It would be fine if they were black roses, but they aren't."

Juniper stood from the grass and patted Cricket's shoulder. "My theory is that you were asleep for over a year. In that time, you couldn't work on your curiosity the way the rest of us were able to right away. Instead of within a week, perhaps it could take as long as when you were asleep to work properly."

Cricket's heart lodged in her throat. "Mistress Eliza won't give me that long. I'm lucky she's given me this much time." If Cricket's curiosity didn't match the necromancer's original vision, she was tainted no matter where they traveled. She would have no use for Cricket.

"Just keep practicing and having the petals ready if necessary. I'm here to help any way I can if you need someone to watch you."

"Juniper!" Mistress Eliza shouted, startling them both as she rounded the tent. "You're about to be up and should've already been backstage."

"Oh dear, I lost track of time." Juniper blew Cricket a kiss before darting off to her performance tent.

Mistress Eliza placed her hands on her hips and limped toward Cricket. "You've been practicing back here for days. Have you managed to bloom any roses yet?"

Cricket bit her lip and shook her head. "I haven't, but I can make my bones be seen at will, and just now, I was able to bring the flowers forward, and they didn't attempt to consume me."

Mistress Eliza rubbed at her chin. "If it wasn't for those deceitful flowers, I might allow you to show your curiosity. But we just can't risk the dahlias being seen. After the spectacle with the grave, I'll only allow you on stage once you hone in on your gift." She paused and tilted her head while tapping her fingers against her thigh. "Perhaps you need to relax your muscles more. Give into a little pleasure with someone. That can always help feed your curiosity."

Cricket's eyes widened, and she choked, coughing. "I'm fine," she croaked.

"For now, see if anyone needs help."

"All right, I'll do that."

"I'll be in my tent with my tarot cards if you need me," Mistress Eliza said, then spun on her heel and limped away.

Couldn't the woman see that Cricket was trying? Even when her mind focused on the murders, she continued to practice day in and day out so she wouldn't have these monstrous flowers spontaneously come out of her.

She pulled back the tent's fabric and watched Zephyr as he sawed across a plank of wood, his taut muscles flexing. He moved with grace, even when not performing and just working.

He wiped the sweat from his forehead and grinned when he looked up at her. "If you want, you can test the guillotine on me once I'm done."

"Ah, I just might."

"Without the blade, of course." He winked.

"Damn," she teased.

As Cricket studied him, her heart beat faster, and for the life of her, she couldn't fathom why. But she knew why—she was finding herself attracted to the one man who would break her heart, the one man who wouldn't want more than a tumble and perhaps friendship. She needed to get her head on straight.

Without a goodbye, she grabbed one of the burlap sacks and left the tent to pick up rubbish around the carnival grounds. Several apple cores were tossed on the grass, and she put them in the sack as she passed through the crowd. Buckets were set everywhere for customers to place their rubbish, but it made no difference.

Up ahead, farther away from the crowd, a flicker

caught her attention. The glistening object became brighter beneath the sun's rays as she approached. Pearls?

Cricket smiled as she plucked up what was indeed a white pearl necklace. She tucked the beads into her satchel and would later gift the trinket to Juniper.

Near the cemetery's woods were torn and crumpled sheets of paper that she shoved into the sack. A trail of orange peels and rotted fruit littered the ground, and she wrinkled her nose while dropping them into the open bag. When she turned in the direction of the carnival, a strong hand gripped her by the arm, fingers digging in, and yanked her back to a hard chest. The sack fell from her grasp as her body jolted forward. The person's other hand clamped around her mouth, muffling Cricket's screams before they could drift to the carnival and be heard.

"Abomination," a deep man's voice rumbled in her ear, his hot breath sticky on her neck as she was dragged into the woods. "You should've stayed dead."

Cricket's stomach coiled into tight knots—she desperately wanted to get a look at the man's face and wriggle out from his firm hold. Her body writhed, allowing her room to elbow him in his ribs. The man groaned, his grip slackening enough for her to break free. Cricket whirled around to kick him between the thighs so she could get her knife and flee. But his face was familiar, and she froze, *knowing* him. Charles. He took her slip-up as an advantage and rammed her into a tree, the wig falling from her head. His hand covered her mouth once more, and her gaze latched onto hateful brown eyes, his peppered mustache lifting as his lips curled into a sneer.

"Why are you doing this?" she tried to ask when his hand left her mouth and wrapped around her throat, squeezing. But her words were as muffled as when she'd tried to scream.

He didn't say anything, only dug his fingers in harder. She grappled with her skirts, attempting to get to her knife as her breaths were cut off. Her fingers brushed the handle, and she finally curled her hand around it. With her remaining energy, she brought it up and thrust it as hard as she could into Charles's chest. A low inhale of breath escaped his mouth while he stumbled back. Cricket no longer clutched the knife in her shaking hand, and speckles of blood coated her fingers.

"Abomination," he rasped again when he slumped to the ground and released ragged breaths until his eyes stared blankly toward the sky.

Cricket stood there, trembling as she peered at the authority's dead body. Not once had she ever come close to hurting anyone, yet she'd just killed a man who'd been trying to end her life.

She needed to tell someone, so she ran to the first person who wouldn't look at her in horror at what she'd done. As she pulled back the entrance to the tent, her gaze found Zephyr, who was chipping away at the wood. Autumn laughed alongside Wilder when Zephyr glanced up.

"Zephyr, I need to talk to you," she said, her voice cracking. Autumn and Wilder stopped laughing and looked at her with worried expressions. "Just you."

"Of course." He set his tools down and came toward her. She brought her hand up from behind her back to show him. "Is that blood?"

She nodded, tears pricking her eyes. "I … killed someone. Not just anyone, though. An authority. *Charles.*

He attacked me."

"Show me where," he whispered, his voice calm.

Cricket led him through the crowd, not looking at anyone directly, too fearful that they would know what she'd done if they could see her glistening eyes. Twigs snapped below their feet as they reached Charles's dead body. Blood stained his white shirt a bright shade of ruby, the knife still protruding from his chest.

"Charles called me an abomination, then started choking me. I had no other choice. Or I did—I could've died, but..." she trailed off, taking deep breaths of fresh air.

Zephyr clenched his jaw. "I should've been with you." He knelt, pressed his hand into one of Charles's pockets, and pulled out a gold watch, the others empty. Lifting the authority's satchel, he opened it and let out a string of curses. He showed her the contents resting inside—a knife and at least ten black dahlias.

"That bastard," Cricket gasped, covering her mouth and dropping to her knees beside Zephyr. "Charles did it. He's the one murdering these innocent women. And what he wanted was for me to die again."

"We need to let Mistress Eliza know, but I don't know if I trust the other authorities after this." Zephyr's expression hardened, his knuckles turning white around the satchel.

Charles had always been a stuffy man, yet she never would've thought he could do something heinous like this. But there was one authority she would always trust. "We can trust Bram. I need to speak with him."

"We'll get one of the performers to bring him here while you wash the blood from your hands." Zephyr closed the satchel and held onto it tightly. "If I'd been with you, the bastard would've gotten worse than a stab to the chest. I would've ripped off his damn head."

## 17

Even though Cricket could've easily washed Charles's blood from her hands herself, she let Zephyr do it for her, comforted by his gentle touch. Her chest continued to heave as she splashed her face with cool water, attempting to rid the memory of Charles's hand around her neck.

After they'd gone to Mistress Eliza's tent, she'd sent Wilder to go into town to fetch Bram. Mistress Eliza closed the carnival, ordering the performers to return to their homes.

She and Zephyr met Mistress Eliza and a group of performers near the woods where Charles's body still lay. The necromancer wanted to ensure no one would venture there until Bram arrived.

It took a little while for Bram and Miles to reach the carnival. Wilder and a carriage trailed behind them.

Bram held his hat in place as he slid down from his

horse.

Mistress Eliza placed her hands on her hips and glowered. "You need to tell me why one of *your* men attacked one of *my* performers."

"Which performer was attacked?" Bram asked.

"I was," Cricket said, and everyone's gazes fastened on her.

"What happened?" He briskly approached her, and she could see the concern flickering in his eyes as he studied her. "Your throat's red."

"Charles attacked me, and I killed him to defend myself," she whispered. "He choked me, called me an abomination, and was going to murder me."

"That's not all," Zephyr said. "Charles is the murderer. We found a blade and black dahlias in his satchel."

Bram turned to Miles. "Question the performers and find out if anyone saw anything. I'm going to take a look at the body. You three come with me." He pointed toward Cricket, Zephyr, and Mistress Eliza.

They stepped into the woods behind him, and he knelt beside Charles's dead body. Cricket averted her gaze from Charles as Bram peered inside the satchel. "I knew he didn't believe anyone should be brought back from the dead, but I didn't know he held such a hatred to do something like this."

"Why kill the other women, then? They weren't brought back from the dead," Cricket said.

Bram held up a hand. "You're leaping ahead. We don't know if he killed the others."

"What other proof do you need?" Zephyr asked, incredulous. "There's a satchel full of black dahlias right there."

"Which are rare and hard to find," Cricket added.

"It doesn't matter at the moment," Bram said. "I need to first compare his writing with the one in the note you gave me."

"What note?" Zephyr's brows pinched together while Mistress Eliza spat, "What are you talking about?"

Cricket winced. Perhaps she should've told the others of the letter, after all. She should've known it would come to this. "On the victim found near the caravans, a letter was written to me with a single sentence asking why I didn't perform. I thought it best to keep it to myself." Only Juniper knew, but she wouldn't mention Zephyr's sister unless she wanted to tell them herself.

"You can discuss the letter later," Bram said before Zephyr or Mistress Eliza could answer. "We have more pressing matters to tend to. Whether Charles is or isn't truly the Dahlia Murderer, he still tried to kill Cricket."

"What else do you need from me?" Cricket asked.

"I need you to go over every detail from the beginning, no matter how small or insignificant it may seem. When Miles finishes questioning the other performers, he'll inspect the body."

Cricket followed Bram out of the woods and fed him her recent stories with Charles, however short, detail by detail while Zephyr waited near Mistress Eliza. Cricket didn't know what would happen with the carnival now. But none of this was the carnival's fault.

Bram ran a hand across his jaw. "I promise to keep you informed on what I find. First, I will compare the letter with Charles's notes at the office."

"I understand if you need to haul me away in manacles

and put me in a cell for the time being," Cricket murmured, fidgeting with her skirts.

"I'm not going to do that. Nothing here shows that you did anything out of ill will. Zephyr and I witnessed his attitude toward you in the past."

"But what if people believe that's why I murdered him?"

Bram sighed. "You did it out of defense, Cricket. I know you wouldn't hurt a fly. Just be careful until I confirm things, all right?"

"All right," she said. "But for now, make sure Anika doesn't come to the carnival. Tell her I'll see her soon."

Bram nodded, then walked toward Miles, where they chatted in low voices.

Cricket slipped past several performers and approached Zephyr and Mistress Eliza, a heated conversation taking place between them by the sound of their raised voices. The necromancer ran her hands down her face. "I suppose we might as well say goodbye to opening the carnival again until it's time to leave." Her gaze narrowed at Cricket. "I won't reprimand you for not telling me a letter was left for you. But you do know that could've put my performers at risk, and it did put *you* at risk."

"I know," she whispered. "Yet it was addressed to me, and I was afraid you would send me away."

"Last chance, Cricket," Mistress Eliza snapped. "I'm relieved you're all right, and hopefully you did murder the bastard that's been doing this, but if you hold on to any more secrets, you're gone. Do you hear me, child?"

"Yes, Mistress Eliza." Cricket lowered her head as the woman nodded and limped away.

"This is my fault," Juniper said, tears beading her lashes as she ran toward Cricket. "I'll tell her it was my idea, and I made you do it."

"Your idea?" Zephyr said through gritted teeth. "You knew about the letter and didn't even tell me? Your brother?"

"I don't have to tell you everything," Juniper bit back. "Besides, the less who knew, the less chance that word would spread to Mistress Eliza. Cricket would've been kicked out that day."

"It was my fault for keeping it secret," Cricket said. "The choice was left to me, and I gave it to Bram since he's the one who could search for a handwriting match." By the way the vein ticked in Zephyr's jaw, he wasn't pleased.

"I would say you're safe now," Juniper murmured. "But death still comes for us all in the end."

"Sometimes twice." Cricket sighed.

Stormy rushed over and grasped Juniper by the shoulders. "What happened?" she asked rapidly.

Zephyr started toward the caravans, his shoulders stiffened. Cricket left the two performers together and caught up with him. Silence stretched between them, even as they entered his caravan.

"You're mad at me, I know," she finally said, sinking onto the bed.

He frowned, tightening his fists as he sat beside her. "Furious, but not at you. More so at that dead bastard. But I get it. You haven't really known me as long as you have Bram."

"I trust you, but I didn't want you to worry or get on Mistress Eliza's bad side after she already knew you dug up the grave with me. Besides, you're the one person I trusted with that, right? Over Bram and everyone else."

He smirked. "You still owe me for that."

"A favor is a favor," she drawled. "If you're itching to take your mind off everything and do something else, you don't have to linger inside with me."

"I think I'm itching to stay right here." Zephyr's warm leg pressed to hers, and he reached toward her, his hand cupping her cheek. "You have a smudge of dirt here." Her breath hitched as he slowly wiped the spot on her chin with his thumb.

Cricket was relieved that, at this moment, she didn't have to think about murdering someone. That it was just him and her in this small space, in this temporary escape. She liked the comforting feeling of his palm cradling her face, and surprising herself, she wanted more of him in that moment. Her gaze trained on his shapely lips while her digits brushed his leather collar. "I never see you take this off. Even when you sleep."

"Only if I'm replacing it with a new one," Zephyr said softly. "I never look at myself in the mirror when it's off, and I've never shown myself to anyone without it." He released her face, making her shiver without his warmth. She blinked in astonishment as he unbuckled the collar at the back of his neck.

Her hands grasped his arms. "You don't have to feel like you need to show me."

"I want to. My head really won't fall off, but I do have a reminder here." He peeled the collar from his throat, then ran his digit across a scar that went halfway around his neck, pink and raised.

Cricket couldn't keep herself from bringing her

fingers up to touch his scar. "Is this from…?" She didn't have to say the words from when he was murdered—he seemed to know what she meant to say as he nodded.

"It is. After raising Juniper from the dead, Mistress Eliza's magic was weakened when she brought me back. She almost couldn't seal the wound shut, but she did. Every day I'm relieved Juniper doesn't have her physical scar because we both already hold onto the emotional ones. The collar still doesn't hide it completely—I know what rests behind it, the reminder of my parents' deaths. That was another thing I would talk to you about when you were asleep and when I was watching over you while we were traveling. You're the one woman I've told all my secrets to, even if you don't remember them." His lips tilted up at the corners.

Cricket blinked, at a loss for words. She wished she could remember the conversations he'd spoken to her, but not even a dream or a nightmare lingered from that time either.

"It may be a reminder of ugly things, but it's not ugly at all. It shows your strength, your resilience, and that's what makes it beautiful. I'm honored you showed me, Zephyr." She lifted his hand and pressed it to her chest, right beside where her heart hammered, then glided it down to her abdomen. "This is where I was cut. The scar may not be there, but I still feel it. Every day."

"There's a part of us that will continue to always fight those demons." His hand trailed to her hip. "Get some sleep. Escape for now, and I'll still watch over you. I promise no one will try and hurt you inside here."

Cricket believed him and scooted back until her head pressed against a pillow. She wanted nothing more than to be held right then. "Lay with me?"

Zephyr stared at her as if she might take her words back before finally saying, "Of course." He slipped off his boots, settled behind her, and draped an arm around her waist. She leaned into his warmth, wondering what it would be like to get lost in his kiss, in all of him.

As Cricket went to bathe, she adjusted the collar of her dress to hide the bruises forming around her neck from Charles. She found Mistress Eliza crocheting a blanket on her porch steps beneath the cloudy sky. The necromancer looked up and beckoned Cricket toward her.

"I thought things over last night, and I want you to understand why I'm only giving you until we leave to hone in on your curiosity," Mistress Eliza said.

"But—" she started and was cut off by the necromancer.

"I know you can dance. I know you have some of your ability down, but those dahlias will be too much of a nuisance. Word will have already spread to the other cities about a murderer here, whether dead or not, who left them as wicked presents, so for the sake of the carnival, that is too much of a risk. The red roses were part of the vision when I brought you back from the dead, and it must be that way. Life and death in your curiosity. Not death and death."

Cricket understood, even if the Dahlia Murderer never existed, a black flower, although living, could still represent death to an audience by its shade. "I'll focus harder." But she truly didn't know how much harder she could sink into her ability when she was trying her damndest. She was frightened of failing, of what would become of her if she couldn't do this.

"Let what happened yesterday, in your past, drive you to become magnificent. Become the talent I know you can be."

"Yes, Mistress Eliza."

Cricket then went to wash up in the lake to clear her thoughts, but she decided to work on her curiosity first. Practicing and practicing until sweat drenched her body, until she desperately needed to clean herself off. But neither the dahlias nor the roses crept from her flesh.

The snap of twigs sounded, and Cricket whirled around to find Zephyr grinning as he neared her. "There you are. I was beginning to wonder if you were hiding from me."

Cricket's cheeks flamed when she remembered waking curled up beside him, his arm no longer around her waist but hers around his and her head nestled into his chest. "No. Mistress Eliza said I have until the carnival leaves to hone my curiosity."

"Ignore her threats. That's all they are." He shrugged. "For now, I think you deserve another break. Juniper wants to go to a pub."

Cricket couldn't practice the entirety of the day, or she would drive herself to the brink of madness. "Let me wash off quickly."

"With me here or somewhere else." He smirked.

She rolled her eyes. "You can stay, but turn around." Even though a part of her was aching to tell him to come into the water with her.

## 18

Laughter and music spilled through the large room of the pub. Smoke combined with the citrusy scent of oranges filled the air. Cricket, Zephyr, Juniper, and Stormy found an empty table in the back corner. Leslie was working the bar and gave Cricket a funny look as she noticed the difference in hair color. Even though the evidence pointed to Charles being the killer, Cricket adorned another chestnut wig until Bram verified that it was indeed true.

"I need to relieve myself," Zephyr said, setting a handful of silver coins on the table. "You ladies get anything you want."

"And what would *you* like?" Cricket asked.

"Oh, you *know* what I would like. But surprise me." He waggled his brows before sauntering down the hallway. Her gaze lingered on the leather collar, back in place around his throat. For some reason, she was a friend he felt comfortable sharing his story with which made her feel special.

"Whiskey and potato soup sound good?" Stormy asked, palming the coins.

"Sure." Juniper smiled, watching Stormy walk toward the bar where Leslie poured a glass of liquor for another customer, then draped her long blonde hair over her shoulder.

Almost everyone sat with a companion except for one pretty gray-haired woman reading a book in the opposite corner, a tall silver mug beside her. A few inebriated men playing a game of cards and dice whistled at a brunette barmaid when she passed. She sent them a vulgar gesture, and they chuckled.

"So," Cricket drawled, running a hand over her wig, "how was the stay with Stormy last night?"

Juniper's gaze flicked to the performer once more before she said in a low voice, "She kissed me."

"What?" Cricket's hands slapped the table. "Were you going to mention it to me or wait until I asked?"

"I don't think people shout it to the stars every time they get kissed, do they?" Juniper grinned.

"I'm sure some do." Cricket laughed.

"And what about you? Have you?" Juniper arched a brow.

Stormy came back carrying four glasses of whiskey. She managed not to spill them as she set them in the middle of the table.

Cricket grabbed a glass and drank the strong liquid down. "Since I've awoken, there haven't been any kisses." She paused, thinking. "Or perhaps one. The kiss on

Zephyr's cheek during our performance." Or two… She had given him another a few nights ago.

"Are we talking about kisses?" Stormy rubbed her hands together, her eyes drifting to Juniper.

Juniper ignored her and asked, "So, how do you feel about him?"

"We're friends." And yet, do friends yearn to press their lips to one another's?

"The look in your eyes tells me differently." Juniper held her glass up for Stormy to clink with hers.

"What look?" Zephyr's deep voice sounded from behind her. He grabbed his glass of whiskey and tossed it back as he sank down in the chair beside her. His arm pressed to hers, and his woodsy scent surrounded her.

The young woman who was whistled at brought out the steaming bowls of soup on a serving tray. She set one in front of each of them, her gaze lingering on Zephyr, and her red-painted lips curled into a seductive smile. "I've seen you before," she said.

"It's possible?" Zephyr smirked, looking as though he was attempting to remember if she was one of the women he'd brought into his bed.

The young woman leaned on the table, her cleavage spilling out farther. "You're the performer at the carnival." She bit her lip. "I've heard about you."

"Good things, I hope."

"Very good things. Maybe I'll see you later." Her hips swished side to side when she walked away, and jealousy crawled through Cricket. Zephyr didn't seem to notice as he lifted a spoonful of soup to his mouth.

"How about a game of cards?" one of the drunk men, with a few missing teeth, shouted toward them.

"Why not?" Stormy shrugged and pulled her chair up to the table. Cricket followed suit—it had been a while since she'd joined in on a game here.

They played for hours until night had cloaked the city, and it was decided to do only one more round. Near the end of the game, Cricket threw the die, then lifted her cards. "3, 4, 7," she said, bluffing about her numbers.

It was between her and Zephyr for the winning hand, and he studied her, his tongue moistening his lower lip as he peered at his cards. He placed them face down in front of him. "I fold."

"I think that's the first time I've seen you lose." Juniper giggled, pushing all the coins toward Cricket to put in her bag.

"There has to be a first time for something." He chuckled.

"You let me win, didn't you?" Cricket said as they walked away from the table.

"Now, why ever would I do that?" Zephyr grinned, pushing open the door and holding it for them. As they started to leave the pub, a man's shouts pierced the air from behind the building. The four of them rounded the corner to find Leslie half-dressed beside a man with unbuttoned trousers. Leslie's hand covered her mouth, and the man cursed as they stared down at something in the shadows.

A dead body.

The chest was torn open and black dahlias rested in the victim's palms. Charles wasn't the murderer, even though Cricket had thought him to be—had prayed for him to be. He'd given his reason why he'd wanted her dead—because he believed her to be an abomination.

Underneath that, she knew he also believed she was the root cause of why the murders were happening.

As she approached the dead body, something gave her pause, her heart speeding in her chest. The victim wore men's clothing, and as her gaze fell to the face with eyes covered by black dahlias, the person wasn't a woman but a blond man.

Cricket banged on Bram's door until he answered, a candle in his hand. "What are you doing here at this late hour? Is everything all right?" He searched from her face to her three friends standing behind her.

"No, Bram, it isn't," she said, her voice cracking. "We were at the Garland, and a dead body with dahlias was found behind the building. Miles and a few other authorities came before the victim was taken away to the coroner. Only this blond one wasn't like the others. It was a man."

He inhaled sharply. "A man?"

"What about the letter?" Zephyr stated, his nostrils flaring. "Did it match Charles's handwriting?"

"We're still digging. Nothing he has at the office or his home was written in cursive. Just to cover all possibilities, I even checked Clancy's, and it doesn't match his. There still isn't a clear answer. He could've also written differently in the letter so someone wouldn't notice."

"It couldn't have been Charles," Juniper piped in. "The murderer is someone else and still on the loose."

"Unless this is another person wanting to mimic again," Stormy mumbled, gripping the ends of her hair. Cricket didn't believe that was the case, not with how the dahlias were strategically pressed inside the rib cage the same way as the two others she'd witnessed.

"Bram, who's at the door?" Anika called as she came down the stairs in her flowing nightgown. "Oh dear, I'm underdressed, it seems."

"There's been another Dahlia Murder, darling. It doesn't seem to be Charles as we thought. I'm going to take a horse to the coroner and see the body for myself." Bram then looked at Cricket. "I don't want any of you walking home. I'll have the coachman bring you there."

Anika grasped Cricket's hand. "You all can come in and stay."

"I would, but we need to warn the others at the carnival about the murder," Cricket said.

"Promise me you won't wander anywhere alone," Anika pleaded.

"I promise."

After explaining to Anika what they'd witnessed at the pub, the coachman took them back to the carnival in the carriage. She didn't know when she would get answers from Bram, but she hoped by early tomorrow.

A group of performers lingered around the fire while Mistress Eliza sat opposite them, sipping from a glass bottle and chatting with Autumn. Cricket and Zephyr went to Mistress Eliza, and a sinking feeling plummeted into the pit of her stomach as she stopped in front of the necromancer.

"The Dahlia Murderer is still out there," Cricket started. "There was another dead body in town, but this

182

one was a man. I think everyone needs to be extra careful. Especially the two blond male performers."

Mistress Eliza's gaze narrowed at Cricket, her voice coming out a slur from having too much to drink. "So that means whoever wrote you that letter is still going to threaten my carnival. Is that what you're implying? That the carnival is going to suffer more because of you?"

Horrified, Cricket was too taken aback to find words in her defense. Because what the necromancer implied was true. This was all her fault.

"You have no right to say that," Zephyr said between gritted teeth.

Cricket didn't wait to hear Mistress Eliza's reply as she took off toward Zephyr's caravan. All she could focus on was that it was her fault. Perhaps she should've sent back the others alone while she stayed with Anika. She was nothing but a waste of time to Mistress Eliza.

The scratching sensation clawed beneath her flesh like an old friend bidding someone a hello. Under the night air, dahlias, black as midnight, rose from their gardens across her arms.

"Cricket!" Zephyr shouted, grasping her by the arm and tugging her to his chest. "Stay calm."

Even though she tried to tuck them away, they wouldn't return to their depths. She opened her locket, finding it empty. "There's more in your caravan," she rasped, her blood akin to a fire raging through her veins.

Before she could stumble toward it, he lifted her into his arms and rushed her inside. As she went to grab her bag, dahlias bloomed from her eyes, darkening the world, and she screamed. Rustling sounded, followed by the press of salty fingers and a petal onto her tongue. The rose flavor filled her mouth.

The black curtain lifted from her eyes as the dahlias hid away, revealing color and Zephyr's handsome face. Breaths ragged, she reached for the blade that should've been at her thigh when she remembered it was plunged into Charles's chest.

"What are you searching for?" Zephyr asked.

"My knife," she sobbed. "Perhaps if I cut them out, the dahlias will stop growing from *me*. I shouldn't have been brought back. Mistress Eliza believes I'm a burden, and I am."

"Fuck her. Fuck anyone who believes that," he spat. "How would they feel if this was happening to them? And if you die again, that's it. Mistress Eliza can't revive you a second time, and I don't know where to find another necromancer."

"I don't care. I want them gone," she said, tears raining down her cheeks. But she did care. She cared quite badly. "Mistress Eliza wasted her necromancy on me."

Zephyr lifted her chin so her eyes met his blazing hazel ones. "She didn't. You will prove her wrong. Show her you can do this. For yourself. You've always wanted to perform. You're so close—I can feel it in you. My curiosity feels yours." He leaned in, cupping her cheek as his forehead pressed to hers. "I've wanted to kiss you ever since I first saw you at the carnival in the front row. And after you woke up to live your second life, I've wanted to even more."

"Is that all?" Cricket asked, her voice husky, her heart pounding from his lovely words.

A wide, devious smile crossed his face, beautiful and dangerous all at once. "No, I'm not sure you want to hear all the things I want to do to you. All the things I want you to do to me. I want to peel this down." His long fingers skimmed across the collar of her dress before trailing down her sides to her hips, then brushing the fabric of her skirt. "I want to hike this up and touch every damn inch of you so I can hear you moan, taste what it sounds like when you do it against my tongue."

Her body heated, aching for his touch. "A kiss, for now, will suffice." She was punishing herself when all she wanted was for him to shed his clothing and feel the touch of his skin against hers, but torture was the only choice until she could think properly.

Zephyr's mouth captured Cricket's, and his lips slanted across hers, tasting of whiskey and mint. His tongue flicked the seam of her lips, prying them open before dipping impishly inside. The kiss deepened, and he drew her closer, his demanding tongue performing with hers. A kiss that created sparks, that if he went any further she knew it would ignite an inferno, blazing and brilliant. He nipped her lower lip, and she tangled her hands in his hair.

Cricket pulled back, her chest heaving as she peered at his swollen lips. "Zephyr, you just gave me a reason to want to try even harder."

# 19

The victims' lips moved, pale blue in color, whispering words Cricket couldn't hear. Their clothing was ripped down the middle, blood pooling from their broken insides to the floor. The drip, drip, drip echoed around her. She edged closer, desperate to hear what they were whispering. Until finally, the words grew louder, becoming a crescendo that beat inside her skull. *Your fault. Your fault. Your fault. Your fault. Your fault.* Her own chest split apart, her ribs cracking open until she watched in horror as her heart beat in sync with their terrifying words.

Cricket's eyes flew open to morning light, and she grasped her chest, finding it closed, her dress not ripped. It was only a nightmare. The victims and their dead blue lips whispering how everything was her fault.

A warm arm draped around her waist, anchoring her

in a way that brought her back to reality. Keeping her from falling into that dark pit of grief. She leaned in closer to Zephyr's touch, letting his deep, steady breaths ground her. The prior night trickled into her mind, and she stilled. The kiss, the feeling of his soft lips against hers, the way his tongue flicked hers as his touch ignited something ravenous within her.

But then the whispers from the victims came once more, and she needed to clear her head. She gently lifted Zephyr's arm to the side, careful not to disturb him, and snuck off from the bed. With quiet movements, she grabbed a cotton dress to change into, then slipped on her boots and strapped the new knife Zephyr had given her, after their kiss, to her thigh. Perhaps she could pretend the kiss didn't happen. But did she want to? *No…* No, she didn't. Not at all.

"You can dress right here," Zephyr purred. His smile was lazy, and his eyes hooded as they pinned to her. "I don't mind."

"Be a gentleman, not a rogue," she teased.

"I can be both," he said in a gruff voice. "Especially when I pleasure."

*Oh my…* Cricket couldn't hold back the heat creeping up her neck and the pool of it swimming through her belly, sinking lower and lower. A knock came at the door, drawing her from any response she might have given. Zephyr pushed up from the bed, snatched the knife from his desk, then shoved it into his pocket before nonchalantly opening the door.

Cricket's heart thumped with how fast he'd moved, and by the way he did it, she didn't think this was the first time. She remembered how he'd mentioned he always carried leaves in his pocket as well. Her chest tightened at the thought that he'd done this every time a knock came since losing his parents when they'd been attacked inside a carriage. But she would never have been able to tell by his easy posture and how he cocked his head as if there wasn't a care in the world.

"Hello, Zephyr, is Cricket with you?" a familiar voice asked. Anika. "Autumn came to my carriage when we arrived and brought me here. After last night, I needed to check on her. I couldn't sleep a wink."

"She's here." Zephyr pulled the door wider so Cricket and Anika could see one another.

Anika wore a bonnet over her hair, and her satin emerald dress showed off the curve of her pregnant stomach.

"What are you doing here?" Cricket hissed, brushing past Zephyr and stepping outside into the fresh air. The scent of meat being roasted for breakfast caressed her nose. "Where's Bram? Did you come alone?"

"He's in town at the coroner's building. Nothing of importance with the death or the killer has been found yet. And no, my mother is waiting in the carriage. You know how she feels about carnivals, but I told her either way, I was coming to see if you were all right."

Anika's mother had always believed that carnivals and circuses were demons' work—their lack of clothing, their sensuality. The necromancy of Mistress Eliza's Carnival accompanied her view as well, and she never would've allowed Anika to go in the past, so when they were younger, they'd always sneak to it while telling her they would be at Cricket's.

"Didn't Bram tell you I didn't want you to come here,

188

though?" Cricket sighed.

"He may be my husband, but he doesn't tell me where I will and will not go, and as for you, if the roles were reversed, can you tell me you would just wait at home, twiddling your thumbs?" Anika huffed.

Of course, she wouldn't. "There's no use arguing with that. Besides, you're already here anyway." Cricket shrugged.

"Good. I brought breakfast. I figured we could picnic somewhere." She craned her neck, peering past her at Zephyr, who leaned against the door frame, his shirt still off. "Your *friend* can join us if he'd like." A wide grin spread across her face.

"I'll let you *lovely* ladies chat while I get cleaned up, unless you need me?" His gaze met Cricket's, questioning.

"We'll be fine. I'll take them to one of the tents." She peered down at her rumpled clothing from the night before. "But let me change first."

"Later, we can go to our practicing spot," Zephyr said as he stepped outside. Cricket's heart swelled at the way he said *our*.

After slipping back inside and changing, she walked beside Anika, past a few performers who told them good morning. "Are you sure your mother will get out of the carriage to come with us?" Cricket cast her a knowing look.

"If not, then she'll be waiting a while," Anika said.

Cricket stared at Anika's dark locks of hair drawn back beneath the bonnet. Respite filled her that her friend's hair wasn't blonde and that her irises weren't blue. But did that matter? The murderer might make a different decision in the way they took the life of a man instead of a woman. For now, the hair and eye color were a repetitious game, yet she wouldn't be as naïve to believe it couldn't change.

"Have you still been feeling well?" Cricket asked, relieved that the past few times she'd seen Anika, she hadn't been pale or nauseous in the way her friend had been when she couldn't get out of bed.

"I did lose my stomach last night several times after you left, but I think that was from how worried I was. As for the constant nausea, it no longer feels as though I'm possessed by a demonic entity."

Cricket laughed softly. "Shh. The baby has ears."

"With my luck, they'll have lingering crying spells, but I already love this child very much." Anika smiled, pressing a hand to her belly.

Cricket remembered Felix, the terrible crying spells during her brother's first few months of life. No matter how irritated Cricket was, her mother would always hush her and hold him until he fell asleep or cooed. Anika would be just as loving as Cricket's mother was.

"You'll be a wonderful mother," she said as she looked toward the carriage where the coachman sat at the front, feeding one of the horses an apple.

"It seems Mother still hasn't decided to step foot out of the carriage." Anika sighed.

The coachman hopped down from his bench and opened the carriage door when they approached. Breeta sat up straight, her unblinking stare focused on her daughter.

"Are you going to join us for the picnic, Mother?" Anika asked. "If you don't want to go inside the carnival, there is the cemetery on one side where we can feast instead."

"Or on the other, where a beautiful lake rests, and I know for certain one naked male will be bathing," Cricket added with a grin.

"Both of you, stop acting like children." Breeta frowned, toying with a lacy yellow sleeve. "I made it here in the carriage, didn't I?" She stepped onto the grass, a deep line still between her brows. Her dark hair was drawn into a low bun, and only a few fine lines creased her eyes.

Anika grabbed a large picnic basket from inside the carriage, and Cricket took it from her. Her shoulders dropped a little from the weight, and she wondered how much food her friend had packed. Anika plucked up a blanket and told the coachman they would be back in a little while.

As they walked toward the carnival tent, Breeta drew a glass vial from her bag and spilled a few drops of water on the ground. Blessed water—her superstitions still held strong.

Breeta's hard face turned to Cricket as she muttered, "Seems the Dahlia Murderer is still taunting Nobel. Just when I thought we'd found relief from this nuisance, it continues. Bram has been on the case without barely any breaks, even when at home. He can hardly focus on anything else since the murders started."

Cricket's heart tightened as guilt knocked on it, yearning to break free of its cage. She wasn't fond of how the woman used the word "nuisance" as if also blaming Cricket, the way the dead victims had in her nightmare... Breeta seemed to like her less than before, and while Cricket had always ignored the woman's snotty words, it was harder at this moment. Even when Cricket was younger, she'd given her annoyed stares. She was a social climber, and because Cricket's family didn't have much either, she wasn't worthy of her time.

As Cricket lifted the fabric of the tent, Breeta tugged her back by the arm. "I'm not going inside a tent. We can eat out here in the open."

Cricket wanted to roll her eyes and tell her that devilish things only lurked behind the stage, but she held her tongue and asked Anika, "Are you fine with that?"

"I'm all right with anywhere," Anika said as she unfolded the large blanket on the grass. "How are the other performers after everything?"

"They're upset about losing money, but mostly just performing for an audience." Cricket set the basket in the center and sat on the soft quilt. "I wish one of the performers at the carnival was a genuine seer. Not like the necromancer who—"

"Brings back the dead?" Breeta hissed, grasping her chest.

"Yes." Only now, she couldn't.

"Hmph. A pity another can't be found to get answers from a victim."

"I thought you believed it all to be the demons' work." Anika arched a brow at her mother.

"To get this demon off the streets, one might need to face another," Breeta said as she opened the basket and took out a blueberry muffin.

Cricket was certain that Breeta would be content if Mistress Eliza could bring back a victim, if only to have Bram at home more often, due to her fear of them leaving one another and her ending up without money once more. But Cricket didn't want to say it aloud and hurt her friend, even though Anika would know that already.

While Anika took out the remaining food, including meat and fruit pies, pastries, strawberries, grapes, and rolls, Cricket could barely concentrate on what Anika and Breeta were chatting about. Now that she was looking at Anika pouring water into glasses, all she could think about was the recent event at the pub. The body behind the building, the man's chest being ripped open, and the desperate need to know if Bram would find out anything at all.

As Cricket forced down a slice of pie and a few grapes, she observed a handful of performers fiddling around on stilts while laughing in the distance. She hadn't seen Mistress Eliza yet, and she hoped to avoid her for the remainder of the day, or until she could hone her curiosity and prove to the necromancer that she could be worth something.

"Do you want to come back with us?" Anika asked once they finished eating.

"Perhaps soon I'll stop by and bring you breakfast this time," Cricket said as she folded the blanket and handed it to Anika. She then accompanied them back to their carriage and watched it until it safely disappeared out of the trees and onto the road. A few sprinkles dropped from the sky, causing her to glance up at the darkening clouds. She was about to turn to go back toward the caravans when she caught sight of a yellow-hooded figure darting between trees inside the cemetery.

Remembering what had happened to her when she was near the cemetery last, she drew out the hidden knife from its sheath. She wasn't going to lose sight of the person, and she wouldn't be foolish either. So while running in the direction of the mystery figure, she screamed as loud as she could to get the attention of the other performers. Breaking through the tree line, Cricket found no one, though the figure had been there moments before. And then she saw it. A folded sheet of paper pinned to a tree.

The others arrived as she ripped the note open.

*Do you think there have been too many bodies, Cricket? Blame no one but yourself.*

20

Cricket trembled as she held the note—it was the same handwriting as the one left for her before. When she stepped forward, a hand pressed down on her shoulder, and she screamed, whirling, knife in her grasp, but Zephyr dodged the blade.

"It's me, Cricket," he said, his voice soothing. "I heard your scream while I was gathering supplies from the tent and rushed over here."

Just as she was about to answer, more sets of feet thumped against the earth. Several performers halted near the edge of the woods where they stood. Wilder, Autumn, and a few of the strong men studied them.

"You were screaming," Autumn said, holding a wooden staff. "What happened?"

"Check the rest of the woods. The murderer was just here wearing a bright yellow cloak with a long pointy hood. They left this note pinned to the tree for me." Cricket handed Zephyr the letter while the others spread out and began searching through the woods and cemetery.

Zephyr furrowed his brow as he read the letter, his expression hardening. "You didn't see what direction they went?" He clenched his knife in his other hand as he surveyed the area.

"No, I saw the yellow fabric slip behind the trees, but I suppose I wasn't quick enough. They vanished as soon as I came in here."

"Let me take a look around."

"I'll go with you." Cricket gripped her blade, her knuckles white. If she had any enhanced strength, she would've easily crushed it.

They trekked through the trees, searching for any sign of movement or even a scrap of yellow fabric that had possibly snagged along a branch. But there was nothing besides the sounds of crunching leaves or snapping twigs from their own feet. The only evidence of anyone being there was the note fisted in Zephyr's hand. She peered at the ground for footprints, but the dirt was too hardened for the murderer to have left any behind.

"We came up with nothing," Autumn said as she and Wilder stepped out from between two trees.

"Empty here as well." One of the strong men sighed, his muscles bulging against the sleeves of his shirt.

Zephyr gave the letter back to Cricket. "The upside is that a left-behind note is better than a dead body, right?"

Cricket scowled. "I suppose. I need to tell Mistress Eliza, then give it to Bram."

"We'll inform the others what happened while you

two do that," Autumn said to Zephyr and Cricket before they went their separate ways.

Mistress Eliza wasn't in her caravan but sitting inside her tent, sifting through a deck of tarot cards. Two candles were lit, and a few crystals rested on the square table draped in red velvet fabric.

"Need a reading that desperately? You know the rules about barging in here," Mistress Eliza snapped, but then her brows rose as she studied their faces. "What is it?"

"I'm telling you this time," Cricket started, an anxious feeling clawing at her insides. "A note from the Dahlia Murderer was left for me in the woods near the cemetery. They were wearing a yellow cloak, but they got away."

Mistress Eliza pushed up from the chair and limped toward them. Her lips remained set in a tight line as she read over the note. "Was anyone murdered?"

Zephyr shook his head. "No, and this isn't Cricket's fault. You won't threaten or berate her for this, or I'll fucking leave right now with her."

"Well then..." Mistress Eliza blinked, seeming unused to this tone from Zephyr toward her.

"It's fine, Zephyr, you don't have to—"

But the necromancer cut her off by lifting a hand. "What I need is for you two to take a horse and tell the authorities to get this solved. We have lost pay, and traveling to our next location is still too soon. Everyone here needs to remain in pairs. No more milling about alone at whatever hours people please."

"I won a good amount of money yesterday at the pub during a card game. Not that it's as much as what could've been earned, but you can have it for the carnival," Cricket offered.

"Thank you, child. That will do."

After telling Mistress Eliza that the other performers were being informed, Zephyr grasped Cricket by the hand and led her toward the horses.

"We can take one together. It'll be faster," he said as he untacked a chestnut mare from the stables.

The last time Cricket had ridden a horse was when she'd first awoken and had borrowed it to take back to Nobel over a month ago.

After placing the saddle on the mare, Zephyr easily lifted Cricket and settled her into it. With one swift motion, he mounted behind her, his strong body pressed to hers as he grasped the horse's reins and brought them down. The mare jolted, then barreled forward. A small yelp escaped Cricket, and she gripped the horse's mane, perhaps a bit too roughly, as the mare galloped at a pace faster than she'd ever ridden. Growing up, she and Anika had never had their own horses—they'd always walked everywhere. Bram was the one who'd taught them both how to ride.

It didn't take long before they reached the heart of the city. Cricket knew Bram wouldn't be at his manor and would most likely either be with the authorities or at the coroner's.

Zephyr tugged on the reins, slowing the horse to a stop as they reached the authority building. He easily leapt to the gravel from the mare and grasped Cricket by the waist to help her down. She didn't hesitate and rushed into the building with Zephyr close behind her.

Miles's eyes widened when he noticed her, and he set aside the book he held. "Can I help you with something, Miss Cricket?" His voice was gentle as it had been each time she'd encountered him.

"Is Bram here? We need to speak to him," she rushed out, looking around the room and finding only two other empty desks and sketches of the city with markings pinned to the walls.

"He came from the coroner's earlier, then had to run another errand, but he should be back at any moment."

Zephyr leaned against the desk, telling Miles about the note left for her when the door opened. Bram walked in, taking his hat from his head, his hair mussed. His gaze fell to hers, and he halted. "Cricket?"

She didn't waste time and took the note from her satchel. "If you had any doubt that the same person was the murderer from last night, this is proof they are. They were in the woods near the cemetery wearing a bright yellow cloak. I followed them but only found this note."

Bram's lips pursed while scanning the message. "What the hell were you doing following someone into the woods alone?"

"I screamed for the others as I went inside, and I had a knife. I didn't just tiptoe in there. I couldn't waste time and let them slink away, even though they did just that." She may not be an authority, but she wasn't helpless.

Bram pinched the bridge of his nose.

"It's fucking obvious the murderer is taunting her," Zephyr growled. "What are *you* going to do about that?"

"What she needs is not to be left alone." Bram frowned.

"I wasn't alone. Anika and Breeta came for breakfast. They had just left when I saw the flash of yellow," Cricket said.

"Anika?" He inhaled sharply, his lips pursing together

even tighter. "A murderer is on the loose, and no one chooses to listen."

Zephyr's jaw hardened. "Cricket has received two letters now, and you've found nothing on the handwriting?"

"Three times," Bram said, releasing a breath. "The coroner discovered one this morning, hidden in a secret pocket of the victim's coat from last night. I was going to leave here and come straight to the carnival to tell you."

Cricket swallowed the lump in her throat down. "What did it say?"

Bram took the letter from the front pocket of his coat and opened it for her to read. *Cricket, it's a pity you stabbed the wrong person.*

Zephyr cursed under his breath as nausea bubbled up her throat.

"I'm going to question everyone at the carnival again," Bram started. "Are you certain you want to stay there still?"

"I'll make sure she has someone with her at all times. She's safe with us at the carnival," Zephyr said.

The murderer had known she was at the pub the night before… "I don't think it matters where I go, but I'll let Mistress Eliza decide," Cricket murmured. "We'll follow you there."

Cricket and Zephyr mounted their horse with Bram and Miles following suit. When they arrived at the carnival, most of the performers were gathered around the fire, only a few eating. Juniper rushed toward Cricket, her red curls tangled from the breeze, while Zephyr returned the mare to the stables.

"You received another letter?" Juniper asked, her eyes

wild with worry.

"Not only that one. Another was left as a vengeful little gift on the victim from last night, telling me it's a pity I stabbed the wrong person," Cricket said, anger now coursing through her instead of nausea.

Juniper bit her lip as she furrowed her brow, seeming to mull something over. "I don't understand the point of these notes being left behind. If the murderer wanted you dead, they would most likely do it. Why taunt? Unless it's part of something bigger and they're waiting."

"Waiting for what, though?" Cricket wondered aloud.

"I don't know, but it's something for us to think about."

Bram was questioning Mistress Eliza and two other performers. The necromancer's eyes found hers, and she sighed. Cricket knew she must've heard about the third note and was holding a strong opinion that Cricket was more trouble than she was worth, that she was luring a murderer into the carnival over and over again.

Once Bram finished with Mistress Eliza, the necromancer limped toward her and motioned Juniper away.

"I can leave if you want," Cricket said.

"I'm not going to yell at you, child. It seems, more than anything, you need to be protected. No one else has been hurt or threatened here, so we'll do our best to take care of you. These sorry excuses for authorities need to move faster. Just watch your back and don't bathe alone either," the woman grunted. "You can stay now, but the same circumstance remains for when we leave for the next town, regardless."

That was more than Cricket expected. "Thank you."

Once Mistress Eliza went to talk with Autumn, Zephyr slid up beside her. "Seems she needs a good night of pleasure to rid herself of that sour mood." He smirked. "In case you thought I was offering myself to be the one, I wasn't. I have my sights set on the lovely blonde female standing beside me."

Cricket rolled her eyes. "She needs her necromancy back is what she needs. But she's allowed me to stay when most wouldn't have."

Wilder and a group of performers approached. "We'll make sure you're safe, Cricket," he said. She'd rarely talked to any of them, but his kind words made her heart swell. Yet she felt as if she'd brought all of this on herself.

Bram pulled her aside, questioning her one more time alone. She had nothing else to give besides mentioning the yellow cloak again. She couldn't even give accurate details such as height and body shape since she hadn't been close enough. But they hadn't appeared smaller than Cricket. It most certainly could've been either a man or a woman. If only she'd caught a glimpse of the hair color or part of their face.

"The person seems to be growing bolder, though," Cricket said. "Since they left a note like this during the day."

"I'm going to have more authorities monitor the roads here. We're going to catch this bastard just as we did with Clancy. I swear it," Bram vowed.

As he turned away, she promised herself that when the murderer was caught, she would be front and center to watch them hang, the way she hadn't been able to witness Clancy's death.

## 21

"**Y**our face is pinched," Zephyr said, tossing his sword in the air and catching it easily by its handle. They'd been in their practicing spot in the woods ever since waking. "You don't want to look like you're holding back vomit."

Cricket pinned him with a glare. "How about you keep quiet? You're the one who wanted to come out here with me. I offered to bring Juniper."

"I know what Mistress Eliza threatened, but you've been working yourself ragged ever since the authorities left yesterday. You will hone in on your curiosity when you're ready. Mistress Eliza brought you back from death, so she has no right to make you lose a place in the carnival. I know most of the performers would side with me on that."

Would they? They may have vowed to protect her

203

while she remained here, but she didn't think they would forever, not when she was a way for them to lose coin and food in their bellies. "It's not for her—it's for me." Cricket pressed her palm to her chest, feeling the rapid pulse of her heart. "Besides, if I stay indoors, I may never catch sight of the murderer if they decide to show up again. Perhaps I should wander around alone like bait on a hook."

"Don't be foolish," he chided.

"Look, if I can at least get my curiosity down, then I don't have to worry about it being a liability if I were to come face to face with the murderer. This is for me—*I* need this."

Zephyr placed the sword on top of one of the rocks and sauntered toward her. He lifted her hands, then pressed his palms flat against hers. She could feel every line, dip, and callus there, his warmth tamping down her raw emotions. "Will you try something with me?" When she nodded, he continued, "Look into my eyes and focus on your breathing. Slow. In and out."

Cricket licked her lips and locked her gaze with his. She took deep breaths through her nose, inhaling the piney scent of the woods.

Rustling stirred as Zephyr's thick vines unraveled from his bare back and curved around them, creating a barrier that made her feel protected. But then she realized something. He hadn't placed a leaf into his mouth, his feet weren't bare as they touched the grass, and she couldn't see any other plant touching his flesh.

"You don't have a leaf hidden in your mouth already, do you?" she asked.

Zephyr shook his head and smirked. "It's because I'm

touching *you*," he purred. "I told you I've been feeling something inside you every time I touch you, and it started to make me wonder if your curiosity could draw mine out. It's not death I feel inside you, but life. I feel the roses in your blood, pumping, aching to be set free. It's your guilt, your melancholy, your fear, and every other harsh emotion you've felt that is making them resist. I've seen the single red one find its way out once, and I know you can bring it out again. You can make them all bloom if you don't let your emotions consume you."

Cricket couldn't feel his curiosity the way he could hers, but oh did she wish she could. However, she pretended as though she did. Pretended she could feel his pull, that his vines were seeping beneath her flesh and grasping her roses. She watched as her skin became translucent, the layers drawn back to reveal her bones. When the scratching came, followed by the soft brush of petals, she kept her breath even. A bright crimson spot formed before a single rose blossomed at her wrist. Beautiful and ruby and shining like glass. Her heart slammed against her rib cage, and she let the power she held draw the flower back to the slumber it had awakened from.

Not breaking contact with Zephyr, she blinked away the tears pricking her eyes.

"Do it again," Zephyr instructed. "Don't let the darkness consume you, lovely Cricket. Think of something that makes you happy."

Before she'd died, so many things made her feel happy, and since then, even if she hadn't let herself truly feel them, there were more now too. The night and its brilliant, countless stars, the first day of winter, her mother's cooking, her father's teasing, dancing alone in front of a mirror, watching Anika paint, Bram's politeness, Juniper's kindness, Zephyr's sweetness and banter. But at that moment, the way he'd said her name made her heart flutter the most. She honed in on that feeling and more. Dancing as a child, when there seemed to be no worries in the world, twirling and twirling, creating her own magical world, a world where she was weightless, free of all care. And she would fall to the floor in a fit of giggles, still consumed with delight from what she'd imagined.

A prickling sensation twitched within her, and she squinted, prepared for the dahlias when red roses broke through her skin, across her hands and arms. Red like cherries, the sweet floral scent caressing her senses. Beads of perspiration slid down the back of her neck as she attempted the final task, to draw them back in. They listened, tucking themselves away for now.

"I did it," Cricket whispered, her chest heaving. She continued to hold Zephyr's intense stare, the dazzling smile that played on his lips. "Because of *your* help."

His smile turned lopsided, making him appear almost boyish. "Now, do it on your own, and I'll watch. I promise I'll keep you safe." He took a step back, his palms breaking away from hers.

Cricket shook out her hands and breathed steadily, then shifted on her feet before focusing. Only this time, when the flowers came, the red roses were accompanied by black dahlias. She fished them back in as best she could, but a few dahlias lingered, so she placed a dried rose petal in her mouth, chewing until her arms were bare once more.

"That's an improvement." Zephyr grinned. "You'll get it."

They took a break to eat fruit and fish caught from the lake while drinking whiskey until she felt relaxed. Once they finished their meal, Zephyr brought her to his caravan to fill her locket with more petals. Earlier, Cricket had seen Juniper carrying a bag of props, but now both she and Stormy were nowhere in sight. She smiled knowing they were somewhere together.

"Are you ready for more?" Zephyr asked, placing his swords neatly on the wall.

"Depends on what kind of more." She laughed. "But I'll do a little more in here."

He sat on the mattress and scooted back against the wall, then patted the spot in front of him. "Come here," he purred, a wide smile spreading across his cheeks. "We're going to bloom flowers wherever I tell you to."

Cricket rolled her eyes, but as her gaze swept up his toned chest, to his strong jaw, to those shapely lips of his, she couldn't deny his request. She lowered herself in front of Zephyr, shifting toward him until her back pressed against his firm chest, and she was settled between his strong thighs.

"I like you this close," Zephyr whispered, trailing a finger down the column of her neck that sent a delicious shiver through her. His digit then skimmed across her arm, to her palm, and halted in the center. "Bloom a rose here."

As she called on her curiosity, it didn't listen. She couldn't even get her skin to turn translucent. All she could focus on was his long finger, wishing it would touch her elsewhere, beneath the layers of her clothing. "I can't," she said, her voice husky.

He inched closer, leaning near her ear, his warm breath heating her cool flesh as he cooed, "I don't like those two words coming from that beautiful mouth of yours." His lips brushed her neck, and she gasped, her back arching into him as he softly nipped.

Light scratching prickled her skin before a deep red rose lifted from the center of her hand.

"See? You did it. Now, how about here." Zephyr touched the dip between her collarbones, and Cricket's mind drifted to flower petals unfurling during the spring beneath the blazing sun's rays. Her skin tickled as a red rosebud broke through her flesh and opened. "Reel them both back in."

Her body trembled slightly, beads of perspiration dotting her brow, when finally, her curiosity took the flowers away.

"Perfect. Would you like to try other places?" he asked, his voice gruff as his hand drifted to the curve of her hip.

"Yes," she murmured. *Please,* she wanted to beg.

"Tell me if you don't like anything I do, and I'll stop," Zephyr said, his fingers on the top button at the back of her dress.

"Keep going."

One by one, he unfastened the buttons down her back, then peeled the fabric from her, letting it pool to her hips. He ran the pads of his callused fingertips across her stomach, halting. Her breaths remained even, just as he'd taught her, until three roses grew. With a smile, she tucked them away and lifted her body so he could bring the dress the remainder of the way down.

Cricket kicked the fabric away, and he chuckled, deep and lusty. Left in only her undergarments, she leaned back into him. Zephyr spread her thighs apart, and a cluster of rosebuds released, disappearing as fast as they'd come. She could barely breathe as she wondered where Zephyr's fingers would venture next. A moan unintentionally left her mouth as his digits skimmed higher up her thigh.

"I'm restraining myself, and I think I may have to stop," he rasped.

"Don't stop," she whispered, arching into him again and drawing his hand up so he cupped her mound over her undergarments.

With a growl, Zephyr lifted her and brought her into his lap so she now faced him. "Tell me you want me as much as I do you. Lie to me if you have to. I don't give a damn."

"I can't lie. Not about this. I want you. *Badly*," she admitted. Her lips crashed to his, and she tasted whiskey and cherries. His fingers dug into her hips as the kiss deepened, fueling her desire. She rolled her hips forward while skating her hands up his chest. Not once had she ever felt this raw want, this need, to have someone, to have all of someone. He loosened her corset, then trailed sparks of heated kisses across her shoulders before he removed it. His intoxicating lips drifted to her neck, and while he kissed down it to her breast, she could feel every inch of him as his arousal strained against his trousers. When he took her nipple between his lips, she pulled him onto the mattress so they faced one another.

"I want to hear the sounds you make when your pleasure peaks," Zephyr said before he dipped his hands into her undergarments. She couldn't hold back a moan as his fingers moved against her, inside her.

Cricket reached between them and unlaced his trousers, drawing them far enough down to free him. His cock was like velvet in her hand as she stroked him hard, then harder.

His tongue found hers, and their mouths exquisitely caressed the other's. His hand's pace matched hers, growing faster as he circled her pearl until a pleasureful bliss stormed through her and she writhed from his touch. Another deep growl escaped Zephyr's throat, his mouth claiming hers once more in a fierce kiss, his warm seed spilling between them.

"I don't want this to be temporary," Cricket breathed, having meant to keep the words to herself.

"Neither do I." Zephyr pushed a lock of hair behind her ear, his eyes slitted. "Tomorrow, if you work just as well with your curiosity, I'll make you come much, *much* harder."

Even after allowing him to pleasure her, she still blushed at his words as she nodded with a content sigh.

For now, she still couldn't use her curiosity on her own in the way Mistress Eliza wanted, only with Zephyr's touch. But she could at least control herself enough if the murderer came near her.

**22**

**M**orning light filtered through the window, waking Cricket from sleep. She smiled as visions of the night before filled her mind. Her head rested in the crook of Zephyr's arm, and her hand lay on his warm chest. His heart beat steadily against her palm. She lingered there for a few more moments, feeling the rise and fall of his chest—one beautiful thing in a sea of horrors.

Cricket finally forced herself to rise and grabbed the first shirt she could find, one of Zephyr's folded neatly in the corner. She pulled it on over a pair of her trousers.

As if knowing she'd awoken him, she peered over her shoulder, where he watched her with hooded eyes and a lazy smile.

"You're wearing my shirt," he purred as he sat up, reaching for a clean pair of trousers. She thought about how she'd unlaced the ones from the night before, stroked him, and that blasted heat crept up her cheeks.

"It's not as though you wear them much," she said with a grin.

"It's yours."

"After breakfast, I was going to see if Bram has any updates. I was hoping you would want to accompany me." If he didn't, she could ask Juniper or maybe Wilder.

"Keep blushing like that when you look at me, and I'll do anything." He grabbed his boots from beside the bed and slipped them on. "If Bram doesn't have any news, then maybe we can find a lead of our own."

"I like that idea. Perhaps we can even track down another necromancer somehow. If not, maybe we'll find something else that can help Mistress Eliza's ability. I know she's mentioned how she's tried everything, but maybe…"

"We'll do it." He paused. "So how did you end up with Bram anyway? He still seems too … stiff for you. Not your type at all."

"That's only when he's working." She placed her hands on her hips. "And what's my type precisely? Do expand more this time."

Cricket's breath hitched as Zephyr backed her into the door, caging her in. "Me."

"Someone who is sweet, funny, protective, caring. And one who will pleasure me until I feel like I'm shining brighter than the stars." She winked, then reached down and opened the door behind her.

He chuckled as they stepped outside. The sun cast its rays over the caravans, highlighting the cloud-covered sky in oranges and yellows. A gust of wind carried the smell of pastries through the air, and she knew Juniper had to be the one either making or eating them.

As they neared the campfire, she searched for Juniper's tight red curls but only found Stormy sitting with a few performers sipping from mugs. Cricket frowned when she discovered Louise's arm wrapped around Stormy's shoulders. Louise giggled at something Stormy said, then leaned forward, flicking her tongue across her ear lobe before giving it a quick nibble.

Zephyr stiffened beside Cricket. "I knew she would do this to Juniper," he growled, "but I'd hoped to be proven wrong."

Cricket thought back to her words, encouraging Juniper to try, that Stormy and Louise perhaps weren't meant to be. But really, she didn't know them as well as Zephyr and Juniper did. They knew how the two women always ended up back together.

"Where's Juniper?" Cricket asked, not hiding the frustration lacing her tone when she approached Stormy.

Stormy avoided looking directly at her as she took Louise's arm away from her. "I told her yesterday that we needed to make different sleeping arrangements and that maybe she should stay with you and Zephyr."

"Was this before or after you pleasured Louise that you told her that?" Zephyr narrowed his eyes.

"That's none of your fucking business," Louise said between clenched teeth.

"My sister has always been too good for you," Zephyr snapped at Stormy.

"Put her up on a pedestal, why don't you." Louise rolled her eyes.

Cricket grabbed Zephyr by the arm and pulled him back before they said something that would cause a physical fight. She could barely control herself from throttling them, then ripping their hair out until they were both bald.

"I think we need to go to her caravan. She's probably been in there since yesterday." Cricket should've checked on her, but she'd thought she'd been with Stormy.

Zephyr knocked on Juniper's door, perhaps a bit too loudly. When she didn't answer, he knocked again. "Come on, Juniper, open up. If you don't, I'll use the key."

A nagging feeling told Cricket not to leave. "I think you should use the key." If they saw that Juniper was all right, that she hadn't hurt herself, she would apologize for making him invade her privacy.

Zephyr unlocked the door, but the caravan was empty. The scent of pastries tickled her nose, yet there was no sign of Juniper. The bag she carried with her whenever she would leave to go somewhere was still on the floor.

"Where the hell is she?" Zephyr ran a hand down his face.

"She's usually one of the first to eat, but maybe she's bathing at the lake or with Mistress Eliza or someone else."

"All right," Zephyr said. "I'll check the woods, then with Mistress Eliza while you ask the other performers. I don't want you going out to that area, and if Mistress Eliza is in one of her foul moods, you don't need to deal with that either."

Cricket nodded, and as soon as he left, Autumn hurried to her. "Is everything all right? I saw what happened with Stormy and Louise."

"I don't know. Can you help find out if anyone has seen Juniper? Or maybe you have?" Cricket asked.

"No, not since yesterday. She looked visibly upset as she went to her caravan, seeming as though she wanted to be left alone. I now know why." Autumn frowned.

"I need to find her."

They went to each of the caravans, checking with the performers there, then toward the tents where several others milled about. No one had seen Juniper since yesterday.

When they returned from the tent, Zephyr was with Mistress Eliza outside her caravan. As he caught Cricket's stare, she shook her head. His hand gripped the back of his neck, and he looked uneasy.

Juniper could've snuck off into town, but Cricket didn't think she would go alone. And yet, one was capable of anything when heartbroken.

She was about to take one of the horses and go to one of the pubs when her chest tightened—there was one place she hadn't searched. A place where she knew Juniper might've gone to if she'd truly wanted to be alone.

Whirling around, Cricket took off toward her caravan with Autumn shouting her name behind her. Once she reached it, she drew open the door to a strong metallic odor that invaded her nose. Her gaze latched onto bright crimson, and she froze, unable to take in the horrible sight resting before her. Blood. So much blood spattered the walls, the bed, the floor. *Juniper.*

Cricket trembled. Juniper shouldn't be here like this. She should've been there waiting for her so Cricket could wrap her arms around her, tell her that Stormy wasn't worth her time, that Juniper was one of the kindest people she'd ever had the pleasure of meeting. Juniper hadn't done this to herself—someone else had.

Decorated in black dahlias, Juniper's body lay torn and broken. A scream ripped from Cricket's throat, and footsteps thundered behind her. Zephyr stood in the doorway, his gaze on his sister, blinking as if he couldn't believe the nightmare before him. But then a guttural cry poured out of him, an emotion she'd never heard from Zephyr, one that most likely hadn't been there since he'd been a boy and witnessed his parents' murders.

Tears streaked his face as he rushed past her, dropping to his knees in front of the bed where his dead sister lay. He took the dahlias from her eyes, her mouth, her hands, and threw them all on the floor.

Stormy approached, a scowl on her face, but as she peered past Cricket into the caravan, a choking sob came from her. One Cricket believed she had no right to have when it was her who should've been with Juniper. Yet as Mistress Eliza limped between two caravans, she knew it wasn't Stormy's fault but her own. The necromancer's darkened expression was proof of that as her gaze found Zephyr sobbing over his sister.

"What happened here?" Mistress Eliza seethed, drawing out the ruby stones from her pouch. She hobbled up the steps and hurried toward Juniper. Cricket stopped in the doorway, praying more than ever that the necromancer's spell would work, would rouse Juniper so she could see her face don a different expression, any other expression than the dead one she held now.

Mistress Eliza pressed a hand to Juniper's shoulder, then an incantation spilled from her lips. Juniper's body jolted, her fingers flexing.

"Please wake up, Juniper," Zephyr whispered.

"Wake up," Mistress Eliza demanded, falling to her knees beside Zephyr while continuing to leave her hand against Juniper's shoulder. "Wake up, child. You have more to do here." But Juniper didn't open her eyes, and her body grew still.

Mistress Eliza stood, then slowly turned around, her gaze blazing as she looked at Cricket. Grabbing her by the arm, she yanked her out of the caravan, where a large crowd of performers had gathered. Autumn studied her, worry shining in her eyes, while Stormy ran away in tears.

"This, this is *your* fault," Mistress Eliza spat as if she were pinning down Cricket with nails. "One of my best performers is dead because of you. I can't revive her because of *you*. Why is it that every time a body shows up, you're there? It makes me wonder if you aren't the one doing these things. Everyone here was protecting you, yet you couldn't protect her."

Cricket's lungs froze beneath her rib cage, and she couldn't find air. All eyes turned to her, but no one said a word until Autumn did, "It's not her fault." Except Mistress Eliza was right about that—it *was* Cricket's fault.

"I didn't murder her or anyone," Cricket stammered and took a step back, her body shaking.

"Get out of my sight," Mistress Eliza growled.

The truth was everyone here had to know if Cricket had never woken up, none of this would've happened at the carnival. Someone intentionally did this to Juniper to hurt Cricket. She couldn't face Zephyr either, not after last night, not when they'd been pleasuring one another instead of making certain Juniper was with Stormy instead of assuming it. His sister was the one he should've been protecting, not Cricket. And that was her fault too.

Spinning on her heel, she ran away from everyone, their whispers, toward Zephyr's caravan. Thankfully it was unlocked—otherwise, she would've just gone. But she collected the belongings that were there, stuffing a few changes of clothing into her bag. If there had been anything of importance to her still in her caravan, she wouldn't have wanted it after seeing Juniper's broken body on her bed. Taking her satchel, she bolted from the caravan as Autumn shouted her name. If her curiosity came now, clawed at her flesh, she would welcome the dahlias, let them reap her of her own life. But they didn't come, not the one time she wished they would.

Cricket didn't look back at Autumn, nor the caravans, or the tents, or anything. She just ran, ran away from the carnival that she never should've been a part of, away from the lives she had ruined.

It wasn't long before Cricket's lungs burned and her legs grew heavy. The more she ran, the more she wished she had stolen a horse when she'd fled the carnival. She wore her wig, though, disguising herself the best she could while darting through the city, bumping into people as she passed. She ignored their stares and curses, taking a shortcut to venture into the poorer side of town. No longer were the buildings freshly painted, their windows free of cracks, or their roofs not in dire need of repair.

"Do you have any coin, Miss?" a young redheaded boy of maybe twelve with dirt smeared across his cheeks and hands asked. Cricket tried not to study the shade of his hair, the same color as Juniper's.

She drew out two silver coins from her satchel, wishing she'd had more, but she'd given the money she'd won from the card game to Mistress Eliza. The boy tucked the coins into his pocket as if they were gold and thanked her when she hurried away. She went by a bakery with broken windows and a faded sign, which appeared to have been unoccupied for ages. Another man and woman, covered in grime, begged her for coin, but she couldn't spare any more, not if she wanted to keep herself from starving.

A building that was clearly a brothel caught Cricket's attention when a partially-dressed woman slurred at her, "You're a pretty thing. You can work here unless you would rather come in for pleasure."

Cricket avoided looking at anyone else as she passed a few more brothels and pubs. Out here, there were more brothels than anything. She finally reached the inn that she never would've considered staying in before, but with how cheap it was, she could remain there for more days if need be.

The inn didn't look as decrepit as the other buildings. Other than being covered in muck, the windows were all in one piece, and black curtains blocked what was inside. Heavy smoke greeted her as she pulled open the creaking door, not just from cigars but something sweeter. She glanced at a mirror on the wall, finding her eyes red-rimmed and puffy.

Straightening her wig, she walked farther into the establishment. The front lobby held three rectangular tables, a few of their chairs missing. At one, a woman, her cleavage spilling out of her faded dress, sat in a gentleman's lap, trailing kisses up his neck while he played cards with another. In the shadowed corner, a man groaned. She looked away as she watched him unfasten his trousers and lift a woman's dress.

Cricket approached the empty front desk, waiting for someone to appear and give her a room.

"Albert!" one of the men at the table yelled. "You have a customer!"

It took a moment before a man smoking a cigar, muttering to himself, hobbled in from another room. His teeth were blackened, and his face tinged with red splotches.

"How long are you staying?" he asked, thick smoke curling from his cigar into her face.

"What will this get me?" Cricket opened her satchel and pushed aside the coin Zephyr had given her when they'd been in Sorel. She'd forgotten she still had it, yet now she never wanted to get rid of it. Slipping out four coins, she placed them on the counter in front of him. The pearl necklace she'd never gotten to give to Juniper was still in there, but she wanted to save it for when she became more desperate.

The man slid the coins around with his pudgy fingers as if he were playing a game of chess. "A few days," he grunted. "But we can always renegotiate after that if you want. I'm sure we can accommodate such a lovely lady. That is if she's willing to be accommodating in return...." His eyes met hers, a ravenous hunger flickering there.

Cricket's stomach churned at what the man would want in exchange. "A few days will do for now," she finally said and took the key from him.

The wooden stairs hidden in the opposite corner of where the couple pleasured one another groaned as she ascended them. There was only the filthy wall to balance against, the banister splintered and missing.

As she turned down the hall, dark stains covered the

frayed carpet, and she found the door to her room resting at the end. A few beds squeaked while eager moans spilled out into the hallway.

She locked the door to her room behind her as soon as she entered. A musky odor struck her nose, but at least it wasn't too pungent. The sleeping space was simple—a small bed without a headboard rested against one wall, a wooden chair cloaked in a thin layer of dust tucked in the corner, and a tall wardrobe, its doors missing, lingered beside it. A dingy curtain covered a cramped nook with a chamber pot.

Cricket propped the wooden chair against the door as another line of defense. Pathetic or not. She dropped her bag beside the bed and sank down onto the mattress. The sheets scratched her bare arms when she leaned back, and she wasn't certain if they'd been washed, but it didn't matter. It couldn't be any worse than when she was still alive, albeit asleep, below ground.

Taking a deep breath, Cricket pressed her back against the wall. She didn't know what her next step would be— she didn't even know what she would do here. The only other place she could've gone would've been Bram's, and she didn't want to explain to him or Anika how it was her fault that one of the kindest women she'd ever met was dead because of her. But they would know soon enough—if they didn't already.

The bastard who did it was still out there, and Cricket didn't know what else to do. She had unintentionally lured them back to the carnival, but it hadn't been to taunt her in the way she'd expected. Cricket sobbed into her hands and drew her knees to her chest, crying harder. She had no right to let these tears fall, yet she couldn't hold them back.

Cricket wasn't certain how much time had passed— she didn't have her pocket watch with her. But she knew it had been a long while since her stomach continued to growl. There wasn't much food in her bag besides a few pieces of jerky and a soft apple that she might need later, and if she'd thought about it more, she would've grabbed a few extra things, including her pocket watch that she knew was resting on Zephyr's shelf.

Before venturing downstairs, she changed out of the clothing she'd been wearing at the carnival, then tucked Zephyr's shirt neatly inside her bag. The inn didn't serve food, so she went across the street to a pub and ordered a bowl of porridge. It was cold and watery, but she polished off the bowl before returning to the inn.

As she pushed open the door to her room, a white folded paper laying on the floor caught her attention. Her gaze darted around the small area, and she drew out her knife while slowly snatching up the note to unfold it. Heart pounding, she read the words scrawled in the same cursive that was becoming achingly familiar.

*I see you fled the carnival, Cricket. But do you really think you can hide?*

Cricket's hand shook, and she tiptoed toward the bed, then yanked the fabric up to peer underneath. Empty. She shoved the curtains leading to the chamber pot aside and discovered the small space clear. Glancing out into the hallway, she looked side to side before stepping out.

She darted downstairs to find the man at the front desk. "Did you see anyone go up the stairs or come down earlier?"

"I saw you, but I wasn't here the whole time. Why?"

"Never mind." Cricket hurried back up the staircase and locked herself in her room. Just as she pulled out her knife, a clawing sensation stirred within her. "Not now!" she hissed.

A single black dahlia bud bloomed, unfurling before her. All she could see were the ones on Juniper's dead body, and she didn't want this wicked thing back inside her, so she took her knife, slicing it clean off. She expected pain to come, but it didn't, only when she tugged on the lingering stem.

Her eyes widened, and she focused, watching as the stem slipped back inside her. She backed away from the fallen dahlia, not wanting to touch it. Clenching the knife, she sat on the bed and hoped to lure the murderer in. Then she would place the dahlia on their bleeding corpse.

A knock came at the door, and Cricket gripped the blade tighter. She hadn't moved from the bed the entire night, hadn't done anything but stare at the one entrance into her room and wait. Sliding from the bed, she kept her feet light as she padded toward the door. The adrenaline rushing through her veins took away any exhaustion she carried from not taking rest.

She grasped the coolness of the metal knob when a knock came again. "Cricket, I know you're here," a man's voice said, deep and familiar. *Bram.*

With a relieved sigh, she cracked open the door, only enough for her to see that it was indeed Bram. He wore his bowler hat and long black coat, his lips set in a tight line. "How did you find me?" she asked.

"It wasn't difficult when people saw a young woman racing through town as if lightning were on her heels. The man downstairs was happy enough to oblige your whereabouts for a few coins."

"What a bastard," Cricket whispered, wondering if maybe the murderer had given him payment and he'd lied about only seeing her.

"You don't think it's dangerous staying in this part of the city alone?"

"I do, but the murderer found me, so I might as well lure them in."

Bram's brows rose up his forehead. "What? Can you open the door fully and tell me what precisely happened?"

With anyone else, he would've already pushed the door wide. "This was waiting for me when I got back from grabbing a bite to eat," Cricket said as she fished out the letter she'd tucked into her bag. She handed it to him without a word when he entered the room.

Bram frowned as he read over the note. "So you received another letter, and you didn't contact anyone? You should've waited at the carnival instead of running to this side of the city."

"I couldn't. I've caused too much trouble already. Juniper is dead because of me—because this murderer is taunting me..." she trailed off, tears stinging her eyes.

"What's this?" Bram asked, furrowing his brow as he picked up the dahlia on the floor that she'd cut from herself. "Was this left for you too?"

"No, it belongs to me." Cricket sighed. She told him about her curiosity after she'd awoken, how she wasn't allowed to perform until she'd honed it, and as she'd been trying, dahlias bloomed from her instead of roses. And then, at first, how the dahlias had almost consumed her on several occasions until Zephyr helped her. "It's been getting better, but last night when one bloomed, all I could think about was Juniper, so I cut it from myself."

"Anika had mentioned you were having trouble with your curiosity, yet I didn't know it was like this." His face softened. "You shouldn't have to see those after what happened to you."

"It's another reason Mistress Eliza wouldn't want me at the carnival now."

Bram inspected the room as he spoke to her, seeming to search for any sign the murderer may have possibly been inside. "She didn't mean for you to leave the carnival. People get angry and say things they shouldn't when they are in the heat of the moment."

Cricket couldn't get the image of Zephyr kneeling before Juniper and peeling the dahlias from her eyes. "There was a right for her to be. For Zephyr to hate me..."

"This isn't your fault, Cricket. As for Zephyr? He's distraught and searching the city for you. You ran off right after his sister was murdered. How do you think he's going to react with no one able to find you and the murderer still on the loose?"

"It's better he doesn't see me and then finally realizes that he should've been protecting his sister instead."

Bram sighed. "Listen, you have two options here since it's quite obvious you aren't ready to return to the carnival. Come to my home, or I'm going to stay here. And you know if I stay here, Anika will follow, and I don't think this is the best place for her while pregnant, do you?"

"Stop weighing on my conscience," she snapped. "If I stay here, the killer will come back, and maybe I can catch them..."

"They knew you were at the carnival the whole time, and they were careful, letting you see only what they wanted you to see. I don't believe they are going to walk through this door when they know you're in here waiting for them."

She hated to admit it, but he was most likely right. If anything, they would send a letter telling her to meet them somewhere or slink up on her from behind the way Clancy had.

"Just come to the manor for now," he continued. "If you decide you want to go back to the carnival, I'll take you there. But waiting around to be slaughtered isn't the best option."

Perhaps there was something else she could do. "I'll come with you, but only if you let me really help. Even when the man was murdered, he was still blond and blue-eyed. So why take Juniper's life? Why the change? Was there a note left on her body?"

Bram shook his head as he studied her. "There was no note found on her. And I'll allow you to help more if you don't do anything I tell you not to do."

"Fine. And don't tell anyone I'm staying with you, only that I'm safe. No one." Cricket said, meaning Zephyr more than anything.

"I won't. But I'll admit, I think that man at the carnival needs you."

What Zephyr needed was to stay far away from her and the danger she brought to everyone around her.

# 24

Arriving at Bram's manor, Cricket stepped from the carriage to find the gardeners cutting hedges and placing weeds into wicker baskets. She'd removed her wig and adjusted the collar of her dress to continue hiding the bruises that were slowly fading. Before leaving the inn, Bram had questioned a few of the people downstairs, to which no one had seen anyone or anything suspicious the prior day when Cricket had received the murderer's letter.

Bram welcomed her into the sitting room, empty but for Breeta embroidering. The woman glanced up, blinking as she stared up at Cricket. "You're all right," she said. "Anika's been worried sick."

"Where is she?" Bram asked, removing his hat and placing it on the rack.

"Stress painting somewhere, I believe." Breeta quickened her pace with the thread.

Bram turned to Cricket. "I'll tell her you're here. Please, make yourself at home, and the servants will bring tea shortly.

"Thank you, Bram." Cricket took a seat opposite Breeta as he ascended the stairs. A few moments later, a servant placed a cup of tea on the table in front of her.

After a long stretch of uncomfortable silence, Breeta finally glanced up from her embroidery, her shoulders rigid as she studied Cricket's bag. "I'm sorry to hear what happened. Are you returning to the carnival?"

"No, Bram invited me to stay here for a little while."

Breeta's lips pinched. "Are you sure that's wise? I don't think you should return to the carnival, but—"

"But what, Mother?" Anika snapped as she entered the room.

"I don't think this is the place for us to have this conversation." Breeta lowered her voice. "But if you insist, it isn't appropriate for Cricket to stay here since Bram once courted her."

"Oh, hush, Mother. She will stay as long as she wishes, and you will make this feel like a home to her." Anika motioned Cricket to follow her up the stairs. "Now, come on."

Breeta didn't argue as she returned to her embroidery, but her shoulders didn't relax.

Cricket wondered if she should've just remained at the inn after all or at least tried to find another one while still helping Bram in whatever way she could.

"It's quite obvious your mother doesn't want me here," Cricket said softly as they reached the top of the stairs to walk down the long hallway.

Bram slipped out of the bedroom, straightening the

229

cuff of his sleeve. He kissed Anika on the cheek as he explained, "I'm going to report the new note to the authorities. We'll discuss matters further when I return."

As Bram disappeared down the hallway, Anika opened the door at the opposite end. "This room is already prepared for you."

Cricket stepped inside and took in the dancing portraits hanging on the wall, the dark purple silk sheets on the bed, the ivory writing desk tucked in the corner— all her favorite things. Her lips tilted up at the edges as she rested her bag beside the desk. "How long have you had this room ready for me?"

Anika grinned. "After I found out you were still alive, I had it done this way for if you ever needed it. This house has so many unnecessary rooms that surely we can spare one for our dearest friend."

Cricket's smile fell as the images of Juniper's broken body drifted through her mind like a lone ship lost at sea. "I don't see how you or Bram would want me here after what happened to Juniper. Wherever I go, something terrible happens. Bram seemed to have already told you about the letter I received at the inn. What if a letter is left here, or worse, a body? Aren't you frightened?"

"None of this is your fault." Anika pressed a hand to Cricket's shoulder, reassuring her. "Servants will be on duty every night outdoors and indoors. If anyone slinks onto our property, attempting to cause you harm, I have a gun, and I will use it. I'm quite a good shot. Bram taught me how to use it when we were searching for Clancy."

Cricket smiled. "Perhaps you can show me after the child is born."

Anika placed her hands on her hips. "I'm perfectly

fine to shoot, and I'll teach you today. But first, I have a question for you. What about Zephyr? Are you truly not going to tell him you're here?"

"No. Bram will let him know I'm safe." Cricket bit her lip, not wanting to think about Zephyr now or remember the guttural sounds he'd made when discovering his sister's slain body.

"I know you have a heart that always wants to run away, but I think he would prefer you run toward him. Especially now. Wouldn't you?"

Cricket honestly didn't know if she would or if she would blame the person and want to be left alone. Or perhaps she would want to be held as she cried, but either way, she didn't want Zephyr to worry about her. When Cricket remained silent, Anika nodded and said, "Come on. Let's paint a while, and then we can go shoot."

Cricket was relieved by the momentary escape as they entered the room across the hall. Canvases decorated its entirety—some finished, others halfway painted or barely holding a few strokes of color. Even as children, Anika could never focus on only one art piece. She would bounce between canvases but always completed what she'd started, regardless of how long it took. The days when Cricket would dance as Anika painted seemed long ago now.

"I want to show you something." Anika gestured to the other side of the room, where a large canvas hung in the center of the wall. It was the art piece that she'd painted of Cricket in mid-pirouette while dressed in a lavender dress from when they were both thirteen years old.

Cricket's breath caught as she trailed a finger down

the side of the golden frame. "You still have it?"

"I've had several customers offer to purchase it, but I could never get rid of this piece or the one of Bram."

She studied the painting beside it of Bram when he was about fifteen years old, running a brush through his horse's mane. "I would love it if you painted me a piece that I can take with me one day." Or at least she hoped she would make it to that day…

"Of course." Anika brought a hand across her growing belly as she pulled out a set of paintbrushes from the desk drawer. "Now, would you like to dance while I paint?"

Cricket lifted one of the thicker brushes. "I'd like to paint this time."

"Then we'll paint."

They sat beside one another and worked on their art pieces, but as Cricket moved the brush, dipping it into various shades of reds, blacks, and greens, she couldn't stop herself from painting vines covered in red roses and black dahlias.

Cricket lost track of time as the hours ticked by. Eventually, Anika stood, stretching, and said, "Should we get something to eat in the garden? Then we can proceed to target practice."

A thrill coursed through her at the thought of pulling the trigger of a gun, and Cricket found herself eager to begin learning to use the weapon as she and Anika shared cucumber sandwiches and lemon tea. Anika proved herself to indeed be an excellent shot, striking the target through the center before handing the rifle to Cricket. "Calm your nerves," she said. "Exhale. Focus just below the center."

Cricket took a deep breath, holding the gun steady as Anika had told her to do. She then aimed, the bullet piercing not far from Anika's.

"Brilliant!" Anika grinned.

They took turns firing shots until Bram's voice echoed behind them. "I suppose asking you both to rest would be too much."

"This was something I should've been teaching Cricket already. She's a natural," Anika said.

"I'm sorry to have to end your entertainment, but there may be a new lead and I need Cricket to come with me to meet with someone who says the Dahlia Murderer attacked her. Leslie specifically asked for Cricket and refused to talk to us without her present."

Cricket furrowed her brow. It couldn't be the same woman, could it? "Leslie? From the Garland?"

Bram nodded. "It happened last night, but she says she was afraid to come forward until today. She doesn't trust us since word spread about the incident with Charles, and she's uncertain what the other authorities are capable of, so she wants you there. The main reason is that you survived your murder."

"Leslie does realize that my murderer was a different person, right? And even then, I only lived because a necromancer brought me back to life."

Bram shrugged. "She doesn't care and is very adamant about it. She just wants to talk to you."

"Yes, of course I'll go," Cricket said. It would be a way for her to possibly find out more and could help the case.

Anika took the gun from her. "Be careful. I'll have the servants prepare a meal for when you return."

Cricket walked beside Bram to the carriage and sat opposite him. He picked up a notebook to read over as the horses took them away from the manor.

"Still no matches on the handwriting?" Cricket asked.

He sighed. "No. Miles and the other authorities have been going from home to home, questioning and searching. But they keep coming up empty. There's also a chance the murderer isn't a resident here. In a city of thousands, a stranger wouldn't easily stand out, it's true— especially if they're attempting to blend in."

There had to be a way to uncover something faster. "And no luck on finding another necromancer?"

"We're still hoping to find one."

If they ever did, maybe they could revive Juniper. That possibility led to hope blossoming in her chest, that maybe a necromancer would come out of hiding and journey to Nobel.

The carriage drew to a stop in front of the authority building, and Cricket followed Bram inside to a room at the end of the hall where Leslie waited. Her blonde hair was pulled back into a plait, and her pale blue eyes lit up as they met hers. She straightened in her chair, blinking with a content expression. "Cricket," she said.

Cricket took the woman's hands and sat. "Oh, Leslie, are you all right? What a horrid trial you experienced."

"Yes, I'm fine. May I talk to you alone first, though?" She stayed facing Cricket, but she watched Bram out of the corners of her eyes.

Cricket nodded to Bram, and he shut the door, leaving the two of them alone. "You were attacked last night? What happened? Was it after you left the pub or somewhere else?" She was lucky she escaped the bastard when no one else had.

"It was late, and I was walking home from the pub when someone attacked me from behind, strangling me until I couldn't breathe," Leslie said, her voice calm, her expression almost dreamy.

Cricket wrinkled her nose as she stared at Leslie for a long moment. "You were walking alone after a murder just took place behind the building?"

Her eyes ticked side to side before she batted a hand in the air. "I don't live far from there and kept on the main street. The others were too busy at the pub."

"Did you get a look at the person's face?"

"No. We were cloaked in shadows, so I couldn't see anything clearly." Leslie paused, wiping her palms against her skirt.

"What else happened after you were strangled?" Her pulse raced, and she couldn't stop from thinking about Clancy's blade piercing her chest, followed by his macabre dahlias brushing her flesh.

Leslie took a breath, her calmness wavering as she stuttered, "The murderer took out the dahlias from a satchel and placed them over my eyes. That was when I had time to escape."

Cricket froze. That didn't make sense… If the person was practically mirroring the way her death had been, the dahlias would've come last. Besides that, the dahlias would've most likely fallen from her eyes as the murderer cut into her body and cracked open her rib cage. Leslie was lying… She could *feel* it.

It wasn't only the dahlias, though… The route to Leslie's home was well-lit—she should've caught some sort of feature about the attacker. It also seemed as if

Leslie had spun the story beforehand of precisely what to say, and now that she was asked questions that she wasn't expecting, she was becoming more nervous.

Cricket studied Leslie's neck—not a single bruise or mark there. If she'd been choked that hard, the way Cricket had been, there would've been at least one by now. "The Dahlia Killer puts the flowers over the eyes after they slice into the victim, not before. If you did suffer strangulation, as you say, there would be a ring of bruises around your throat. But yours appears as blemish-free as a baby's bottom. And if it did happen in the way you described, regardless, the murderer wouldn't have just let you flee. They would've gone after you and made sure you were dead. Now tell me the truth, did you encounter anyone, or is all this an elaborate game to seek attention? There have been victims. *Real* victims." Cricket's chest tightened as she spoke the next sentence, "And one I was very fond of."

Leslie chewed on her lip, her eyes flicking side to side again before her body trembled. "It happened. Maybe I imagined the dahlias…"

"Please tell me the truth, Leslie. I need to find the person who is doing this. So tell me, did it really happen?" If Cricket hadn't previously known Leslie, she might not have noticed the small things that didn't seem right with her and her story.

"I made it up," she whispered, her lower lip wobbling. "It was a charade."

Cricket inhaled sharply, loosening her clenched teeth. "Why?"

"There's nothing truly special about you or the others, yet you were chosen, and so were they. I have blonde hair and blue eyes, so why not choose me?" Tears beaded Leslie's lashes.

Cricket stared at her in horror, taken aback by this revelation. "You want to be slaughtered?"

"I don't have anyone who truly sees me," Leslie sobbed. "Day in and day out, my life is at the pub, and for once, I wanted to be seen as something special."

"As a victim, I wouldn't consider myself special—I would consider myself unfortunate." Cricket couldn't sit there any longer, or she would shout things that would get her put in manacles. She pushed up from the seat and glanced over her shoulder before opening the door. "And not all of the victims have been blond and blue-eyed. Each of them is very different from you in that they will never have the opportunity to laugh, cry, sing, or dance— or enjoy a single drink in a pub. Ever again."

# 25

Cricket sat alone at the dining table, sipping on tea between bites of her biscuit. She'd been at Bram's for three days, and since the supposed lead with Leslie, there had been nothing more from the Dahlia Murderer.

Footsteps echoed from the hallway, and she glanced up as Breeta entered the room, her skirts swishing. She sat across from Cricket, her spine tall and rigid.

"I owe you a sincere apology for how distant I've been the past couple of days." She let out a breath as if it had been hard to speak those words. "Or, I suppose, all the years I've known you. I'm just a bitter woman whose broken heart never healed and who wants the best for my daughter. I always have."

Cricket knew little about Anika's father except that Breeta had been his mistress before learning he was a married man. Once he found out Breeta was with child, he started to come around less and less until he no longer did.

"You raised a daughter with the kindest heart, and that's what matters. Besides, experiences sometimes turn us into something different than we were before. I'm not the same either."

"I will never be sweet like my daughter, but I'm trying to be less bitter." Breeta looked toward one of the servants. "Well? Did someone forget my tea?"

"Sorry, Miss," the servant said and hurried out of the room.

Breeta's brow lifted as she peered at Cricket and said, "What?"

"Kindness, remember?" Cricket smiled and finished her breakfast before finding Bram in his office, looking through various sketches. Anika was still asleep, but she would most likely wake in the next hour.

"You can come in," he said, waving her inside. "They're just sketches I did of the victims to see if I could put something together."

Taking a deep swallow, she hardened her heart as she lowered herself into a chair and reached for the stack of sketches. The first victim was one of the bodies she hadn't seen in person. The woman's chest was broken apart, just as all the others. "Your drawings have vastly improved."

"That's all Anika's doing. She teaches well. Before her pregnancy, she'd done some sketches for us of other crimes, but it stopped her from being creative. And when she found out she was with child, she didn't want to do the task any longer."

"I won't fault her for that decision." Cricket's

attention fell to the next sketch. She held her breath as she studied Juniper's body. If the sketch had been in color, to where she could see red curls, she wouldn't have been able to hold back her tears.

When the killer made their next move, would it be a man with red hair this time? Or would they go back to a blond victim? A different color entirely? Perhaps leave Cricket another note? Maybe the murderer had decided it was her turn to be next and was just waiting in the shadows for her.

Bram lifted his pocket watch and looked at the time. "I need to go. I'm going to be late. You're welcome to continue analyzing the sketches if you'd like."

"Thank you, Bram."

Once he left, Cricket took the sketches to her room, spreading them across her bed to study. She lined them up one by one and inhaled sharply on the last drawing. It was of her, except this one she could tell wasn't done by Bram but Anika. Everything appeared more real, the lines smooth, her features prominent. Looking at herself this way was strange, seeing how she appeared in death. The dahlias must've already been removed because they weren't in this picture, and she was glad for it, even though her chest and stomach were slashed, the fabric of her torn and bloody dress still there.

She noticed nothing else similar besides the dahlias that weren't in the sketches. The flower wasn't a simple one to find, but somehow the murderer had easy access to them. All the flower shops had come up empty—not a single midnight black dahlia had been in any of them, not since Clancy had bought them to use for the death of his choosing.

Cricket thought of herself, the black dahlias from her curiosity, and she shivered. *I'm not the one doing these heinous acts.* She stared at the drawings until she thought she would go mad and decided to bathe.

Filling the bath, she peeled the dress from her body and sat in the warm water. She thought about how Zephyr had helped roses peek out of her instead of the dahlias. Each day she'd continued practicing, and each day she'd gotten better. She held her hand up, focusing, her skin becoming translucent.

"Come on. Grow for me," she whispered.

In answer, tiny dots covered her arm, not obsidian but crimson. She watched with bated breath as the flowers bloomed. Red. All red and no black. She then reeled them in, letting them sleep beneath her flesh for now. Her lips lifted into a smile before falling. This was the moment she'd been waiting for, to master her curiosity, but did it matter now?

It did. Even if she wasn't at the carnival, or performing, this was for her, what she needed to protect herself.

As the water grew cold, her teeth chattering, Cricket wrapped a towel around herself and slipped on a dark purple dress from the wardrobe of things that Anika had bought for her. She glanced at the sketches one more time, knowing there had to be *something*.

But there wasn't...

Cricket left her room and descended the stairs to see if Anika was up yet so she could show her friend that she was able to hone her curiosity. Voices echoed from the kitchen, and she stilled. Anika and a ... man... A man she knew well. Zephyr. What was he doing here?

"I watched you perform when I would go with Cricket to the carnival. We went every year together. Your performance was always her favorite. She would talk about how wonderful performing on stage alongside you would be."

"Did she? She never told me I was her *favorite*." Even though there was sadness in his voice, she could hear the smile in there too.

"And handsome," Anika added with a soft laugh. "Although she didn't say it aloud, I could always tell."

Cricket's cheeks heated, and she almost fled back up the steps, but she wouldn't be a coward. Not after he was already here.

Cricket slipped into the room, meeting Zephyr's eyes, and she instantly regretted not telling him herself that she was safe. She was far from perfect, and hurting him was another mistake to add to her list of them.

He stood from his seat, dressed in a white collared button-up shirt tucked into dark trousers, making him seem too proper but beautiful nonetheless. "I searched the city like mad for you. Then Bram told me you were somewhere safe, and I'm not a fool. I knew you were here, but I kept hoping you would come to me. When you didn't, I decided to come to you."

"Everything is my fault," Cricket whispered.

"I'll give you two some time alone," Anika said, standing from the table. She pressed a gentle hand to Cricket's shoulder. "Let me know if you need me."

Once Anika left the room, Cricket made the first move and stepped toward him. It was the least she could do when she wanted to do so much more. "I'm glad you're here."

"Two of the servants tried to escort me away when I came. I was lucky Anika was out in the gardens—she told me you were here."

"Anika's good at confessing things when she deems it necessary," Cricket said.

"At first, before Bram told me you were safe, I thought—I thought something happened to you." Zephyr's voice cracked on the last word, and she grasped his hand, intertwining her fingers with his.

"It's my fault what happened to Juniper. I was too ashamed and didn't want to see the blame in your eyes." But as he stared at her, there wasn't blame, only melancholy.

"Don't think for one more moment that it's your fault. It's that murderous bastard's fault." He ran a hand through his hair and unclenched his jaw as he blew out a breath. "Will you go for a walk with me?"

"Anything you want," Cricket murmured. If he asked her to walk with him to the ends of the world and leap off right then, she would.

"I never thought I would hear those words fall from your pretty lips," he said softly, tucking a loose lock of her hair behind her ear.

"I mean them." Cricket didn't release his hand as she led him out into the gardens, the serene quiet enveloping them.

"Autumn told me what Mistress Eliza said to you, and she had no right," Zephyr said, shattering the silence. "If you're not a part of the carnival, neither am I. I go wherever you go. You want to start a new carnival? I'd be your first performer."

A smile tugged at the corners of her lips. "My *only*

performer."

"The *only* handsome one you'll ever need." A smirk played on his lips as his eyes found hers. "So, is it true what Anika said? I was your favorite."

"Yes," she huffed, "you were my favorite."

"It didn't always seem that way."

"I have a terrible confession." She bit the inside of her cheek. "In a sense, I blamed you for my death, blamed the carnival, for losing the life I'd had, which was something I had no right to do. You were the main reason I was at the carnival. I wanted so badly to see you perform, to pretend I was dancing on that very stage, getting to travel with the carnival from place to place. But as I've grown closer to you, I knew how foolish it was. And if I can fault you over something as ridiculous as that, then you certainly have the right to accuse me of causing Juniper's death."

Zephyr halted and drew her to him, slowly lifting her chin, their breath mingling. "I don't blame you. You were kind to Juniper, brought her out of her shell when no one else could. I don't blame Stormy either, even though I wanted to. I'm just desperate to find the murderer and tear them apart worse than they did my sister. I want their blood spread by my own hands for this city to see that the killer is dead."

"I want the same." Perhaps she would even tear them apart worse.

"Come with me somewhere quiet," he said, a plea in his voice. "Just for a while. I'll take you back here any time you wish. Just you and me—that's all I need right now."

Cricket wouldn't deny him anything in that moment.

She cupped his cheek. "All right, but let me tell Anika so she doesn't come searching for me." Before they left, she grabbed her satchel from her room and let Anika know that if she didn't come back today, not to worry. She knew the perfect quiet place they could go.

Wrapping her arm around Zephyr's waist, she led him to a cozy inn where her father used to work. Of course, her father wasn't at the front desk any longer, though. Before she could take a few coins from her satchel, Zephyr placed three on the counter and took the key from the young woman.

Once they entered the small room, filled with scents of vanilla and lavender, she sat beside him on the edge of the bed. The rooms, or at least this one, were the same as they used to be. Succulents rested on shelves hanging on the wall, two paintings of the city were above the bed, and an ornate quilt covered the mattress along with several knitted pillows.

A small smile crossed her face. "I have something to show you."

Zephyr leaned in close, his breath hot on her neck, before he whispered in her ear, "My answer is yes to anything you say."

Cricket brushed a hand down his cheek, letting several red roses bloom across her palm without even needing to make her skin translucent. "Because of you, I have control of myself. Thank you, Zephyr."

He took her hand in his, trailing his fingers over the roses as he smiled. The feel of his digits touching the velvety petals was the same as if he was touching her bare flesh. "You're beautiful. Life and death combined." Zephyr's eyes grew hooded, and he captured her mouth with his. "We're not leaving this room until morning."

Cricket's heart pounded, and she knew her eyes were as dilated as his. "I…"

He lifted her into his lap so her legs cradled his thighs. "This isn't about fucking, although dear gods do I want to, but I only want you. Whether it's you lying beside me or me making you come until you quake with pleasure."

Her lips twitched, and she studied him with wide eyes. "If you fulfill your promises, good sir, I think we'll never leave this inn."

Zephyr's hands trailed down her sides to cup her buttocks, his fingers deliciously digging in. "I want you. It's undeniable." His voice came out gravelly as his hard length pressed against her softness.

"Show me." She brought a finger to his mouth and caught it on his lower lip. He gave it a gentle nip and rolled her hips into his. "Give me the performance I've been waiting for."

"I accept the challenge," Zephyr growled, capturing her mouth once more, their kiss eager and desperate.

Cricket helped him bring his shirt over his head, only briefly breaking contact between their lips for mere moments. Piece by piece, they shed their clothing until nothing remained between them but thin undergarments. He slowly peeled the undergarments away, taunting her until he began worshiping her body with his tongue and hands.

Zephyr lay her gently on the bed, kissing down the valley between her breasts. He flicked his tongue over her peaked nipple, then sucked it between his teeth before trailing heated kisses lower and lower. As her heart pounded, he spread her legs, his teeth grazing her inner thigh. He slowly ran his tongue up her center, making her gasp and yank on his hair for more.

He released a low chuckle. "I'll make it so you're ruined for anyone else, so that you'll only ever want my head between your thighs, my tongue lapping up your sweet flavor. Do you want that?"

"Yes," she breathed, willing to surrender to him if he would just keep touching her the way he did.

Zephyr slid two fingers inside her as he stroked and circled her. He did as she'd asked—he *performed*, using whatever tricks he had hidden in his exquisite movements. A whimper escaped her, and her body quaked from the way he feasted on her, from the way his tongue and lips made love to her core.

When his mouth found hers, she brushed her fingers along his collar.

"Remove it," he rasped, rolling them so she was on top of him.

Her heart sang at the fact that he wanted absolutely nothing between them. Cricket unbuckled his collar and took off her locket, resting them both on the night table. Pulling him from the bed so they were both standing, she skimmed her fingers across his scar before replacing them with gentle kisses. Using her tongue and mouth, she traveled down his chest until she reached his length. She licked the salty pearl from his tip while skating her hands down his back to his firm buttocks. Needing no urging from her, he slid his manhood between her lips. Zephyr growled as he moved, deep and lusty, his fingers tangled in her hair. She worked him with her tongue, licking and sucking him from base to tip until she desired all of him.

Zephyr seemed to know precisely what she needed

when he groaned. "It's time to move on to the next act of our performance." He sat on the bed and pulled her into his lap with her facing away from him. Using deft fingers, he stroked her center while kissing up the column of her neck. His other hand cradled her breast, kneading it as she arched into him.

"No more teasing," she whispered. "Show me the finale."

As if she weighed nothing, he lifted and turned her to face him. There was no pause when his length pressed fully inside her.

"Zephyr," Cricket moaned in delight.

He gripped her hips, urging her to move. She ground her core against him, and it didn't take long before the pace picked up. Harder, faster. Her fingers tugged his hair, making him groan. Their movements grew frantic as they both savored the pleasure they were receiving from one another.

"Come for me," he purred. "Let me hear that beautiful sound you make."

Her eyelids fluttered, the inviting feeling inching closer. Then, as if her roses were brushing all her nerve endings, bliss shattered inside her, and she screamed his name.

Zephyr didn't hesitate to flip her onto her back to thrust inside her when she wrapped her legs around his waist to bring him in even deeper. She dug her fingernails into his back, and he relished the moment as he let go, growling her name while spilling himself inside her.

"That was..." Cricket breathed. She gazed into his bright hazel eyes, unable to stop smiling. "That was..." She couldn't get the words out, what she was feeling as they lay spent and relaxed.

"The most amazing performance we've ever put on together," he said between kisses that traveled along her neck, his teeth gently nipping her ear. "I don't think the stage curtains need to be drawn shut quite yet, though. I think the performance deserves an encore."

"Endless encores," she drawled, bringing his mouth to hers.

## 26

Cricket brushed a lock of hair from Zephyr's cheek, and his eyes turned slitted. A smirk crossed his face as he wrapped his arm around her waist and tugged her closer. "Looks as if my wish came true. I got you in my bed," he purred.

"This isn't exactly your bed, now is it?" she teased, trailing a finger over his lower lip.

With one swift motion, he lifted her atop him as he rolled to his back, and Cricket gasped. He pressed his forehead against hers. "This one is sufficient. If I had enough coin, I would make it so we never left this room again," he said gruffly, nipping her neck.

"I think we would die of starvation or thirst." Cricket arched a brow and rolled, squeaking as they fell from the bed and collapsed on the floor.

Zephyr caught himself before his weight crushed her,

and she couldn't hold back the loud laughter spilling out from her. A laugh she hadn't released in ages.

"Oh, fuck." He balanced himself on his arms while his body shook from his own laughter. "Are you all right?"

She threaded her fingers through his hair. "I will be once you wake me thoroughly." Neither one of them had been able to sleep much during the night. There'd been lovemaking, touching conversations, and more lovemaking. Darkness still lingered behind the curtains, the sun not yet risen.

Zephyr captured Cricket's lips and brought one of her legs around his waist before giving a heavenly thrust inside her depths.

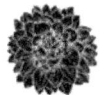

When the sun filtered in through the window, Cricket and Zephyr eventually had to wake from this dream of ecstasy and return to the world of horror that threatened to consume them.

Cricket slipped her dress over her head while Zephyr drew on his trousers. He left them unfastened as he buttoned the back of her dress.

"I'm leaving Nobel later today to let my aunt in Sorel know about Juniper and to prepare a burial for her body once it's released from the coroner's," he said softly. "My aunt never tried to take us from the carnival when we'd chosen to stay with Mistress Eliza, and I haven't talked to her in a long time, but I know she cared about Juniper."

"Do you think if Mistress Eliza's necromancy returns,

or we find another with the ability, that you would want to try and bring her back?" Cricket didn't know if she should give hope, but perhaps it was something good to hold on to.

Zephyr shook his head. "Juniper had a harder time than me when she was first revived, and I don't want to pull her away from peace. She once told me if something happened to her again, just to let her be."

Cricket thought about her family years ago. Her playing with Felix, the sickness spreading through their household, worsening for him. "I had a little brother once. He died when he was four from a plague. I still miss him and wonder what he would be like now if he had lived."

Zephyr circled his arms around her, holding her tightly as he rested his chin on top of her head. "Maybe Juniper found your brother in the afterlife and is telling him all about his wonderful sister."

The thought made her chest swell. "Once this murderer is brought to justice, I should find my parents and let them know I'm alive. Just like your aunt, they deserve that much." Tears pricked Cricket's eyes as she wrapped her arms around him, finding comfort in his touch. "There's one other thing I need to do before returning to Anika's—I want to talk to Mistress Eliza. Not that I need you attached to my hip to do so, but I was hoping you could walk me there?"

"I'll walk you anywhere you want."

After Cricket placed the locket back around her neck, she grabbed Zephyr's collar from the bedside table. She trailed a finger across his scar, beautiful even though it held a horrific memory. He closed his eyes, inhaling softly at her tender movements. Gently, she reached to buckle the collar around his throat. "There," she whispered.

"Thank you."

Before leaving the inn, they ate breakfast downstairs, a bowl of oatmeal and strawberries, along with chamomile tea. The day was bright, and the warm rays crept across her bare arms. As they walked the path toward the carnival, Cricket tried not to let her nerves take over. But if this was the last she would see of Mistress Eliza, she wanted to offer the necromancer the locket back and thank her once more for giving her this second chance at life, even if the woman wasn't pleased she'd given Cricket life after death. From what Bram and Zephyr had said, Mistress Eliza hadn't thought Cricket would run off and would've just been out of her sight for a little while.

Not too far from the caravans, Autumn and Wilder carried armfuls of logs. Autumn looked toward them and stilled, a smile spreading across her face. She dropped the logs and ran in their direction.

"You're back." She grasped Cricket's hand and pulled her away from Zephyr. "Everyone's been wanting to make sure you're all right. Hearing that you're safe isn't the same as seeing it for oneself."

Cricket blinked away tears. "Thank you for standing up for me that day. It means a lot." She was frustrated with herself for not giving Autumn a chance at first, for being more envious of her and Zephyr. But the truth was, even though they hadn't been close friends, Autumn had stood up for her before anyone else.

"Mistress Eliza knows what she said was wrong. Juniper was like a daughter to her. We all are family. And sometimes families get along, and sometimes they don't, but we have one another's backs." Before Cricket could respond, Autumn leaned in closer, whispering, "Take care of Zephyr. He needs you."

Cricket's heart clenched. "I promise. I hope I see you later." She went back to Zephyr, and they trekked toward the caravans. Her gaze fell to Juniper's home, and she wondered what would happen to it now. Who would fill it? And what about Cricket's? Had anyone cleaned it? Even if someone had wiped away every drop of blood, she could never step foot inside there again. She kept her thoughts to herself because they didn't matter at the moment—she would be at Anika's after talking to Mistress Eliza.

"I need to do this alone," she told Zephyr when they approached the necromancer's home. "Can I meet you at your caravan after?"

Concern filled his eyes. "Are you sure?"

"I'll be fine."

Zephyr nodded, walking backward and watching her with an intensity that made her want to press her lips to his to calm her nerves. But instead, she stayed glancing over her shoulder at him as she took the steps to Mistress Eliza's home. Once he disappeared from view, she knocked on the door. She waited a few moments, and when the necromancer didn't answer, Cricket knocked a little louder.

"Are you looking for Mistress Eliza?" Stormy asked, and Cricket whirled around to face her, unable to hide her frown. "She's inside her tent." The performer stood there, looking as though she hadn't changed her clothing or brushed her hair since Cricket had seen her last.

"If Mistress Eliza was going to yell at anyone, it should've been me," Stormy said, tears filling her eyes. "Yet, I ran, even when I could hear her shouting at you. But I did tell her what happened, how I shouldn't have hurt Juniper, how I at least should've made certain she'd gone to stay with you and wasn't alone somewhere."

Cricket's face remained hardened. "Juniper loved you, you know. You're the only person she'd ever felt that way toward. You weren't the one who murdered her—however, you were the one who left her alone. I don't hate you, Stormy, but I hate what you did."

"I hate myself, and I knew Juniper was special, that she was more special to me than Louise ever was. That part frightened me most of all, so I turned my back on the one good thing in my life because I was afraid. Now that she's gone, I'll never get to tell her how I feel, how sorry I am, how this was the biggest mistake of my life," Stormy sobbed, then took off running. Before Cricket could call her name, she was already gone.

Cricket didn't want to have sympathy for how Stormy felt, but it was there. Pushing her emotions away, she skirted around the caravans toward Mistress Eliza's tent.

Standing at the entrance, she could hear the necromancer shuffling her cards. Cricket inhaled and exhaled through her nose before she spoke, "Mistress Eliza? May I come in? It's Cricket."

The sound of the cards stilled. "You can come in, child." Her voice didn't sound angry but more resigned.

Cricket pulled back the fabric of the tent and entered the small space. The necromancer sat in her chair, smoking her pipe with several decks of tarot cards in front of her. At each of the corners of the table rested a

255

crystal and a lit candle.

"So, you finally decided to return home?" Mistress Eliza said, leaning back in her seat.

"I took your words as though you wanted me gone from here."

"From my sight. Not the carnival." Mistress Eliza sighed. "Regardless, I shouldn't have yelled at you the way I did. But out of everyone I've ever brought back to life, Juniper was different. She clung to my skirts as a child, so shy at first, frightened to live again. My heart has always held a special place for her. Juniper was the one performer who always listened, always did what was asked of her, never argued back with anyone. She was like my own. But all of you are. And yes, so are you."

"I miss her too," Cricket said softly. "And I understand why you shouted at me. I've blamed people for things before when I shouldn't have." She thought about Zephyr, the carnival, how she never should've blamed either one when her death had been because of Clancy.

"Stormy told me what happened, and she's working on her punishment to continue to stay." Mistress Eliza paused, inhaling smoke from her pipe. "There's still been no sign of the murderer, and these authorities haven't done a damn thing. We'll be leaving in a few days since the land in the next town will be ready for us."

"It's better I not linger around then … so the carnival can continue. But I did want to show you something. That I wasn't a failure when you reignited my heart." Cricket held up her hands and kept her breath even, focusing on her curiosity until the prickling sensation stirred beneath her flesh. The buds rose, and a garden of red blossomed across both arms, not a hint of darkness to be seen. "Your vision, it was real."

Mistress Eliza's lips parted, and she stood from her chair, limping toward her at a brisk pace. She lifted Cricket's arms and ran her finger across one of the roses. An appreciative look formed on her face. "They're beautiful as I always knew they would be. I do want you to stay, Cricket. To travel with us, to perform, to dance, to blossom. I'm not the only one here who wants that."

Cricket blinked, surprised by her words. This was what she'd always wanted, to dance on the carnival stage, yet something more important needed to be done first, so for now, she would put her dream aside.

"I'll come and stay as long as you'll have me, but I will remain here until the authorities don't need me. And if the murderer is found while we're traveling, you'll allow me to leave so I can see them hang. For Juniper and the other victims."

"As you wish, child."

27

Cricket left Mistress Eliza to her cards and found Zephyr outside a nearby tent sharpening his blade.

"Did you follow me over here?" she asked, sinking down beside him.

"Possibly," he drawled.

She rolled her eyes. "At least you didn't barge in."

"A thank you gift will be sufficient." He chuckled, then sobered. "How did it go?"

Cricket recounted the conversation between her and Mistress Eliza, how the necromancer wanted her to travel with the carnival. And that Cricket decided she would return to them after helping the authorities in any way she could.

"I'll stay here with you until you leave," Zephyr said.

She shook her head, placing her hand on his arm. "Don't. You and the carnival have lost so much, and I know performing is an escape for you. You need it. I promise I'll come to you."

"That's a promise you'll have to keep then." He winked. "After I take you to Anika's, I'll leave for my aunt's. I won't be back until late into the night, but can I take you on a picnic in the morning? I still owe you one."

"I would love that. And I still owe *you* a favor."

"Oh, it will come soon enough." He smirked.

She went with Zephyr to collect his pack for the short journey to Sorel before taking a horse back to the manor together. He helped her down from the mare, and he didn't hesitate to pull her close, his arms folded around her. With those shapely lips of his, he kissed her, worshiped her mouth as he backed her into one of the pillars.

He slipped his tongue between her lips, and the kiss deepened. She never would've stopped kissing him if it wasn't for a meek voice gasping, "Oh my," behind them.

Heat flooded her neck and cheeks as she stepped away from Zephyr to find one of the servants, Nettie, carrying a basket of lavender. Zephyr didn't appear embarrassed in the slightest. Instead, his hooded eyes peered at Cricket as if he wanted to devour her again.

"See you tomorrow morning, lovely Cricket," he purred, capturing her lips once more.

Somehow, she forced herself to peel away from him, and as soon as she brought her hand up to knock on the door, it flew open to Anika, the widest of smiles lighting up her face. "Now *that* is what I call a kiss."

Breeta sat in the chair, appearing flushed herself as she stitched at a rapid pace. "Perhaps it's best you not do that again in front of a window for all to see."

Cricket fought a smile as Anika motioned her inside, then she took a seat across from Breeta. A servant brought them sandwiches and tea, and they spent a long while chatting. Cricket shared every detail of the carnival's inner workings with them until the sound of a horse's hooves filled the afternoon air, and Bram returned. He shoved the front door open, his normally calm gaze wild. When his eyes met hers, he sighed. "Cricket, you're all right. I didn't know if you would be back yet."

"I'm fine. What is it?" she asked, exchanging a worried glance with Anika.

"I need to talk to the two of you." His gaze drifted to Breeta. "Alone."

Breeta didn't argue as she gathered her things and hurried out of the room.

Bram took off his hat and raked a hand through his disheveled hair. "Miles has been working on something in secret. It's about the dahlias. He kept the ones Charles had with him and then the others after that instead of disposing of them."

"Is he the one doing this?" Anika hissed.

"No, he suspected that the dahlias found in Charles's satchel had belonged to one of the more recent victims, and he wanted to find out if his theory was correct. I wish he had told me, but after the incident with Charles, he wanted to ensure he could do this without someone turning on him."

"What did he find out?" Anika asked.

Cricket bit her lip, wondering if it had led them to where the flowers were either grown or being sold.

"I don't believe the dahlias were purchased from anywhere. These flowers aren't withering as they should.

They remain in full bloom as if under a spell of some sort," Bram said, taking two from his satchel.

Cricket flinched, praying these flowers weren't the ones that had been on Juniper. But she had to touch one for herself. She ran her fingers across its petals, which were soft to the touch, perhaps even familiar. The hair on her arms rose like needles at the strange feeling.

"I believe the murderer is someone at the carnival," he continued. "I didn't before, but even when the carnival was in Sorel, there would be enough time to journey here and back if they rode fast enough."

A horrific thought crossed her mind—she was the only performer who could bloom dahlias, ones that she recently found out she could cut from herself.

Bram held up both flowers. "The dahlia in my right hand is from a victim, and the other in my left is from *you*. I saved it after the inn but hadn't looked at it again until today. Without water, it hasn't withered a fraction. It's as if it's just been plucked from a stem."

"It's not me. I didn't do it," she said, her voice hard.

"Of course she didn't." Anika glared at Bram.

"I don't think you did anything, Cricket," he started, lowering his voice. "For one thing, you were never alone at the pub when a murder occurred. I believe someone took them from you without you knowing. You told me you passed out several times, and Zephyr was alone with you."

"Zephyr?" she hissed. "Are you mad? He has nothing to do with this."

"You've also been sleeping with him at night," Anika murmured. "Could he have? Don't think about it with your emotions."

Cricket covered her mouth as she remembered Zephyr carrying her when the darkness took over. She supposed he could've taken some then, but what about before that? Another image struck her like lightning, cracking a tree in half. His curiosity feels hers, and if he'd been around her while she was the Sleeping Darling, could he have done something then? Drawn them forward, then snipped a few off? Thinking back to the pub, he'd also been there when the victim was murdered... Could a blond man have been relieving himself at the same time as Zephyr, and he'd chosen to kill him? Had dahlias been hidden in his satchel? Then there was the incident when she'd found the note pinned to the tree. He'd been the first to arrive, and she hadn't seen him enter the woods. Would he have been quick and sneaky enough to do these things? Perhaps even rip their rib cages apart with his vines?

Cricket's hands shook, and her lungs clamped—she didn't think she could breathe. "His curiosity might be able to pull mine forward... But it can't be. That would mean he murdered his own sister."

Bram pursed his lips. "People murder family members all the time. I've seen unbelievably gruesome things done to them."

"Were you awake with him the whole night when Juniper died?" Anika asked.

Cricket had blamed herself for Zephyr being with her instead of his sister, but they had been asleep for most of the night. Or perhaps it was just her... Would she have heard him sneaking out if she was deep in sleep, exhausted from him pleasuring her and with everything else that had been going on? "Not the whole night, no.

262

But it couldn't be," she finally answered. "What about when the carnival was in Sorel? What of those dahlias?"

Bram gripped the back of his neck. "The flowers from the earlier victims were disposed of, and perhaps those had been ones from somewhere else. It's another reason I need to question him."

"He won't be back until late since he went to Sorel to meet his aunt and tell her of Juniper's death. I don't know her name or where she lives."

"Bloody hell," Bram grumbled.

Cricket bit the inside of her cheek, part of her not wanting to tell him this, but the sooner Bram questioned Zephyr, the sooner they could all move on to the real murderer. It was impossible that Zephyr had killed his own sister… "He's meeting me here in the morning for breakfast."

Bram jerked his head up. "That's perfect. It doesn't give him a chance to run, and I want to question him before anyone else at the carnival in case they were to warn him."

"I'm going upstairs to bathe, if that's all right?" Cricket whispered, needing to think.

"Of course," Anika said, taking her arm in hers and helping her up the stairs as though Cricket might collapse at any moment.

"I'll be fine." But would she really if Zephyr had done it? No. He'd even helped her unbury a body. That would mean all along, he knew he was the one who murdered the victim. The very thought was absolutely preposterous.

Cricket remained in the bath until the water turned cold. She couldn't get herself to eat more than a few bites of fruit, and she avoided everyone for the rest of the day as she tried to sift through her thoughts. None of it was making sense, or was it? If Zephyr needed to be questioned, she concluded that she would be the one to do it. The way he was with his sister, bringing her trinkets… He couldn't have. She was starting to loathe herself for doubting him for even a second.

Pulling back the curtains, she peered out at the night. Zephyr said he would be home late, so she would go to him and wait if he wasn't there yet. The halls were silent, and Bram and Anika had already gone to bed. Only two servants stood in the sitting room, watching over the manor. She descended the steps, and no one said anything as she passed. After all, she was a guest.

Cricket quietly drew open the door and slipped out into the night. She waited for a servant outside guarding the home to round the side of the manor before she hurried through the garden. Making certain her footfalls remained light, she kept to the shadows and went out the gate, then down the road to the carnival.

# 28

The torches lit up the night at the carnival, but no one lingered outside. The only soul she'd seen was one solitary authority, passing by on horseback as he patrolled.

Cricket hurried to Zephyr's caravan, praying he was already home. She thought about the yellow cloak that the murderer had worn in the woods, and as she knocked on his door, there was no possible way Zephyr could've taken it off and hidden it in time. Especially when there'd been the other performers searching the woods. Someone would've been bound to spot it. That still would mean someone had practically vanished into thin air.

As for the night she'd fallen asleep with her head on Zephyr's shoulder, him leaving Cricket's caravan to go into town to murder Joanna at the inn and somehow carry her bloody body back didn't seem feasible.

Zephyr wasn't home yet, and she didn't have a blasted

key or know how to pick locks. An idea came to her then—Mistress Eliza had spare keys to all the caravans, but she didn't want to disturb the woman. However, she wouldn't wait outside when the murderer could be skulking around, watching her at that very moment. A shiver ran up her spine, and she hurried to Mistress Eliza's. It took the necromancer several moments to answer the door in her nightgown while holding up a lantern in one hand.

"Are you out here alone, child?" Mistress Eliza asked, her eyes wide as she glanced out, searching to confirm her answer.

"I decided to come back and wait for Zephyr, but he isn't home yet. I was wondering if I could use the spare key."

"I'll go and wait with you until he arrives." She frowned and waved her inside. "Come in, but don't touch anything, and stay where you are."

Cricket nodded and inhaled the smoky scent of Mistress Eliza's home. The necromancer limped past the velvet curtain, and the clank of metal sounded as she sifted through her belongings. Besides the couple times Cricket had been inside here, only Juniper had been allowed. She was trusted enough to tidy up the front area and leave pastries on the table for her.

Mistress Eliza drew back the curtain with a huff, and Cricket stilled. Lying on the floor in a heap was something made of bright yellow fabric, a shade she recognized.

Cricket swallowed the lump in her throat, her body trembling. She blinked, praying she'd imagined it, that a woman she trusted wasn't holding onto the key to the murders. Mistress Eliza had the yellow cloak from the stranger in the woods, and she was *hiding* it for them. Perhaps it wasn't the same cloak though. Perhaps she was getting ahead of herself. But Cricket had to be certain.

"I found out something interesting today," Cricket began, hoping her voice sounded calm, flippant. "None of the dahlias found on the victims have withered. They remain vibrant blooms, just like the ones from my curiosity."

"Is that so?" Mistress Eliza seemed uninterested while fiddling with her jewelry.

Cricket watched her closely as she added, "Someone took them from me somehow."

The necromancer arched a brow. "What a wild imagination you have."

Cricket couldn't wait a moment longer—she shoved past the necromancer into the space behind the curtain. Ignoring the cluttered surroundings, she snatched the yellow fabric. Her breathing hitched as her chest tightened. Hope that she'd been wrong disintegrated. It was the same cloak—dried mud on the hem and the long, pointed hood—she'd seen that day in the woods. She held out the cloak, her jaw tightened. "You know who's been doing it, don't you?"

Mistress Eliza's eyes turned to an icy glare before she regained her composure. "Come now, child. You aren't honestly foolish enough to believe I would allow someone here to murder people?"

The blood in Cricket's veins boiled—Mistress Eliza was trying to make her appear foolish. "You're helping someone!" she seethed, taking out her knife and pointing it at the necromancer. "Who? And *why*?" Zephyr's face flashed before her, but she wouldn't speak his name in case the woman blamed him to hide the real murderer.

Mistress Eliza's lips curled up into a sneer. "Since you won't let this go, open the drawer beside you. Flip through the book there, and you'll see."

Cricket didn't remove her stare from the woman as she yanked open the drawer and took out a thick notebook, yellowed with torn edges. She flipped through each page, one performer after the other with their curiosities. Some she hadn't seen before, the ones who'd already passed away, but most were the faces she saw every day, only younger. There was Zephyr and Juniper as children. Autumn. Stormy. Page after page, she flipped, then she halted on a familiar face. *Her.* It was of Cricket with red roses, her bones showing beneath her flesh.

"I don't know what any of you look like before you're murdered, but I always feel the pull, then I see the curiosity that guides me to save you all. Yet yours did something to me," the necromancer said through gritted teeth. "What did I do to deserve this when I didn't murder anyone? I only ever saved lives!"

Cricket's hand shook as she turned the page, then the next, and the next. They were all in the same pose as Cricket's was, and they were all the victims who'd died by the Dahlia Murderer's hand. Roses and translucent skin. Except one victim was missing. "You don't have Juniper in here."

"Like you, Juniper became too nosey. She discovered what I was doing when she looked through my book. *You* are the reason that sweet child is dead! I was left with no choice. Then just when you gained your curiosity and would've been joining us to perform, you do this."

The letters written to Cricket all made sense now, a

way to taunt her into bringing out her curiosity. She clenched her teeth so hard they might break. It would be simple enough to knock Mistress Eliza to the floor and tie her up. But as she bolted toward her, the woman moved swiftly, no hint of a limp in her step, as she grabbed Cricket by the shoulders and slammed her head into the wall.

The room spun, and something hard struck her skull, the world darkening to nothing.

Cricket opened her eyes, and a muffled sound tore from her throat as she tried to scream. A piece of fabric was between her teeth and tied around her head. Her wrists were bound behind her back, and her ankles confined in front of her.

"Don't scream when I pull the fabric down, or Zephyr will face a worse fate than his sister," Mistress Eliza warned, trailing the tip of a blade down Cricket's cheek. *Her* knife.

Once the necromancer lowered the fabric to her chin, Cricket whispered, "Why have you been murdering people in the same fashion that I was killed?" But as she recalled flipping through the book's pages, the pieces slid together, becoming clearer.

"I'll let you believe you're distracting me with your question." An all-knowing smile crossed Mistress Eliza's lips. "When I used my necromancy on you, I lost my ability. I believe that prolonged your curiosity or twisted it into something else. You were meant to be one of the great acts here. But I couldn't wait, and I needed to find another where the curiosity would perform the way it was meant to, so I had to make a decision. Either your dahlias would help bring another the gift you were meant to have, or it would help yours come forward. As I killed, my necromancy almost roused each one but still failed. Yet each time a victim was discovered, you tried harder to hone your curiosity, and it's the reason it now works perfectly. *You're* perfect."

Cricket swallowed the bile drifting up her throat. She wished she had a curiosity like Zephyr's, one that could reach out and strangle this wicked woman. Blood pounded in her ears, and she wanted to break free of the binds and run outside to scream to everyone in the carnival. Yet she wouldn't make a sound until she could escape to protect Zephyr.

She studied Mistress Eliza's leg, the way she easily moved about the room. "Why did you pretend to have a limp? How did you carry the victim here? How did you get to the pub? Did someone else help you?" There were so many questions, which led to someone else helping her.

"I have many gifts, child. Gifts you couldn't even begin to understand. This whole world is open to me— all I have to do is… Here." Mistress Eliza took the ruby stones from her pouch, then moved her hand, and the air shimmered. Cricket gasped as a triangle of deep crimson light filled the space, glowing in the caravan's gloom. "Open a door, and I am anywhere I choose to be in the world. As for the limp, I did have one, but as my leg healed, it didn't put on as good of a performance, so I've kept it hidden all these years."

"You're mad," Cricket whispered.

"You, my dancing flower, will now face the same fate as the others." The glowing light vanished, and she opened a box filled with dahlias. "When you were the Sleeping Darling, I felt them in you but hoped they wouldn't come. As you slept, I drew them forward with my stones and cut as many away as possible, hiding them in my caravan. But more grew inside you. When you woke, and your destined curiosity didn't rise, I knew why I'd secretly kept them all along. So one night, I left Sorel through one of my doors and went to Nobel. I think you know what happened after that, child."

Cricket stared at her in horror.

"What? No more questions?" Mistress Eliza chuckled. "We'll find out if my necromancy returns by killing you. And if not, it's too late now. I would do it here, but we can't very well get my home bloody."

If Cricket was going to die regardless, she needed to find a way to let Zephyr know that Mistress Eliza was the one who'd murdered his beloved sister. He couldn't wander this world for the rest of his life not knowing that he was performing for the woman who'd been the cause of it. Only, Cricket had to be careful so the necromancer wouldn't kill him.

Mistress Eliza pinned her with a heavy stare. "Now, I'm going to unbind your ankles. Follow my rules, or you know what will happen to Zephyr. You don't want another death on your hands, do you?"

Cricket wanted to stab her in the throat, but she couldn't while tied. So she didn't fight back when Mistress Eliza untied the fabric from her legs, then returned the one to her mouth. Once outside, it would be the right moment to do so.

However, the necromancer didn't open the front door as Cricket expected, but instead, she made another glowing triangular door once more. "Get up!" she snapped, grasping her by the shoulder and yanking her through the room.

No longer were they in the caravan but outside in the woods. The air was calm, and the night dark, save for the light of the moon. This wasn't good at all. She'd hoped when they left the caravan, she would've been able to get the attention of someone still awake.

As Mistress Eliza took a step toward her, blade raised, Cricket shifted her hands, trying to loosen them from the fabric bind to no avail.

The bushes rustled, and they both stilled as a voice hissed, "What are you doing? Why do you have Cricket tied up?" Stormy stepped into the low light, holding a bottle of liquor.

"She's the one," Mistress Eliza ground out, the lie coming easily from her lips as all the others had. "She killed them and *Juniper*."

Cricket shook her head furiously, widening her eyes at Stormy to leave, to warn anyone she could.

Stormy's gaze sharpened. "You aren't limping," she said.

"I suppose I'm not." Mistress Eliza rushed forward, but Stormy dodged out of the way. She slammed her bottle against the necromancer's head, and the woman fell to the ground. Stormy snatched up the knife and darted toward Cricket. She sliced through the fabric tying Cricket's wrists together just as Mistress Eliza produced another blade from her waist.

"Duck!" Cricket shouted. But the blade was too fast, piercing Stormy's chest. Blood bloomed to the surface of the performer's white shirt while she swayed on her feet, pale in the moonlight.

As Mistress Eliza reached for another blade, Cricket didn't hesitate to barrel forward and slam her boot against the necromancer's face before she could stand. Mistress Eliza collapsed back to the ground, allowing Cricket to rip the dagger from her hand, then shove the blade into the woman's chest. She tore it free and thrust it in again, this time the heart, a sickening squelch sounding. The woman slumped to her side on the sparse grass, her eyes staring blankly toward the trees.

Stormy groaned, and Cricket rushed to kneel beside her. She placed the fabric that had bound her wrists over the wound. The performer's chest heaved as Cricket pressed on the material firmly.

Ripping the bind from her mouth to speak, Cricket murmured, "You're all right."

"I'm all right," Stormy repeated, her voice a thick croak. "Perhaps now I can tell Juniper I'm sorry." Her head lulled to the side as her ragged breaths stopped, her eyes just as empty as Mistress Eliza's.

Cricket released a high-pitched scream and whirled around to Mistress Eliza. She tore the dagger from the necromancer's chest, and even though she was dead, Cricket thrust the blade deep into her throat.

# 29

With blood staining Cricket's hands and dress, she stumbled toward the caravans. She knocked on Zephyr's door, but he still hadn't returned. The thought of the other performers not believing her terrified her. But Autumn had defended her before, so she hurried to her caravan, knocking on her door a bit too hard.

"It's me. Cricket," she called.

A lantern turned on behind the curtains, and the door drew wide. Autumn blinked in surprise, wearing a silk robe with Wilder hovering behind her in unfastened trousers that he must've hurried and slipped on.

"Cricket? Why is there blood on you?" Autumn gasped and pulled her inside the caravan, holding the lantern closer to inspect her. "Are you all right? What happened?"

"I'm fine. But the Dahlia Murderer isn't. I killed her.

It was Mistress Eliza." Cricket sobbed and wrapped her arms around Autumn, needing someone, *anyone*, to hold onto before she collapsed.

"Mistress Eliza?" Wilder asked, furrowing his brow. "Are you sure?"

Cricket took her arms from Autumn and explained everything that had happened. How Bram had discovered the dahlias belonged to her, that suspicions led to Zephyr, and when she'd gone to Mistress Eliza for a spare key, she'd discovered the yellow cloak. Then she told them about the book containing the drawings of all of them, the triangular doors Mistress Eliza created, how the woman didn't have a limp at all.

"Stormy was there," Cricket sniffed. "If it weren't for her, I wouldn't have gotten free. And Mistress Eliza … she … killed her." She brought a hand to her mouth, muffling her choked sobs, and Autumn led her by the arm to sit on the bed.

"Wilder, can you go to Bram's home and round up the authorities? Don't wake anyone else yet. I want to make sure they know first. I'll stay with Cricket," Autumn said.

"I'll be quick." He slid on his tunic and boots before rushing out the door.

Autumn wiped the blood from Cricket's hands with a wet rag and offered her whiskey. Even though she wanted to drink the entirety of it, she couldn't get anything down right then.

Cricket didn't speak—she just stayed on the bed beside Autumn and stared at her hands until the authorities arrived. As Cricket and Autumn stepped outside, a few other performers must've heard the horses, too, and opened their doors.

"What's happening?" Louise asked a small group of performers.

Even though Cricket wasn't fond of Louise after what happened to Juniper, she didn't want to see her expression when she discovered that Stormy was dead.

Cricket left Autumn and ran toward Bram and Miles as they got down from their horses. "It wasn't Zephyr," she said hurriedly. "It was Mistress Eliza." She recounted what happened before Miles retrieved the keys from Mistress Eliza's dead body. A moment later, the sound of a carriage drifted through the air, coming to bring the bodies to the coroner's.

"You know how risky that was sneaking out of the manor and coming here?" Bram sighed. "What if Stormy wouldn't have been out there?"

"What if Zephyr would've been taken into custody and hung for something he didn't do?" she bit back. Tears stung her eyes, and she couldn't keep them from raining down her cheeks.

Bram wrapped his arms around her. "I'm just glad you're safe. Next time, take better care before you plunge headfirst into danger."

"Hopefully, there isn't a next time," Cricket said. She would pray every night that there wouldn't be.

Miles returned and unlocked Mistress Eliza's door, then went inside with Bram close behind him. The two other authorities had gone to the woods, remaining near the bodies until the carriage took them away.

It didn't take long before Bram came back out. "Is this what you were referring to?" he asked as he held up the withering book and the yellow cloak.

Taking a deep swallow, she nodded.

A horse whinnied, and she whirled around to find Zephyr approaching. When he spotted her, the mare drew to a stop not far from them. He hopped down from the mare and darted toward them.

"What are you doing here?" he asked, his chest heaving.

Bram nodded his head in Zephyr's direction. "I'll give you two a little time, then we must question you further."

Tears pricking her eyes, she threw her arms around Zephyr and could barely get the words out. "You're going to hate me for why I was here, and I'm sorry for that. But I found the Dahlia Killer. It was Mistress Eliza who murdered Juniper. Your sister had discovered what she was doing, but before she could do anything about it, Mistress Eliza killed her." She took a shaky breath and confessed the rest.

"That bitch," Zephyr spat, pulling her close.

"But the reason I was here," Cricket continued, "was because the evidence pointed to you. I came to talk to you because I couldn't bear to let anyone else do it first. So if you hate me for thinking there was even a possibility that you could have anything to do with this, I understand."

"I could never hate you," Zephyr said gently. "And I vow on my life, I would never hurt you. I would hurt myself before I'd let that happen."

Cricket brushed a lock of hair from his face. "Will you come back with me to the manor until we figure out what to do from here?"

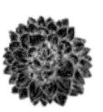

"Is he still sleeping?" Anika asked the next morning, taking a sip of her tea.

Cricket pulled her cup close, peering at her friend across the dining table. "He is. Thank you for letting him stay here." Once they got to the manor, they washed up separately and fell into a deep sleep beside one another after everything. Perhaps it was because the murderer had finally been found.

"I feel as if we owe him more than a night's sleep here after accusing him of committing such horrible acts," Anika said.

"I suppose breakfast will do," Zephyr drawled from the doorway, wearing a mostly unbuttoned shirt.

"Come in, and I'll leave you two alone to chat." Anika stood from the chair and glanced back over her shoulder before leaving. "Perhaps I'll paint you something too."

Cricket smiled softly at her dearest friend as she left the room.

"What else did you say about me?" Zephyr smirked and took a biscuit from the plate before sitting across from her.

"Just what's going to become of the carnival." She shrugged, unsure if it had a future at all. Last night they hadn't talked much—exhaustion had consumed them both.

"Someone can take it over. Change the name of the carnival." His intense gaze stayed locked on hers. "I go wherever you go."

That gave her an idea, one that was akin to hope. The carnival they all loved would survive—she wouldn't allow that to be taken away from the others, even after what

Mistress Eliza had done. "A name change is a good way to start. I don't want the performers to lose their homes, and I know how the carnival can start fresh."

He leaned forward, his eyes sparking with curiosity. "What do you have in mind?"

"Together, we'll burn Mistress Eliza's caravan before we leave."

## 30

Cricket stood at the edge of the carnival stage, peering out the velvet curtains at Autumn as she performed. Wilder's flesh was now wooden and resting in pieces beside her. Autumn scrunched her face, pretending to be confused about how to put him back together. The crowd laughed when she attached his hand instead of a foot to his leg. Then she gave a false pout, held up her hands, and shrugged.

Mistress Eliza's Carnival was now the Carnival of Curiosities, led by Autumn and Wilder. Neither Cricket nor Zephyr had wanted the responsibility on their shoulders—they'd only wanted to perform.

Before leaving Nobel, Cricket and the others had set Mistress Eliza's caravan on fire, along with Cricket's own—a funeral of sorts. No one needed a reminder of where Juniper's body had been found bloody and broken.

Juniper and Stormy's homes remained unoccupied for now.

Cricket's heart pounded as she glanced out at the large audience once more. This was the first performance where she would show her full curiosity.

Warm lips pressed a soft kiss to her neck, and she leaned into Zephyr's touch. He lifted her chin toward him. "Breathe. You have your act perfected. Just focus on what makes you happy."

"I'll try." She would give it her all. Tonight's dance was for Juniper.

Zephyr's eyes became hooded as he studied her. "If you do well, I'll reward you after." A devious grin spread across his handsome face. "But I would do so anyway."

Cricket mirrored his smile as heat spread through her. "I won't deny that."

"Good," he purred.

Zephyr had finished his turn on stage, his performance more brilliant than ever before. It had been his first one since Juniper's death, and she could tell with each step, each toss, each thought, that he was doing it for his sister.

Cricket had begun her search for her parents, hoping they would hear that she was a performer at the carnival and find her. Bram and Anika had also promised to send letters to the other cities to see what they could find out.

"Don't break a leg," Autumn teased as Wilder wished her luck once they left the stage.

"You're up," Zephyr said, his hand drifting down the curve of her hip to her backside, giving it a gentle squeeze.

"Are you trying to make me stay here?" Cricket laughed softly. He chuckled, and she took a deep breath, then stepped forward. And for the first time, she walked onto the stage alone. Her curiosity remained tucked away, not a prickle or stir until she decided to will it.

Two violins played a somber tune, slow and steady, then gradually picked up their pace. She stopped in front of the middle of the stage. Thinking of Zephyr, Anika, Bram, her parents, those she'd lost, and the love they'd brought to her, Cricket lifted her right leg to the ceiling to form a perfectly straight line with her body. She held a hand forward, letting her skin lighten, the bones brightening. The audience gasped in delight, and she lowered her leg, then spun across the stage, doing one swift pirouette after another. Above, two performers unraveled from their hidden white silk fabric that resembled cocoons. They both wore split-colored costumes of white and black while crimson masks adorned their faces.

Cricket honed in on her curiosity, and the rest of her exposed skin became translucent, to where the audience could see her skeleton. At that moment, she was death while she twirled faster, danced harder to the rapid music the bows created against their strings. As she dipped into her curiosity, the prickling crept forth, the roses awakening.

The two female acrobats reached toward her, and she brought her arms up, grasping their hands. They lifted her just as the red roses unfurled from her flesh, proving that death could bring life. The audience roared with applause when her feet touched down once more.

Cricket leapt across the stage, dancing as she never had before, allowing her roses to close and reopen, their petals reaching toward the ceiling. Her limbs seemed to move of their own accord, perfectly in sync with the song. The roses swayed to the melody and fluttered with each motion. Then using a trick she learned recently, Cricket released some of the petals, the music guiding them like magic, showering the awed crowd as they reached to catch them with delight, the remainder floating to the stage in crimson velvet. When the violins slowed, she drew the flowers back beneath her flesh before coming to a whimsical halt and raising her arms to bow to the crowd. Applause filled the tent, and she spun once more until she was away from the audience's view and behind the curtain.

Two arms caught her by the waist, drawing her to his firm chest. "You were brilliant," Zephyr said in a gruff voice as he turned her around to face him.

Elation washed over Cricket, and her chest heaved from dancing, but she wasn't tired enough to not capture his lips with hers. Zephyr deepened the kiss and walked her backward until they were hidden in the costume closet behind the stage. Shutting the door behind them, he pressed her against the wall.

"I think you owe me something," Cricket said, her voice breathy and not just from her performance. She reached between them and unfastened the button of his trousers, freeing him.

"It seems I do," Zephyr purred, lifting her so her legs circled his hips. He slid her one-piece to the side and stroked her arousal with his fingers as she tossed her head back. With one exquisite motion, he buried himself inside her heat, making them both moan. She gripped his shoulders as he thrust, as she ground against him. At that moment, she didn't care if the closet door opened and the curtains fell so that the audience could watch their performance—she just wanted to keep feeling Zephyr.

And then, as if the stage had split in half, pleasure roared through her, and her body writhed. She bit the inside of her cheek to keep from screaming his name.

"I think I've decided what I want you to owe me," Zephyr rasped, still trembling with bliss.

"Anything." She smiled, tangling her fingers in his hair. "Well, maybe not *anything*."

He pressed his forehead to hers, gently placing her back onto her feet. "Tell me you love me as much as I love you."

Her breath caught, and her heart sang at the most beautiful words ever spoken to her. She brought her mouth to his. "That's too simple. I love you, Zephyr."

"Mmm, now let me worship you somewhere else properly." He took her hand and led her out into the night when Autumn ran toward them.

"I have something to tell you. I was with Wilder when we came across something rather interesting," Autumn started. "Deeper in the south, there's word of a witch. One who can gift curiosities. Only this witch can do it without bringing someone back from the dead."

Cricket worried about what else this witch could do and if she was anything like Mistress Eliza. But if others existed who wanted to join the carnival with their gifted curiosities, it could be just what they were looking for. "We're journeying that way next, so I suppose we can see if we find her there," she suggested.

"Then that's what we'll do. I need to get back to Wilder, but we'll discuss more tomorrow." Autumn turned on her heel and left them alone once more.

No matter who they found, no one would ever replace Juniper or Stormy, but perhaps there were performers like them who were looking for a home and a new dream.

"We'll keep our guards up if we find the witch," Zephyr said, encircling his arms around Cricket. She rested her back against his chest as they gazed up at the flickering stars. "On to more important matters, tell me about the first time you saw me and what went on in that pretty little head of yours."

"You're so vain," she teased, rolling her eyes and smiling. "But if you must know, I thought you were the most beautiful thing I'd ever seen. Nonetheless, I've also come to learn that your heart is just as beautiful."

Rustling sounds drifted around them, and Zephyr's vines unraveled from his back. "For that, I'll show you what else I can do with these vines. However gentle or rough you want."

"What are you waiting for?" She grinned, anticipation unfurling within her.

He leaned closer and whispered in her ear, "You, my lovely Cricket, are mine."

"And you, dear Zephyr, are *mine*."

With a wicked grin, he took her by the hand and led her into the woods, where they could be as loud as they wished.

**Did you enjoy Her Cruel Dahlias? Authors always appreciate reviews, whether long or short.**

**Want another deliciously dark story? Try out And Then There Was Silence**

Sadie Hawkins wants nothing more than to find success as a screenplay writer. But when she discovers the love of her life hanging from their bedroom ceiling, Sadie gives up on her dreams.

Until she receives an unexpected gift.

Sadie has become the sole owner of the cabin in the woods she always adored. A secluded place where she can resurrect her dreams and drown her sorrows.

Yet the woods are not the same. The days are still and lifeless. The shadows seem to follow Sadie. And the air holds the scent of her dead husband.

As the days go by, Sadie will either have to accept that her sanity is in jeopardy or uncover the mysteries hidden deep within the past. Mysteries more terrifying than she ever imagined.

**Scientific name:** Dahlia

**Family:** Asteraceae

**Kingdom:** Plantae

**Order:** Asterales

**Subfamily:** Asteroideae

**Tribe:** Coreopsideae

- There are forty-two species of dahlias.
- Dahlias can be found in nearly every color except blue.
- The peak blooming window for dahlias is Mid-Summer.
- They are native to Mexico and Central America.
- Sunflowers, zinnias, and daisies are relatives to dahlias.
- Black dahlias symbolize betrayal and sadness

# MORE FROM CANDACE ROBINSON

## Wicked Souls Duology
Vault of Glass
Bride of Glass

## Marked by Magic
The Bone Valley
Merciless Stars

## Cruel Curses Trilogy
Clouded By Envy
Veiled By Desire
Shadowed By Despair

## Cursed Hearts Duology
Lyrics & Curses
Music & Mirrors

## Immortal Letters Duology
Dearest Clementine: Dark and Romantic Monstrous Tales
Dearest Dorin: A Romantic Ghostly Tale

## Campfire Fantasy Tales Series
Lullaby of Flames
A Layer Hidden
The Celebration Game
Mirror, Mirror

And Then There Was Silence
These Vicious Thorns: Tales of the Lovely Grim
Between the Quiet
Hearts Are Like Balloons
Bacon Pie
Avocado Bliss

**Faeries of Oz Series**
Lion (Short Story Prequel)
Tin
Crow
Ozma
Tik-Tok

**Vampires in Wonderland Series**
Rav (Short Story Prequel)
Maddie
Chess
Knave

**Once Upon a Wicked Villian Series**
Spindle of Sin

**Demons of Frosteria**
Slaying the Frost King
Frost Mate
Frost Claim

# Acknowledgments

Come one, come all, and enter the Carnival of Curiosities. This was a story that had been resting inside me for a while and had been aching to be told. I thank you so much for reading Cricket's story!

It's always hard to not repeat the same thing over and over in these, but I'm seriously bad at them! However, I would like to thank Jackie for editing this book and helping so incredibly much. To SiriGuruDev for improving this story and really help bring it more to life.

Amber H., you continue to save me again and again with final proofs and making the story complete. Hayley, you find stuff that I somehow completely miss! Ann and Vic, you guys are amazing!

I absolutely adored Cricket and Zephyr with all my heart, and just know that they might just so happen to travel a town near you one day!

## About the Author

Candace Robinson spends her days consumed by words and hoping to one day find her own DeLorean time machine. Her life consists of avoiding migraines, admiring Bonsai trees, watching classic movies, and living with her husband and daughter in Texas—where it can be forty degrees one day and eighty the next.